BRINGING OUT
THE BEAST

Aaron Melnick

Brainwashed Media

Nothing like a little pain to remind you that you're still alive.

-NUCLAE PROVERB

PROLOGUE

Any resemblance to any corporations past or present is purely coincidental.

Dark Visions

The maw of the corridor gapes, darkness biting at the light. Small cracks spider-web from the edge of the black void and spread into crumbling rubble outward through the old concrete surrounding it. Shadows float towards the opening, silent and nameless, gliding over the earthen floor of the old unused sewage containment chamber. Fingers of yellow sunlight stab through holes that have eroded somewhere above but somehow fail to pierce the darkness of the tunnel entrance.

One shadow pauses at the opening and gauges something the other shadows do not. It turns to the others without words, without even a whisper.

Another shadow remains at the opening and the others noiselessly enter, distortions in the black lightless tunnel. The others follow the leader that only differs from the others because it is at the front of the group. Darkness in darkness, for some time they follow the meandering channel purposefully, lightless but not stumbling over the uneven dirt and only stopping at forks in the corridors where the leader pauses, clearly divining their way.

At a fork, after a pause, the leader powers forward. He has a scent. The others hurry to keep up, still silent, still almost invisible. There is light up ahead. Not the sweet yellows and reds of sunlight but rather a more cold synthetic hue. The shadows split from the light as if burned and edge up the sides of the corridors in the semidarkness. A faint noise of children playing reaches their ears.

A shadow enters the light and becomes a distortion. Immediately, the distortion is smashed by a quarter ton six legged armored creature bursting from the light. The shadows shoot silent projectiles at the armored being. The creature attacks them but cannot find its elusive almost invisible enemies. Silent projectiles find the creature's head and body and it goes into death throes. More of the large insect-like creatures enter the tunnel blocking out the light and more are slain. Some smaller bipeds come from behind the shadows from a tunnel that the shadows missed. Their knife-like fingers slay a shadow and the ghost bleeds, sanguine spray appearing from its smoke like body. But then the knife hands are put down as the remaining shadow's projectiles find them as well.

In the end, only the shadows remain, and the light from the chamber illuminates strange inhuman corpses swimming in pools of blood fading into the darkness beyond the light, flesh and shadow joined in death. When the shadows get to the entryway they become distortions in the light. The leader stops, regarding the 300 meter diameter round chamber. A path leads through it all threading and branching up a slope that contains about 30 round concrete dwellings. The shadows fan out and begin searching the small buildings. When they find a hexaped they kill it outright, without mercy. They silently shoot all of the bipeds with the knife like fingers.

The shadows fade back into the darkness as if they have no other purpose but to massacre the strange creatures. They march back through the faintly metallic smelling carnage of blood towards the gaping maw of the old sewage chamber. They take nothing, no spoils, no samples, silently fading both out of and into the dark underground night.

TRANSCRIPTION
TRAN·SCRIP·TION
TRAN(T)ˈSKRIPSH(Ə)N/

noun: **transcription**; plural
noun: **transcriptions**

1. a written or printed representation
of something.

   o the action or process of transcribing
   something.
   o an arrangement of a piece of music for
   a different instrument, voice, or number of
   these.

   o a form in which a speech sound or a
   foreign character is represented.
   o the process by which genetic
   information represented by a sequence
   of DNA nucleotides is copied into newly
   synthesized molecules of RNA, with the
   DNA serving as a template.

The Mounds

They are a bunch of teenage techies. Half humans, half circuitry and programs, crowding around us and jeering right in our face. They crowd around us so we can't see the buildings and the streets around us, their hot sour breath spewing from angry metallic masks, hiding most of their faces.

"Get the fuck out of here, freak!" One of them tries to push us down to rob us.

"You don't belong here!" Their metallic silhouettes are framed by the pallid yellowing sky above us. We jump to our feet.

"Don't fucking touch me, Viperhead!" one says, backing away, guard up.

We hurry past trying to escape, blows raining off our head and arms.

"Get his money!" one yells but we go for an opening between two of them and hit it as hard as our small body can, sprinting through and bumping one of them on the way out. That one's mechanical mask falls off showing it was human and his friends laugh at him but still curse at me.

Fake ass cyborgs.

Their insults echo off the gray concrete buildings and hang in the gray air. We want to get away from them and their stupid circuitry implants. Away from this cesspool of humanity. We need some Viprex™. At first it makes you gnash your teeth a little but you don't care much about that after a little while. Anyways, you can always grow new teeth if you grind them down; it only costs a 100 thou in the Clinic City Incorporated™ Gene District. Who needs teeth anyway?

They don't want to let it go. Angrily, mock following, they alternate between laughter and yelling threats behind us, following at a distance. But we are far past them now and we just ignore them. But they don't follow, not this way. And not this late in the failing day.

Why don't they just go back to virtual like most cyborgs do.

Not us though, we like it in the real world where the crowd is starting to thin out and the buildings are getting smaller and more busted up.

We like it in the real world where we can get high off of real drugs, not a bunch of digital code.

The people we pass look more and more disheveled and desperate and wild. Their eyes are trying to meet ours but we stare straight ahead, focused on our mission, all greetings ignored. We turn down an old alley flanked by old flaking brick warehouses exuding odors of decay and mildew. A darkened entrance beckons us inside with a threat of the unknown. Hiding behind this façade of desolation are drug dealers and addicts.

And animals.

Humans are far more dangerous than animals.

OK, humans, but there are a lot of dangerous animals down here too.

We feel the urge to get lost and hide in this dark labyrinth, never to resurface from the gullet of the dead leviathan but we continue down the alley.

There'll be someone around here with some.

We hear a rapid *tap tap tap* behind us. Claws on cracked up concrete. Three mangy strays, trailing behind us green eyeshine catching the spare streetlights. They must have broken through somewhere because they aren't allowed to be on this side of the fence. Strays aren't always violent, but around here...

Get out of here!

We burst into a sprint and they close in on us, barking threats. Cursing.

"We just want talk."

"Come back bitch!"

They are about thirty paces back. We whip around a corner and another and tear down a dark alley, our feet sloshing in sludge. We sprint even faster but they are closing on us, four legs are faster than two with their trotting gaits. Gasping for breath, our lungs begin to burn and we can hear them cursing and howling, they are so close. We hit another corner at a hard angle, bounce into a fence and clamber up it. The fence biting our hands and the strays biting at our legs, demonic growls in their throats.

"We kill you."

"Fucker you!"

Strays don't speak very well and lucky for us, they can't climb either.

We clamber the rest of the way up the fence. The strays are still trying to leap up. One of them bites us on the calf, but not deeply. We swing over the top, cutting our hands on the rusted away barbed wire protecting one unused sector from another. The dogs bark at us and angrily slam themselves against the fence with loud rattling, hoping the rusty links might break. We flip them off and this gets them going even more. Growling, they slam against the fence even harder, their mouths frothing. We pick up some rocks and bricks and start lobbing them over the fence at the dogs, thunking loudly when they hit the ground. We hit one and it whimpers. They get wise quick and back out of range, still barking and cursing.

Why are we wasting time here? Let's get Viprex™.

We turn and start walking. We are in a

small junkyard, a few rats here and there but they are only dangerous in larger numbers. It's the lurkers you don't want to run into. They are ghosts, legends, rarely heard and even more rarely seen, especially in the city.

The piles of broken up rusted machinery are dwarfed by the crumbling carcasses of brick buildings rotting away into the distance. Mutants, cyborgs or automatons now built everything depending on who was cheapest. And they didn't like each other much because of it. Modern buildings are glass, steel and concrete creations efficiently devoid of any soul, but we are far away from that part of the city. We are in the crumbling ruins of the old brick buildings that used to be built here in the past.

Even most humanoid mutants avoid this part of the city unless they have a reason to be here. It is known whose territory it is. In the early part of the century, humans had done a lot of genetic testing on animals to make them "better." Some of the animals became intelligent enough to realize that they didn't want to be caged up and ran off to the more deserted areas, near the warehouses. Eventually their numbers grew, as did the area's reputation as a place that you wouldn't want to get caught in, day or night. The animals claimed their land and the Corporation Government™ fenced it in rather than going on a massive and costly project of extermination. The C.G. created the Hunter

Incorporated™ Extermination "Parties" in which gun owners were allowed to go in and shoot any animal they saw as a form of population control.

Petcorp™ engineered pets are all vying for survival in this place. Petcorp™ has a monopoly on intelligence-enhanced pets because of patent rights. They are not liable for runaway pets and these runaways often form gangs, often based on species, but that isn't always a solid line. Species, in the technical sense, don't necessarily exist anymore as some products are so heavily edited, they are no longer recognizable as a true dog, cat etc.

The mutant animals have lost their naiveté and became more like humans. You know, aware enough to fuck each other over if they could. Aware enough to lie for their own gain.

All the other Petcorp™ creations hate the birds because they can fly free. But the birds are smart, they don't really mess with humans, they keep to themselves, except for occasionally shitting on your head if you piss them off. People generally leave them alone.

The dogs and rats sometimes become drug addicts. If they get money, they find dealers who transdermal them for a fee. They aren't your usual Petcorp™ intelligence-enhanced pets like Fluffy or Moomoo who cater to a human owner's every whim. Unnatural selection compounded with natural selection transformed desirable traits into undesirable traits in these animal addicts.

We navigate through the maze, mostly moldy plastic towering over our head, the metal picked clean long ago. We climb the fence on the far side of the junkyard away from the *strays*.

Gather a few rocks and brick pieces so we can defend ourselves.

We are now officially outside of the modern city limits, but still within the ruin of the old city. We see lights of fires in the distance on the walls of buildings. We shiver, our sweat from the chase dripping down our body and chilling us. We head towards the firelight and stumble over a corpse of a *stray,* partially burned after being suffocated in a clear trash bag. Nonplussed, we continue.

A smell of burning plastic radiates from the yellowish brown haze that hangs in the air. There are walls of rubbish and scrap everywhere, a testament to the wastefulness of the human race. About a half dozen figures silhouetted by the flames bar our way and more move around other fires, arguing, fighting and joking with each other, their faces hidden by gas masks, they openly carry weapons strapped to their backs or stacked up against each other.

Bottle bombs of gasoline mixed with little chunks of Styrofoam line like landscaping at their feet. The animals know better than to attack, having seen their peers burned alive with napalm-like fire; fire that would not go out, with a stench of burning fur, feathers and flesh.

The masked figures still themselves and face us as we approach the fire, the light shining on their black masks.

"What do you need, junk?" one of them asks us, his voice muffled by his mask.

"I got 10,000 bucks for 99."

"That's one point seven."

"mL? No Way!"

"Yeah Motha Fucka! Be glad we don't just take your money and fuck *you* up!" growls the gas mask further back. That masked figure stares at us hard, framed in the yellowish fire, its words hanging in the air, with the smoke.

Just buy it.

"Alright."

We hand the dealer our money, ashamed by our weakness and disappointed by our desperation. They will take our money and beat us or kill us and burn us if we cause trouble. The dealer almost grudgingly hands us a small silver cylinder with some buttons and a small computer screen on it.

"Now get the fuck outta here!" it almost yells.

We spin around and scamper away like a roach. We head towards an area we hope will be deserted. We walk until we find a rusty old train-trestle bridge surrounded by underbrush. We climb up, the fires of the dealers off to our left .

We sit in the trestles and lie back on the rotted wood and corroded metal of the unused tracks, hopefully free of danger. We hit some buttons on the transdermic and a spray is injected onto the skin of our neck. About a third of the Viprex™ 99, produced utilizing enzymatic replicating polymorphs, crosses into our bloodstream and after a few moments, into our brain.

We become so high that we don't feel anything at that point. The sun blindingly bursts through the gray clouds, a rare sight at the horizon, the red giant bleeding its plasma drops into the horizon. The last vestiges of rosy light caresses and warms us along with the drug as the shivering cold of the coming night settles in upon us.

We come back from a dreamless black sleep. In the late night sky the waning gibbous moon looks misshapen and unbalanced. We grab our autohypo and read the meter. We have 1.17 mL left. The odor of burning trash fills our nose. Eerie clicking, squawking and a bovine bleating come from an overgrown hill close by to the south. We shiver, not just from the cold of night. It isn't safe at all here. The mounds burn down below with a perpetual fire and the figures of the dealers huddle together in the light.

We don't want anyone to take our Viprex™.

It's better if we get out of here by the highway bridges. Climb the side and walk on the ridge.

We stand up and start to climb out of the trestles, to girders that tower above us, to the highway bridge. We hear a sound we have heard only at a distance and never this close. The backward whisper makes our body hair stand, electrified. We crouch down and try to become part of the trestle's structure. Another, louder this time, almost sucking the noise out of our ears.

Down by the mounds, the dealers grab their bottles full of gasoline and unshoulder the projectile weapons. They form a defensive semicircle around the burning piles of junk. Their dark silhouettes framed by the yellow red flames. We can't hear their commands over the deafening whispers of what is approaching. The voice of the gods makes the dealers back away. A couple rip their masks off and get on their knees praying and showing their gods the true face of worship.

Then we see something we have only heard whispering in the dark, but never seen with our own eyes. Down below us, three dark shadow figures move slowly, unevenly, and disjointedly through the junk of the mounds.

Two seem large and one small, though size is hard to determine. Darkness manifested, the shadows seem torn from another dimension, sucking in the meager light like their whispers suck in sound. They move gangly, pausing to gasp back in their screaming whispers, voices in reverse, painful to the ear, pulling all sound out of our head. Then they move toward the mounds. The rhythm of their movements, hideously off beat, yet somehow also smooth and organic. Fast to slow and back again. Parts of them fade in and out of existence. They appear simultaneously in the mounds and yet also somewhere else. They vibrate the matter and the air around them. They flow through space carving forward in an inexact path, breaking like waves.

What are they doing inside the city walls? Hide

Holding our breath, we crouch lower and try to shrink into ourselves. The small one freezes and looks up at us, its shadowy featureless face flickering, framing iridescent eyes while systematically probing us with hissing whispers. A madness floats up at us, a panic. Sloth-like, yet not slow, it grabs the trestle and starts to climb toward us. Adrenalized, we begin to shake and scope out escape routes.

Get ready to climb and run like never before back to the ruins.

One of the larger lurkers hooks a shadowy limb over the small one's shoulder. Where they touch resonates with interference bands. The larger one pulls the smaller one down off the trestle. With one last glance up, the small lurker lets out a stinging whisper that makes us cover our ears before turning to join the other lurkers approaching the dealers.

We hear gun fire. Some of the dealers throw their bombs but the explosion and resulting fire have no effect on the lurkers. The lurkers continue to move forward through space, jerkily and then smoothly defying physical laws. They jump in huge orbital arcs, flickering as an ancient movie skips a few frames. The dealers throw bombs. Flames rear up around the beasts, but they keep advancing. The dealers fire bullets, missing or passing through the targets, maybe even bouncing off the lurkers, it is hard to say. They emit a darkness that extinguishes the light from the fires bursting around their hideous forms. The dealers break ranks and start to sprint away but one of the lurkers jumps an impossible distance over the mounds and cuts them off at varying speeds.

The dealer closest to the lurkers shoots himself in the head. The small lurker grabs the body and pulls it back,holding it close in a lifeless embrace. Another dealer is grabbed, her skin starts smoking, her empty husk floats to the ground. The two kneeling dealers, impaled by long curved claws, are pulled close to the amorphous form of the other lurker. They dessicate into kneeling mummified supplicants. The largest lurker grabs a struggling gas-masked dealer as her mask is ripped off exposing long black hair, fading in and out of existence influenced by the lurker's pulsing frequency. She is taken struggling back into the night, her stifled scream echoing in the cold night air. The other dealers sprint away and the lurkers seem to dissipate with a whispering wheeze and fade into the night.

Hiding above the culling, we finally remember to breathe for the first time in a while. We have never seen lurkers before and we are not even sure what we have seen. We have heard rumors of them, the whispering shadows haunting and worshiped and occasionally seen in outlying communities. But we have never, ever heard of them in a city. A faraway whispered screaming teases our ears.

They are gone. Maybe the dead dealers have some Viprex™ on them. Go down and see. Hurry, before they come back.

But what if they come back? They are still whispering.

Do it now so we can get Viprex™.

We slowly climb down the trestles, our heart beating faster and faster. We run over to the bodies. The dry corpse's eyes stare at us accusingly. We wonder if they can still see us standing over them, a thief in the night..

Take the pack now. They have no need of it anymore.

The masked shrunken body carries a

backpack and we turn them over to strip it off. The husk falls apart into little pieces that float around us.

Holding our breath so as not to breathe in the dust from the husk, we grab the pack hurriedly and put it on our back. We hear yelling far away so we jerk around and we feel a burning on our abdomen next to our right hip. There is dust from the husk on our shirt where the burning is.

Running towards the trestle bridge we reach down and try to rub the dust away from our stomach and climb up the bridge on the opposite side as fast as we can. A few pings ricochet off the metal of the bridge, sending a spray of rust into our eyes and we almost lose our grip but we get to the top and crouch/run on the ruins of the old bridge till we reach solid ground. More shots echo in the distance but we are too far away. Scratching at our abdomen we run along the tracks until we run into the base of an even higher highway bridge and start climbing the cracks in the support. The low animal noises suddenly excited below sound hauntingly spectral, they have seen a show that one doesn't often see.

Sweating and near the top, our limbs are exhausted and feel like rubber. We find a particularly large crack and buttress our arms and legs in it so we can rest. Up here, the smell of burning plastic and flesh is fainter than down below. Now we smell the ozone scents of electricity. We hear whirring sounds and wind being displaced.

We gather our strength for the final ascent and when we reach the top we pull ourselves over a meager guardrail to a small maintenance walkway. Next to us, eight lanes of autocars and buses are whizzing by. They are driverless and float elegantly above the roads, the only friction wind resistance. Everything is controlled by central computers. The passengers inside are either eating, getting drunk, screwing, generally enjoying themselves or some combination of those things in virtual. This is up to your imagination, since all windows are tinted black, their headlights flashing us in zoetrope parody.

Tailgating is the rule. Trains of cars, all seamlessly stopping and going as one unit, navigate through the maze of buildings, giant holo-ads and video billboards. If you walk along the road you would get smashed by autocars. There is no stopping the vehicles once on the highway and trespassing on the Clinic City Incorporated™ highways is an international offense anyway so there isn't usually much of a problem, except for people that want to kill themselves. Since there are so many extra people it's usually not a big deal unless an actor or a really rich person offs themselves.

We slink along the service ramps next to the roads itching our abdomen. Some assholes with their windows open drive by leering at us and yell something about their dicks. They throw an empty bottle at us. We duck and flip them off, their car disappearing into the endless train. We hate how people in autocars suddenly become twenty times tougher when transients.

The dark sky begins to dump rain on us and the clouds of water scintillate and flash with the lights from the cars and the city . We rush on, uncomfortable on the skyway. After a kilometer we find a service ladder. We climb down. It ends about five meters from the ground and we hang from the bottom rung and jump down, landing hard in a crouch in a dirty puddle. We sit down on some crumbling concrete rubble under the bridge to take shelter from the rain.

We lift up our shirt and our side is a dark bruise, but no open wound. We scratch at it, pour some of our water on it and try to clean it up as best we can. We feel a sense of deja vu, but this has never happened to us before. We have never been around lurkers before.

Open the backpack.

Inside are some clean underclothes, magazines filled with projectiles and what looks like some circuit detonators for making bottle bombs. Also, there are about five normal silver autohypos along with one autohypo made out of a golden type metal.

This is more Viprex™ than we have ever had. We need to do some and see how it is. We should do a big dose!

How much?

0.99 mL.

That's a lot. Should we do this gold one?

I bet that's top shelf, maybe the dealer's personal supply. We should definitely try that one. That's fancy!

We set the gold autohypo to 0.99 mL, more than we have ever done before. The drug always affects the senses in a different way, shifting to become what the user desires. This time it is visual. The bridge seems to be sweating and breathing, vomiting dirty water out of its downspouts. We realize the bridge is alive and it is gurgling at us in the language of falling water.

The clouds begin to light up with dawn and we see abstract visions in them. Sometimes an amorphous face. Sometimes angelic and then nightmares. We become restless and feel uneasy. We stand up and avert our gaze from the visions to try to snap out of it. The walls of rain on either side of the bridge close in on us. Then the visions become even more disturbing. We see husks of corpses floating to the ground like dead leaves. We see mutants gunned down. We see fires with strange jellyfish-like creatures floating above them vomiting energy. The energy turns into figures that appear out of the walls of rain as if being born from the storm seeking shelter.

This isn't a vision. These are real.

The figures are humanoid and they move

toward us in groups of two or three. They start loosely gathering in our general area, wiping the water from hard poker faces and squeezing out shabby clothes. They mill about each other, gray countenances set in immovable bluffing masks.

"You got Viprex™?" They ask each other. "I don't have that shit." Everyone denies that they have any Viprex™ knowing that it will become a game of smear the loner that eventually breaks down to an everyone for themselves battle to the bloody pulp. People will fight for Viprex™. They would kill for it.

The bums begin to circle around us forming a slow cyclone of loose confederations and some of them are openly eyeing us, being the perpetual loner. Viprex™ addicts have a knack for smelling out the drug.

We casually walk toward one of the bridge supports reaching for our groin as if to take a piss. Hard eyes return our quick furtive glances. The groups begin to amble towards us. We pretend to take no notice and reach down to unzip our zipper. The closest addicts slow for a moment deciding whether or not to rush us now and get pissed on or wait and jump/search/beat us when we are done. In our peripheral vision, we see one of them reaching for the pack on our shoulder.

We spin around with a kick to his midsection and break into a hard sprint and burst through the curtain of rain into the storm, hesitating movement behind us punctuated by cursing. Wet streets slap at our feet and the sound of hard rain in our ears is disconcerting along with the moisture we continually have to wipe from our eyes so that we can see. We move quickly but leave a little in reserve and steal a glance behind us. They are all following us and one of them is fast, maybe 20 meters in front of the fastest group and only about half that distance behind us. The rest of them have no chance, they are too slow.

We turn it up a bit but he still is gaining, running like a madman, his feet kicking up clouds of moisture like steam from a locomotive. We speed up and start towards the more populated areas of the city hoping to get lost in the morning rush hour crowd but this guy is too close. We can hear his pounding feet and even his ragged breathing, he is so close.

Lungs on fire and soaked with the rain and sweat and we brake and spin. Bull-like, he is barreling down full speed and we sidestep and trip him. He rolls like a pinball into the wall and we kick him in the face stunning him. We turn and keep running.

The others are breaking towards us like sharks for blood, about 15 meters away.

They are not going to catch us. They are too slow and easy to trick.

Encouraged by our easy victory, we burst off into the more populated areas near Clinic

City Incorporated ™. We pass through the long lines snaking back and forth where most people need to wait in line for Government Inc.™ food. Mostly dirty people who only get mass water showers a few times a year, wait while getting preached to about how lurkers will punish anyone who doesn't follow the rules of staying in virtual and obeying hololaws.

We push through these more lawless hoods trying to get to the area where the masses are looking for work and the crowds mill about so we can get lost in the dark wet throng of anonymity. We dodge around the vagrants at top speed, narrowly missing several people and almost losing the other addicts in the dirty crowds.

We are sprinting hard and the buildings are turning from rotted brick to glass and steel and the people are getting more well dressed when we almost collide into a smartly dressed old lady walking her dog. We slide around her but our shins knock into her dog at full force.

"ROW!" screams the dog in pain as it gets smashed to the ground.

The dog gets up and they both start cursing at us. A foul stream of words belching from their mouths. Regaining our balance, we keep running and glance behind us. The addicts, who we had almost lost, take notice and renew their pursuit. We whip around the corner, the dog and old lady's curses fading away, drowned out by the rain.

The blast of an autohorn fills my ears as we get blindsided by what must be an autocar. We bounce off the Tesota™, slam to the ground, and lurch to our feet, in pain. We look at the driver, bitterly. She looks panicked but pissed, like we ruined *her* day, her wheeless autocar still bobbing up and down from the impact. We try to keep going but only manage a feeble limp. Our pursuers bound over cars and knock over anyone in their way. They are like rabid dogs. Wet smelly rabid dogs.

So much for getting lost in the crowd.

This is it. They are gonna try to fuck us up. Get them first or we are done.

The car that hit us isn't sticking around. She tears off over us in a whoosh of panic. Where the car was hovering the first addict appears above us and pounces, covered in sweat and rain. Foaming at the mouth, he jumps and plants a flat foot right in the center of our stomach and tumbles down onto us wheezing. Winded, we roll out of it but we get kicked in the face by the second scar-faced addict who is waiting for us as we try to get to our feet. Hazy, we scamper back belly up, crab walking and trying to get our feet while one of the other addicts is trying to rain down stomps on us with her soggy boots.

We jump to our feet and try to block the wild haymakers from the first foaming-at-the-mouth addict. We try to keep him between us and the femme, who is also doing her best to take our head off with kicks. They spit rain and curses in our face. We back hard into a parked autocar floating behind us. We've run out of room. The scarred addict finally gets to us again and throws left hooks to the back of our head behind our ear. Our legs start to give out and the haze sets in with a green tint.

The addict with the foaming mouth is starting to connect on every punch to our head and face. Our legs fully give out. We crumple against the autocar and see the driver staring at us in horror. We collapse and turtle up into the fetal position but they are still getting in kicks and stomps all over our body. We taste blood in our mouth and we hear someone grunting in pain. That person is us. The kicking stops and we cannot move. Our field of vision shows the wet bloody road and their feet. They turn us over, their possessed faces framed by the cloudy gray sky. Sirens begin to echo in the background.

"Get his Viprex™." They try to pull the backpack off of us by turning us over again and we don't let go. They grab our shoulders and slam the back of our head on the ground and we go out.

They try to pull our backpack off of us. Our left hand shoots out and we grab the foaming-mouth one's foot with both hands and twist, breaking his ankle with a sickening snapping sound. He lets out a high-pitched scream, clutches at his ankle and falls to the ground. The femme is pulling the backpack with the Viprex™ off our shoulders so we hook our arm to it and let her pull us up to our feet. Trapped by her lust for the Viprex™, we turn to her and smash her in the face with repeated elbows and then as she falls, knees. Blood pours from her nose and mouth. Her face rearranged, she goes down. The scarred addict attacks from behind but we duck under his slow punch. We land punches to his stomach. He backs up in disbelief that we are even still standing. He hesitates but charges us so we sidestep and grab the back of his neck and pull his teeth down to our smashing knees. He falls to the ground following his teeth and his fellow addict into a pool of all our blood mixed with rain. We spin and kick the broken ankle in the face and he goes down.

Slower addicts on the periphery hesitate after witnessing the beating and sirens pulling closer have them fading back to less gentrified areas.

Bent over, we grasp the pack and half run, half limp down a darkened alley towards the border of the business district and the mounds where the police don't want to go. There is no pain, there is only sprained and torn muscles. The sirens are closer now. We find a pile of rubbish and burrow deep inside letting the darkness take hold.

The first thing we become aware of is a rotten stench and then crust in our eyes. As we wipe our eyes, we become aware of a bruising pain all over our body. Then we remember the beating we took. We begin to panic but the pack is still here, clutched in our hands.

What happened?

Don't worry about what happened. We took care of it.

In pain, we open the pack and spray some of the new Viprex™ and fall into a trance. We stretch and burrow into the trash bags like a maggot in Synthmeat ™ and doze off. We wake up and it is night. We are feeling better but stiff and still sore from the beating. During this time the Viprex™ has changed our genes, this time making us regenerate. We realize that in our confusion, we sprayed more of the gold autohypo.

Wonder what that did.

Seems to be fine. We're still here, aren't we?

Guess so.

We stand up and stretch through the stiffness. We test our legs and we can walk. It is painful but we can move around. It is a cloudy night and there is a starless moonless sky. Our stomach is itchy and discolored where we got bit but we are in one piece. We are in a deserted alley filled with trash in the business section of the city. We need to get somewhere to rest and take more Viprex™ and clean up.

We can trade Shaya some and stay in the Pleasure Flats till we heal.

We hobble from the alley shivering and rubbing our arms, trying to get some blood flowing. The shivering turns to shaking. Soon we come to an old railroad embankment and climb up the side. The shiny metallic tracks razor away into the distance reflecting the city lights. Cricket songs time our steps from the underbrush. Our body aches and our head aching is only mitigated by the Viprex™.

Strange, how they didn't get our Viprex™.

Above all else, we need to keep our Viprex™. No matter what.

No matter what?

Yes. Everything we do, mutations or otherwise, we need to do to survive.

But which one of us is really surviving?

Everything we have done, we have done together. If we go down, we'll go down together.

That's what I'm afraid of.

Hard choices need to be made and we made them. We are alive because of us.

We grunt. No reason to argue.

We keep moving, as we warm up, the stiffness subsides a bit the more we move.

The desolation is totally dark now except for the meager glow of the dusty street lamps. The roads, old asphalt, are worn with deep potholes. Howls and screeching punctuate the chatter of the insects and rodents. Occasionally an animal will cross our path or we will pass by a humanoid wanderer but we stare straight ahead and they leave us alone.

We turn a corner away from the desolation of the tracks and gradually see the signs of civilization. More and more people are walking around. Some couples holding hands. Some synthetic ad-birds endorse their products in their singsong voices. The night is hot and we are sweating profusely from the heat. We play a game and unwaveringly look straight into the eyes of everyone we pass. Most people quickly drop their eyes when looking into ours. We are not physically intimidating but we know our eyes are wild.

We hobble around the corner and approach a pretty girl with silver hair and pale skin. She is wearing an iridescent purple mini dress. A beginning of a smile forms on her lips but it never fully forms as we get closer and she looks away. We are a mess, disdain frozen on our face and mirrored by hers.

Warmed up, we are moving faster now up Carnegie Avenue Level Zero, itching the discoloration on our stomach. Autocars whiz by and almost no one is walking on the sidewalks. We pass by glass and steel constructions with enclosed pedestrian bridges between them and the sky platforms connecting them at top. Usually festivals are held on the building top parks to weed out the poor and street people. Ground level is dark due to the endless press of buildings.

Starving, we go into a lighted Quickstore™ and get a Meat People™ industrial strength synthetic burger. We wolf it down while watching some vagrants milling about in front of the store trying to wipe down some windshields with the customers nervously shooing them away as if they were insects.

Spying some dumpsters between the Quickstore™ and another building we cross the parking lot and head for them. We crouch in between the dumpsters. Looking around nervously we make sure we can't be seen from the street by the windshield wipers. Our pulse quickens but we see nobody in the immediate vicinity. We pull out the gold autohypo from the dead man's pack.

The gold again?

This is good stuff. Definitely was a personal supply.

We set it for only 0.35 this time to conserve. It affects us almost immediately. First we begin to feel….nothing. Our pain is gone. The lights get brighter all around us. The dumpsters start to shine and sparkle. We are aware of the noises of people talking in the distance at the quickstore. *"Can I get a 500?"* says a windshield wiper. The hum of a plane shining high in the sky grabs our attention away from the street.

Sensory enhancer.

"No shit," we say out loud to ourself.

This time. We used it to heal us last time.

We put the hypo back in the pack and lift our shirt up to look at the abrasions from the lurker dust. Though no longer bothered and red, where our hip meets our abdomen is dark as if in a shadow cast from nowhere. Otherwise we feel fine.

We take a hard right and start walking down the hill towards the river and the Pleasure Flats, the sweat dripping off our brow in the humid night. In the Flats, people would often get their DNA altered to give themselves tighter bellies, larger breasts, shapelier legs and buttocks. They smoothed their skin and even their bone structure could be altered. Higher cheekbones were popular as well. So was increased vaginal muscle control. So was altering biological sex.

These genetic procedures were catching on to middle class people also. A beautiful and androgynous holocommercial projected over our head incessantly tells us that, "you have the right to appear on the outside how you feel inside," followed by images of beautiful, sensual people. Now earning power finally did translate into good looks and gluttony was only reflected in people's actions, not their appearances.

The inverse was true as well. These alterations could be used to earn money. Pleasure people always got genetically altered for greater pleasure in copulation, physically and visually. They were usually addicted to Viprex™ or some other drug and often took a female form. The police would often look the other way because they would also visit the places where these services were provided and take a piece. Doctors, cops, husbands, fathers, priests, uncles, sons, brothers and even other females frequented the clubs in town known to provide prostitutes to their clientele. Anything was on sale here. Any fantasy no matter how lurid or perverted. Someone got their genes altered to fulfill it. Even the virtuals, people normally afraid to leave their electronic lairs, will sometimes visit *in the flesh*.

Mutants are sometimes among the prostitutes as well. They are often the most coveted with their sideshow looks and strange body parts. The parody of nature is somehow sexually exciting to the denizens of Clinic City™, bringing about lurid sexual fantasies in the dark rooms.

Flashing lights and sexy holograms adorn the buildings in the Pleasure Flat down the hill by the river beckoning lustful clients like moths to light. Unlike the night before it is so hot that we are totally covered in sweat by the time we reach the flats. There are people everywhere. Men, women and everything in between are ogling scantily clad people walking around in the neon lights of the district. Everyone appears coated in a layer of sweat. People are laughing and talking and we can't make out individual conversations. Strangely, we *can* smell individual people. Even more strangely we can smell a background odor of sexual attraction that we have never noticed before.

Pheromones.

Cops with their stone faces and tech over one eye survey the crowded streets. Multicolored lights make people into garishly painted vamps and tramps. Faces distorted in the blue, yellow, red and black light are in our face as we push our way through the sweaty, smelly throng.

We become one of the swarm, possessed by pheromone-induced lust to copulate with the beautiful and otherwise unattainable creatures. It has become another addiction. Sometimes if we have extra money after buying Viprex™ we come here. Tonight though, we will need to give up some of our ample supply of Viprex™ so that we can be safe and recover from the beating we took. We eventually get to an old building with a neon light that says "Meow's" in huge letters and sneak by the doorman when he is checking a big group. The pheromone smell is even stronger inside the dark interior and lasers adorn the nude female figures dancing on the stage. We ask the bartender if Shaya is free, yelling over the pulsating music. After a hard look he says, "Go up to room 7," in a voice that sounds like he's chewing broken glass.

We begin walking up the stairs.

Hold on a second. We need to hide how much we have. What if Shaya tries to take our autohypos?

Should we put some in the big compartment of the back pack?

Yeah, just put the autohypo with the least in the little pocket.

We put the autohypo with only about 5 mL in the little pocket and the rest, along with the gold autohypo in the bigger compartment, burying it in some clothes. No need to show how much we actually have. We go up to room 7 and buzz.

Shaya opens the door. This week she has blue brown speckled predatory eyes. Her full pouting lips are framed by a pretty oval tanned face, one of the most beautiful designs. Her body is full and shapely and her breasts strain against her scant, sheer black clothing. Her only flaw is a hard look that flickers across her face that says "*Fuck you*". Her long dirty-blonde hair cut to frame her pretty light brown face, drops down around her bare shoulders. Her bright blue eyes shine inquiringly. "What's up?" She smiles and speaks in her quiet way. Her look turns sour. "You look like shit." She laughs and she screws up her nose disgusted. "And you smell like shit! No wonder you don't have a girlfriend."

We pull off our back pack. "Calm down baby," she coos, smiling sensually. "Slow down. Ever hear of a shower?"

I pull the autohypo out of the pack and hit the button so she can see the 5 mL it contains. Her eyes light up.

"I need a place to stay for a couple days till I am well enough to cross the city. Will this be enough for me to stay here?"

"What is that? Viprex™? No way!" She looks excited, then her look changes.

"Wait, how much do you have?" She knows that we must have more if we are willing to give her this much. She knows something's up and suspicion flickers across her face.

"Besides this, just enough for me. I could go somewhere else."

"No, no, no. I just need to talk to the boss about this form of payment. Let me sample it first. Where did you get it?"

We don't answer. We turn to the mirror and look at our reflection and hers behind in the sparsely furnished room. Light plays on her face and she meets our eyes in the mirror. We hold each other's gaze in this other dimension.

"You stole it, right?" her twin in the mirror seems to ask.

"Don't worry about it."

"From who?"

"You want some or not?"

Her reflection doesn't answer but her eyes squint at mine before she turns on her long legs to get another autohypo so she can skim some before she gives it to her boss. "Go take a shower!" she yells from the back room. We take the pack to the bathroom and lock the door. We undress our filthy sodden clothes and look in the mirror at our naked body. We are nothing but skin bones and small muscles that are bruised and aching, though less than they were when we woke up in the trash pile.

Because we have been healing us.

The dark spot on our stomach seems to have faded to a whisper of a shadow.

Take the pack in the shower with us.

You think she would take our Viprex™?

Trust no one.

The shower is set for 5 minutes, a luxury that is à la carte when you buy pleasure in the Flats. When we get out of the shower she gives us a clean shirt and pants. "I spoke to the boss. This will buy you a shower and 12 hours with me."

"OK."

"You don't have to put these on yet," she smiles and drops her clothes off of her body, all curves in the dark light of the bedroom.

Our sweating bodies pound together with rhythmic gyrations, her legs spread wide and her chest heaving. We cum inside her knowing full well that she will never allow herself to bear a child into this world.

We always pick Shaya if she is available. For some reason, over our handful of visits to the Pleasure Flats, she has developed a type of affection for us. Maybe it's because of camaraderie stemming from our mutual addictions. Lying in bed after sex, she asks us if we ever desire a different sort of life.

"What do you mean? You mean not doing drugs ?"

"Yeah, I guess so. I mean feeling like you belong. Not necessarily a job and family, more like having a purpose and other people that share that purpose."

"What's our purpose? To be looked down on by everyone else? Even if they are scums themselves?"

"No," she laughs. "I mean something more important than that. I've never told you this before but I am a hybrid."

"You're a mutant? No shit?" we say purposefully and ignorantly.

Her face tells us that the word mutant must offend her and she clams up.

"I guess I always knew you were different somehow." We try to break the ice, not sure how we feel about her being a mutant.

That hard look softens after a moment. "I am what my people call a Seer."

"How did you end up in Clinic City? I thought mut- I mean hybrids live in the sewers."

"No, we don't live in the sewers. Our city is underneath Clinic City and it is called Subterra. We have everything you have up here and more."

We laugh. "Why don't you go back there then if it's so good?"

She drops her vivid blue eyes. "Viprex™ is not tolerated."

Nothing more needs to be said but we are

curious. Mutants are supposed to have powers that humans unaltered by genetics or tech don't have.

"So you are a...see-er? What's that?"

"A seer. We have augmented senses."

"Like ESP?" we ask.

She laughs.

"More like a radar. We can "see" things that humans need machines or tech implants to see."

She lies.

"Bullshit." We sneer. "Prove it."

"Look out the window behind me. There are two large males walking with a smaller female. They are passing a group of 3 girls. Looks like the girls aren't responding to their cat calls." We watch this play out as she is narrating it, her eyes firmly focused on our face.

We stare at her for a moment. "That's kind of scary. Remind me never to talk shit about you, even if you're far away." She laughs, a rare real smile on her face that makes us smile back.

"So you are a Seer. Is that for security or something?"

"Security, ore recovery, reconnaissance, self protection."

"Oh shit, so you can beat me up?"

"I will if you keep being a smart ass," she laughs, her eyes twinkling.

"You were trying to tell me something before. You asked me if I want a different life, what about you?" we ask.

She tilts her head to the side as if she is trying to dislodge a memory from her head. Or perhaps trying to forget.

"When my body became a woman's body, but my mind was still a child's, I snuck out of my city, Subtterra, with some friends. This is forbidden as humans are not kind to our children."

"Why?"

"The tunnels are dangerous. Full of gods or demons depending on your perspective. Gods that many of your people worship."

We shudder.

Don't mention the lurkers.

"You don't worship them?"

"Not much of a religious guy, but they do scare the shit out of me."

"You've seen them?"

We change the subject. "This is your story. You just left your city…"

She stares at us strangely for a moment and continues.

"I was able to avoid other creatures because of my abilities as a seer. We were curious about Clinic City, a playground for us. We tried to disguise that we were Nuclae and-"

"New clay?"

"Nuclae, our name for our people. We do not call ourselves mutants or even hybrids. Our people are the Nuclae. True humans without tech."

"Humans? You guys change your DNA."

"So do you 'humans.' And you use tech. We call you borgs."

"Not me. My family couldn't afford either tech or DNA augmentation."

Now we are more curious about Shaya than we have ever been before. In the past, we just thought she was beautiful and mysterious. Now we are realizing she has a complicated past.

"We keep getting off subject. Hybrids in Clinic City. Didn't people mess with you?"

"A little, but we were pretty girls and it was not totally obvious that we were Nuclae as it is with some of the other strains of my people.

"We walked around your city in the open wind and even saw the sun sometimes which is a true gift for those in Subterra where we only see artificial sunlight. We went to tech houses and used tech for the first time and experienced virtual. We messed around, went to bars and drank alcohol with humans. People would always buy for us. I met a good looking human boy and we hit it off. I started sneaking up above to see him. I thought we were in love."

"My brothers and sisters caught me sneaking back in one time and they locked me up and told me it was forbidden to go above until I was older."

"What did your parents say?"

"Nuclae don't have parents. We are raised by our older brothers and sisters."

"But what if you have kids, you know, through intercourse."

"It is forbidden. We are implanted in female hosts. No child is unplanned. We only have a limited carrying capacity below ground and we need different kinds of Nuclae to do different jobs. We have no mechanical augmentation like humans do up here. It is forbidden. The closest we have are bioprograms and even those are limited production."

"That's strange."

"It is less strange than having so many children that you overwhelm your city's ability to support your population or having a complete stranger birth your child for the rich?" she sneers.

"Touché."

"Anyways, they eventually let me back to my job as an assistant horticulture aid growing Nuclae dark flowers. But I couldn't forget Clinic City and my boyfriend. After a couple weeks, I found the most beautiful dark flowers I could, wrapped them into a bouquet and snuck out alone through the tunnels to the city above. I went to the bar we often met at and took some flowers to my human boyfriend. I surprised him up above and he was with some human females. He looked at me dead in the eyes and asked me if he knew me from somewhere. He was embarrassed of me because I was clearly different, if not obviously Nuclae, I was something different with my dark looks and dark flowers.

"I was so angry that I threw the flowers in his face, stormed off from his district and ended up down here in the Pleasure Flats drinking alcohol at a bar. An older man sat next to me and struck up a conversation. He was charming and said he had the cure to my ills and it would make me happy so I tried Viprex™ for the first time. I think I did it because I was so angry not only at my boyfriend but also at my people. I felt like they were too weak to be able to come above. I swore that I would never go back. Then I wanted Viprex™ so I stayed with the older man. He taught me the ways of things up here in human cities. He showed me your virtual, holomovies, your news cycles, your foods, your customs. As most humans do, he worshiped lurkers which I found ridiculous but I never told him.

"He was charming and he told me I was so beautiful inside, why can't he help me be that beautiful on the outside. He promised me all the Viprex™ I wanted so we had my DNA altered to be beautiful like the models in virtual."

"They are hot, but they are probably sweaty middle-aged men."

"Probably." She smiles halfheartedly. "First, I got my nose changed, then my breasts enlarged. I became blond. I wanted to look like a human beauty because I saw how much power it gave me, especially over men. But I needed more money for more augmentations and he cut me off. One night after a lot of Viprex™ he told me I could earn money and all the Viprex™ I wanted. That was the first time I had sex for money. From then on he made me earn my genetic augmentation and it became an obsession for me."

"Well, you look good."

Why is she telling us this?

"It isn't just looks. I started getting augmented muscle control, not just for sex but for protection from men who would try to rob me or worse."

"We are sick. I mean men in general, especially when it comes to sex. Not me, of course." We stare at her body lewdly.

She hits us. "Listen to me!"

We focus on her hypnotic blue eyes again.

"I became beautiful like I always wanted to be. Like a human. And as a Nuclae I was already tough, but now I am even tougher." She smiles and flexes her ripped voluptuous body in the mirror on the wall and then slowly the smile changes as if she is listening to a voice and her reflection's eyes focus on mine again. "I don't know. I just feel like something is missing. I am not sure what."

We are not sure what to say. She turns towards us and looks us up and down as an awkward silence follows and she changes the subject.

"You are different from the other times you have been here. I am not sure what it is, you seem …."

"Better looking?"

She laughs, holding our gaze. "No, your eyes have a different light in them than usual. You seem stronger. I can't explain it."

"I don't know why, I got beat up before I came here," we scratch at our stomach. "But, you were trying to tell me something before?"

She hesitates but then she speaks slowly with emotion, almost confessing. "Before I started doing this, I felt like I was meant to do something. When I was young and finally beautiful I felt like I could change the world. That was when I was young and naive and before I was fully addicted."

"So, you answered your own question."

"A lot of help you are!" She looks annoyed.

"What are you saying to me?" We ask.

Shaya looks away and looks back again, her eyes moist.

"As beautiful as I am, I disgust myself. I hate what I have become.".

Why is she opening up to us? We should get away from her.

She must feel bad about herself. She must want to unload to someone.

Or she's trying to make us feel sorry for her so she can get something from us. So we let our guard down.

Doubt it.

We hold her.

"You are a beautiful woman, a talented woman who can do things I have never seen anyone else do."

Why the fuck are we saying this bullshit to her?

Stay out of this.

"You're just saying that because you like fucking me," she says, half sobbing.

We don't say anything because there is nothing to say. We cradle each other in our arms for a while, pretending that we love each other and finding cold comfort in that. After a while her sobbing calms and she talks, quietly and seriously.

"Viprex™ is the only thing that makes the hate go away for a little while. My people have a cure for Viprex™ but I don't want to stop." She pauses and then stares right into our eyes: "We don't want to stop."

We lower our eyes, stung. Embarrassed that she has the courage to admit what we can't out loud.

We don't know what to say so we settle for the truth. "You're asking just about the most fucked-up person you know for advice on a problem that he has too, will never solve and go to his grave with."

It's not a problem.

She looks ready to cry again, her defense

destroyed for a moment but then her eyes harden and she rolls over facing the other way. We do the only thing we can. We get out our autohypo and spray 0.25 mL on our neck.

"This one's on me." We say. She turns back around and presents her neck to us, a cold look in her eyes that looks right through us. We give her the same dose and she turns to us ready to complete the transaction with more sex.

As low as we are, after our verbal exchange, for once, we turn her down.

"I am going to go outside and get some air." We say to both our relief.

We grab our backpack and go down and outside passing by the semi-crowded bar full of naked people and clothed people all having a good time shouting in the chaos. A white-haired girl with all white eyes comes up to us and grabs our crotch. "You want to fuck?" she says.

"No thanks," we push her hand away and turn towards the exit.

"You homo!" she yells after us.

We push the door open to walk outside. It's like walking into a sauna, the streetlights are huge heat lamps beating down on us. It's about four in the morning and there is no breeze. A stink of garbage permeates the air as beeping automatons wheel it around the city. A few people are on the streets walking around but things have definitely slowed down since we came in.

The Viprex™ is making everything look wavy as if the air is refracted by intense heat. We probably will quit after this batch is finished. After so much of something, usually someone would get sick of it. We make a promise to ourself that we are going to sell most of this Viprex™ and pay for some training so that we can get a steady job and live a normal life, we were never meant for this. We can always get our appearance altered so that we will be hard to track. A new life could be waiting for us.

Why? We are content with our life.

We are?

We feel no pain.

Six goths pass us in the poorly lit broken street. A strange dark aura surrounds them. Maybe Shaya's Seer abilities rubbed off on us because we have never been able to sense auras before. Maybe it's just the Viprex. The goths are wearing black capes and they have slicked back hair. Goths alter their DNA to have white skin, black hair with widow's peaks, sharp teeth and altered digestion for synthblood. They are headed for the all day dance clubs where they can be in the dark before the sun rises. They eye me peculiarly and one gives me a menacing smile to show off her enlarged canines.

"Bite me," she grins. The others cackle evilly.

She is taking her role serious.

She smells diseased.

We ignore her and keep walking. Goths have been known to attack people and bleed them, especially loners that they lure using sex.

As we walk above the riverbank, we pass by some hard-looking beings and they eye us. Some are punks, some are mutants. Mixed crowds are dangerous because they are usually Viprex addicts. The only reason mutants and humans would hang out.

Keep walking.

We keep a bitter sneer on our face just to let these people know that if they fuck with us, it's at least not gonna be easy, but we don't challenge them with continuous eye contact. That would be stupid. Instead, we keep them in our peripheral vision.

We walk down to the river, the dark water emanating the smell of sewage. Seagulls are shitting on the piers and rats dodge between our feet. We sit down on the pier looking around and when it is clear we get the hypo out. This is probably one of the last times we will do Viprex™. We have made up our mind to sell most of what we stole. We know this guy Trevi who will buy it from us, no questions asked. We will hold back maybe a couple autohypos for personal use to wean ourselves off. Maybe Shaya will quit too and we can help each other stay straight.

Shaya is a mess.
She really wants to change.
Once a whore, always a whore.

That's not fair to her.

Too much drama.

She's never been so emotional before.

We've never spent this much time with her before.

She's never crossed us.

She will always put herself before us. We can never fully trust her.

Maybe so, but we could give her a chance.

That would be stupid.

We lay back on the pier and dose our neck again. The wood is uncomfortable on our back and head but we need to decompress. The sky has a greenish cast to it and the full moon looks brown. The pollution that there are now so many laws against has done its job on the earth's atmosphere. We find ourselves floating into the green clouds and up into space and the great chasm of the solar system. The planets are great spheres of gas and colored dust. The stars are jewels scintillating against the black. Nebulae cloud the view and we are floating in the vacuum with a feeling of unbalance. From our vantage out in space, we spy planet earth and telescope some action near the pier in the Pleasure Flat. Our view zooms to near our supine figure. The gang of punks and mutants we passed earlier approach another lone straggler upon the river bank. They don't see us lying in the shadows. They attack the straggler and knife him to death before our eyes before rifling through his pockets. The gang seeps back into the shadows, their victim bleeding and dead on the riverbank. Our consciousness hovers above him, his bland staring fish eyes meet our gaze and we shift our focus quickly, stung by the staring of the empty orbs. You should never look the dead in the eyes.

We return to our body and pick ourself up, wanting to escape the vicinity of the corpse's staring eyes and the gang. We go the opposite way that the murderers took. There is no moon in the dark of the early morning and you can't see the stars in the cloudy skies. You can almost never see the stars in the city.

We walk back to Meow's, the Viprex™ beginning to wear off. The bar is mostly empty and silent. The old bartender is watching the robots polish the bar and do their cleaning routine amid a couple of hanger-ons that can't stop drinking, drugging or are just passed out, cheek to the bar. He doesn't seem to notice us slip up the stairs to her room. We open the door. The room is dim with the curtains drawn. Shaya is laying on the bed sleepily mumbling regrets to her dreams. We take one more dose of Viprex and kick off our shoes before stowing our pack under the extra pillow and lay down beside her. The weight of our head guarding our stash, the dark takes us quickly.

Are you uncool? Do you feel that all your friends are better looking than you? Are you always the fifth wheel at the party?

Pro.Pharma has developed a product that will alleviate these symptoms of insecurity from you forever.

Cosmetic Recombinant Somaticon™

Are you the wrong gender?

Do you have bad skin?

Cosmetic Recombinant Somaticon™

Your face will become better looking.

Your pallor will improve from that pasty white or charcoal black to that of a bronze god or goddess.

Your muscle tone will improve.

You will become the most popular person in your crew.

(Results may vary)

Not only that but each Cosmetic Recombinant Somaticon™ treatment is tailor made to fit your unique karyotype.

You will get that beautiful skin you always wanted. That shimmering hair. That button nose. You will be the envy of all your friends.

There is a minimum of side effects and no risk associated with CRS.

Side effects can include nausea, diarrhea, headaches and double vision. Do not operate heavy machinery during treatment and stay away from all animals due to pheromone alteration. Please consult a doctor before taking this or any drug.

Cosmetic Recombinant Somaticon™

Let your outside match your inside.

Results may vary. Consult one of our doctors before using.

A loud banging on the door makes us sit bolt upright. Shaya sits up too and looks at the clock on the wall. It is morning. Gray daylight hangs outside the windows.

"Thought we got 12 hours?" we say, our mouth full of gravel. We rub our eyes and get the pack from under the pillow.

"Didn't trust me?" Shaya nods at the pack in our hands.

The knocking reverberates through the apartment again. Pushy. Insistent. We slide the Viprex™ back under the pillow.

Shaya jumps off the bed naked and gracefully slides over to the door to open it. Four helmeted and visored soldiers dressed in black military garb are standing there armed. The bartender from last night is behind them.

"That's him," he says in his scratchy voice.

"Wade, you asshole. We had a deal." Shaya's eyes are flashing.

"Clinic City Incorporated ™ Police. Put your hands on the wall where we can see them and spread your legs," says one of the men. We do as we are told.

"You too, bitch," they say to Shaya.

"She didn't do anything," we protest. Shaya puts her hands against the wall and does what they say.

"Shut up. Tell us where the Viprex™ is," says the cop behind me in an emotionless voice.

Don't say a word.

The agent behind us puts us in a choke hold.

"You thought you could just take what you took and get away with it?" He says in a menacing whisper in our ear. "Don't you know who I am? You don't know what I'm capable of?" He cinches his arms tighter, choking us. Consciousness begins to fade.

"It's right here on the bed, just let him go!" screams Shaya.

"OK." He throws us to the ground and we gasp for air. "You made me take a risk by coming here. Suffer for it." He kicks us in the face and they start kicking and stomping us. For the second time in 48 hours, we go black.

The armored doors of the Tesota™ Robotic Police Transport are opaque so we can't see out. Sourceless dim light radiates through the cabin. Our arms and legs are strapped down to one of the two stretchers and we are staring up into the robo-medic hanging from the ceiling, its many mechanical arms dangling like an angular octopus' bejeweled with different medical tools ready to inflict medical treatment after a short warning. Its sensors beep at us as it watches us out of dead camera lens eyes. "Engaging head restraints," it says in a robotic voice. A headlock flows up out of the stretcher to fully immobilize us.

Stay calm; we can get out of this.

Like before?

This is not like before. This is the law and they have us cornered with back up.

So we can't go into overdrive like before??

We will have to play their game, until we don't.

Our face and body raw and bruised, we can feel the RPT in motion. We know now that we are under corporate government control and hope that they are taking us to a regeneration unit to fix us up. After that, our guess is that we will be incarcerated until liquidation. They will probably charge us for murder of the dealers and possession of Viprex™. Payment will be our raw materials in lieu of insurance.

"Blood sample. Please hold still." Says the robo-medic in a dulcet yet metallic voice devoid of personality. We try to twist in the restraints to see the needle.

"I repeat, please hold still."

"I am, tin can!"

A skeletal metal arm containing an autoneedle lowers down towards us and punctures a vein in our neck with perfect precision. Viprex™ is dangerous not only for the user but addicts have been known to commit extremely violent acts rather than allowing themselves to be captured or killed. Thus the restraints. We begin to feel content to just lie under restraint. It must be the drug they gave us.

We can feel the RPT come to a stop. In the semi-darkness, a crease of light appears by the floor towards the feet end of the cabin and gradually grows until the robotic stretcher we are strapped to rolls down the ramp into the robotic emergency room. They park us in a small cell-like medical chamber with another robo medic in it.

We can hear someone grunting in pain through the curtains separating the chambers. It is a female voice. The beeping of the heart monitor sounds uneven.

"Please send a human medic, it's been hours!" The desperate voice says.

The disinfectant smell mingled with human smells combine to make us feel giddy and lightheaded. The woman's pleading continues between grunts and half screams.

After an hour, finally, a woman in white scrubs with an abundance of eyeshadow passes us without a glance.

"I'm Doctor Falia. How are you feeling, Ms. Barnes?"

"I'm in a lot of pain, I've been calling for a medic for hours. It hurts when I breathe in."

"I have to prioritize by insurance levels

and you are a low tier. Let me get right to the point. From your ultrasound we believe your spleen is ruptured.   We need you to make a decision quickly. There are a couple things you can do. One is a synthetic spleen printed by Johnston Corporation ™. I believe your insurance covers most of this procedure."

"I heard that Johnston products have a high failure rate," the woman sounds defeated.

"Well, The other possibility is a Microgene ™ targeted gene module. This would completely rebuild your spleen and is very quick and does not require surgery. However, your insurance company World Family Insurance™ doesn't cover this procedure and it is very expensive."

"How much is it,   Doctor?" She sounds very scared.

"130   million.   The   therapy   is   very expensive because of R and D."

"Praise lurkers, but I don't have that kind of money," the patient says under her breath.

Dr. Falia hesitates but only for a second. "Then it's settled, we will do the 3D option. A bot will be in shortly to prep you."

The mechanical noises and voices of the bot remove the grunting Ms. Barnes to a different location and we drift off for a while into immobilized sleep. The sound of our curtains being pushed aside wakes us and the open curtains frame a helmeted tall muscular figure who takes a step in. He is armed with a shockstick. Behind him steps another tall figure with a white doctor's coat. His good looks are young and old at the same time and he has an inquisitive tan face with a calculating stare framed by young black hair.

"Release head and arm restraints," says the doctor.

We sit up, face throbbing from our beating, rubbing our arms, our legs still bound.

"Quite a mess you have found yourself in. And quite a bad beating as well," says the doctor in a young-sounding voice.

We say nothing.

"I am Dr. Varius and I run the Regen unit in Clinic City ™. I must say I am quite interested in your case." His voice is steel. His age is somewhere between 40 and 200. He is good looking and that means he is rich. The rich are the best looking because they can afford the best looks.

Play Dumb.

"These mutants jumped me in the Meow and stole all my money. They beat up my date pretty bad also," we say.

"You don't say? Your date?" he says sarcastically.

"I'll patch up quick, Doc. I'll be out of your way in no time. Just fix me up and I'll pay you right after I get my next paycheck, as soon as I can get back to work."

"Hahaha, paycheck?" He laughs heartily

looking at the cop. The cop laughs too, but in a cold way. The doctor's voice hardens: "Our records indicate that you haven't been employed in years."

"My records?" we ask, incredibly surprised.

"Yes, in fact, *our* records indicate that you spent 3 years in the Prison Facilities Below Kansas City Inc." He frowns, disapprovingly. The visored officer's jaw chews air, like he wants to eat us for breakfast. The robo-medic beeps reproachfully.

"FBKC? Not me. Not me, you guys got the wrong guy."

"Actually your genetic fingerprint, though somewhat altered, confirms it. You are inmate number 02-273-197-22. You did time in FBKC for possession with intent to distribute for 10 mL of CCI Viprex Neurophasia ™, a felony. In fact your blood sample shows that you still use this drug and that it is currently in your bloodstream." He pauses surveying us with his eyes and lets out a breath in disgust.

"Yeah, I'm trying to quit doc. Really I am. I can control it doc. I really can. I just need the right treatment." A smile fleetingly is on the doctor's face before returning to expressionless.

"In fact your problems are much greater than this 197-22. You were in possession of over 30 grams of Viprex™ which is a felony."

Deny everything.

"It wasn't mine. I swear."

"Worse than that, a few days ago, a person very closely resembling you was on camera beating up some *citizens* the morning of the 25th. One of them ended up passing away." He chews on the words.

"Not me, doc!"

"I am not a cop. I leave that to Captain Mahan." He nods towards the stone-jawed Corporate Military™ officer. "I make no assumptions whether you are innocent or guilty. I am here simply to offer you a deal, a chance to be useful to society. You say you need treatment? We are here to give it to you. You have a choice: A full pardon for the felony and no pursuing of your other 'case' if you join our treatment research group or, you can stand trial. I imagine a convicted Viprex™ addict will face a harsh sentence and, after all, it is your second and possibly third offense." He gives us a very hard look.

We look towards the military cop or whatever he is, as if he can somehow help us. There is a grim half smile set in his hard jaw but the top half of his face is hidden by his metallic visor. "You're fucked," he smiles and slaps his holstered weapon with his palm and humps the air. We recognize his voice. He is the cop that put us in a choke hold at Shaya's. We know he likes to inflict pain so we nervously shift our gaze back to Varius.

"Not necessarily," says Doctor Varius. "We

are fair people and I am willing to give you this second chance and so is Captain Mahan and the Corporate Military™. The treatment program is only up to a year but it depends on your *full* cooperation. Any deviation from this major rule will land you back at FBKC."

We tremble slightly.

Let's get a hold of ourself.

"The program involves substitution of other drugs geared to replace Viprex™ and relieve you of any withdrawal symptoms. There are also rigorous psychological and emotional evaluations and consultations. This is to reacquaint yourself with, well, yourself, if that is someone you really want to know."

Take the deal.

"That sounds like a great deal, doc. I really want to kick the habit."

Smile.

We smile. Mahan chimes in, his chin rock hard. "If you successfully graduate the treatment you will be introduced to the general population with a servo-implant that we can monitor you with for as long as we see fit. You stay alive in gen pop for a year and we will release you and erase *all* records, for good."

"Yes sir sounds good to me. Anything to stop doing this shit to myself," we say mindlessly. "I just can't live my life like this anymore."

They don't buy it.

It is too good to be true.

They are letting us off scot-free. No prison, and drugs.

We think about it for a second and we know somehow, we are screwed.

"Its agreed then, we will start right away," Varius smiles at us. It was the smile of the devil.

Evaluation

Their research starts immediately by a bunch of flat-faced fleshbots shaving our head, hosing us down and throwing us into the "Allele Sequencing Chamber" for a complete genetic scan under full physical restraints. We are told, "that some mutations in your chromosomes have developed new phenotypes in your brain" and that to monitor the effects of the corrective drugs they are giving us we will have to be scanned twice a day to be sure "that the expressions of your genes are not belying the facts of what is really happening in your body and mind."   A team of doctors and scientists supervise our treatment. It's a lot of attention for one drug addict.

In our cell the robo-medic is in charge of administering our injections. The cell is all white with no way to see out. There is a burning electric smell of over used circuitry.

"Please lie down on the stretcher 197-22," says the medic in its expressionless voice, saying the numbers separately. In our orange hospital smock, we obey and lie down on the firm white cot, feeling exposed and vulnerable. An androgynous fleshbot, dressed in scrubs, appears from nowhere checking the plasmetal arm and leg cuffs that seem to grow out of the table.

"Relax"

"Engaging arm and leg restraints." The soulless nurse's empty eyes survey our limbs, its cold hands checking that the restraints don't accidentally crush our limbs.

"Engaging head restraints." It says as it attaches a wire skull cap to our head.

"Please try to relax 197-22."

The arm with the autohypo descends down towards the side of our neck and injects their new drug near the brainstem with the bioprogram nurse hovering next to us with a false expression of concern on its face. Nothing happens at first. As we lie there a feeling begins to wash over us. Rather an absence of feeling. Emotionlessness

These treatments continue for a few days without us seeing anybody else. From our supine position, we focus on the metallic arms of the robomedic and artificial fleshbot above us and eventually the room around us disappears. Soon the robomedic disappears along with any want or craving for any need, emotion or feeling. For anything, including Viprex™. Eventually, the room and the bioprogram robot come back, but not our cravings.

After a few days the Clinic City Incorporated™ virtual psychological analysis begins supervised by Doctor Rawson. Short haired, and dark tan, he looks about 28 years old but carries himself as someone who is older. He has modeled himself after a famous actor that I recognize from holomovies but can't remember the name of. Strange that an older, successful professional would want to look like someone else but that is what many people do now. They pay for a "look."

The session usually starts about an hour after my morning injection and scanning while I am still in restraints. After a few times we begin to think that he has some sort of script he follows day after day. Maybe he always wanted to be an actor so he has a script. Or maybe he has no imagination. We wonder if he has a script in life also. Does he go home to his partner and say the same thing to him or her everyday, then to his kids? When the Clinic City™ mail-bioprogram comes, does he have a standard line for it also? He must fancy himself a character in a holomovie. To us he is the main character in our holomovie as we only see him virtually. For us, he is playing a doctor.

> Doctor: How do you feel today?
> Patient: No craving today.
> Doctor: How about before the treatment?

Patient: A little sick, but I think I've made a lot of progress already.

Doctor: (Laughing heartily) You've only been here for a few weeks.

He varies his fake script.

Patient: (Obviously lying) Yeah and I already feel like I don't need Viprex™ anymore.

Doctor: I don't believe you, 197-22. Recovery is not that easy. Besides, your scan still shows that you have mutations expressing themselves in your brain and body.

Patient (Beaming) That's so strange because I feel normal now. Like I am cured!

Doctor: (looking annoyed) Do you have any urges?

I have the urge to slap your face.

Patient: I guess I have a little still. Though much less than before.

We half tell the truth.

Patient: After the treatment I feel much better.

Doctor: After the treatment you seem less excitable, more willing to cooperate. Why do you think that is?

Patient: I don't know, Doctor. You guys know what's best for me. After treatment what you guys tell me to do always ends up making a lot of sense.

Doctor: We know best what's best for you.

Sounds like he is convincing himself.

Patient: (after a pause) Why is that Doctor?

Why does everything you guys say make more sense to me after treatment?

Doctor: (awkwardly) Do you feel different lately?

Patient: What do you mean?

Doctor: Compared to when you first came here do you feel stronger? More virile?

Patient: Virile, what does that mean? I guess I feel stronger.

Doctor: That's kind of what it means, but it also has to do with sex drive.

Patient: I guess, but there is no one in here to have sex with. Can you tell me what happened to my friend when I got arrested?

Doctor: You could go virtual. It is no shame to have sex in virtual or even to take care of other baser needs.

Patient: Like what, doc.

Doctor: If you feel the need to kill in virtual, it is better than doing violence in the real world.

Patient: I'm good. With killing and sex in virtual.

Doctor: So you will kill in real life. You will have sex with a prostitute but not in virtual?

Patient: I don't know. Not here where I know you are monitoring me.

Doctor: Virtual living is perfectly good for everybody else in the world but not for you?

Patient: It's not real.

Doctor: Neither is a prostitute's love. But

you can get a real job in virtual. You can earn real money. You can even have a virtual girlfriend or boyfriend. These are normal things. You don't want them?

Patient: I would rather live in the real world?

Doctor: By doing drugs?

Patient: Virtual never seems real.

Doctor: (showing concern) Is there something telling you not to be virtual?

Be careful

Patient (pause) There used to be but now I think maybe I should go into virtual more. That's strange. How can I schedule a session?

Doctor: We can plug you in.

Patient: Cool. It suddenly makes so much sense. Why does everything you guys say make so much sense to me after my treatments?

Doctor: That is a question for Doctor Varius.

Audition failed

After a few weeks of plugging us into virtual we still are not sold. The drug they are giving us seems to be working against all addictions, including the one we have seen develop in frequent users of virtual. So their own drug is working against them trying to domesticate us.

The darkness on our stomach, though still itchy, has almost totally faded away, along with our craving for Viprex™. Now we only see the doctors and the techs when we are on the security wing of the Regeneration unit at the southern end of Clinic City™ sub basement 317, sector 6C. In transit between units, our arms are bound with plascuffs and a bioprogram walks behind us, our footsteps echoing over the white tile floors. Occasionally, in these pristine metallic halls we see another patient with a shaven head in pale blue pajamas also led by a bioprogram.

"Hey man, what's up?" we say. We look into his eyes and they stare through us and past us.

That is what's in store for us.

An emptiness looks back at us, an emotional vacuum, his reddened and lumpy skin showing signs of irritation. His bioprogram handler has more personality.

We shiver. As far gone as we are, we still feel like we have some sort of a bitter shell of personality that we want to keep. The only time seeing one of the mindless addicts doesn't really bother us is right after a treatment, then they are much less of a concern and we just do as we are told.

After a few more weeks of treatment in the nondescript white rooms and corridors, we care less and less about the other patients and come to just care about our injections.

We need to get out of here.

Where have you been? I haven't heard from you in a while.

They are suppressing our mutualism.

Is that what you call it?

We have always helped each other.

Have we?

We have.

What about lately?

We will be here when you need us. They can't suppress us all the time.

One morning the robomedic engages our body restraints but withholds our shot. We begin to feel sick and sweat starts to pour out of us. The robo's whirring and beeping continues for an hour, running scans and observing our behavior along with the almost featureless automaton that passes for a nurse. We start to shake uncontrollably and voices echo inside our head. Sweat starts to pour off of our body.

"I need some help in here!" we yell.

The only answer is the whirrs, clicks and beeps above.

"Come on, I need something," our voice shakes. *"I'm fucking sick!"* we shout.

We turn our head and vomit on the floor. The bile burns our throat and we begin to dry heave.

"Please calm down, 197-22. Please try to relax," says the bioprogram.

"How the fuck can I calm down. I can't even keep fucking food in me. I swear I am dying and

you're just watching, you fuckers! Fuck you!"

We start banging our head against the stretcher.

"Calm down, 197-22. Engaging head restraints." The bioprogram firmly guides the restraints to our head along with the skull cap.

We wish we could vomit and choke on it but there is nothing left in our gut. The autohypo and the silver arm descend like a gift from some sort of many-armed metallic god finally bestowing mercy upon our soul. The autohypo sprays its gift upon our neck and the robomedic withdraws its arm as the bioprogram nurse watches silently from our right. We wait for the absence of all feeling to hit us. However, though we feel better, eventually we realize that this isn't like the other drug they have been giving us. The door slides up and Varius walks in, his white coat blending into the white walls behind him so that he looks like a floating head.

"Doc, why don't I get my regular treatment today? I don't feel so good."

"We need to deprive you of treatment once in a while and study your responses to see how you are progressing. The drug we gave you is a sedative. It will calm your nerves."

"What's the shit you usually give me, Doc? That stuff is way better. I feel really sick and this fucking bioprogram robot tandem is useless."

He laughs. "The drug is like Viprex™ but in reverse. It changes the mutations that you have developed in your hypothalamus. We know that Viprex™ causes a form of split personality or dissociation. This drug relieves these symptoms and gives the subject more of an even keel."

"One of the effects of Viprex™ is that it changes your genes. It makes part of your brain develop new neurons and this physical change manifests itself with a symbiotic consciousness that shares your psyche. This consciousness is almost parasitic to your mind. This can be dangerous because it succeeds in controlling your thought processes to perpetuate its consciousness. And, of course, your addiction," says the handsome know-it-all, pompously.

"Our drug also mutates your DNA like Viprex™. Again, this mutation is expressed especially in the hypothalamus and blocks the synapses to the neurons created by Viprex™. We take away the sway Viprex™ has on you and you get a fresh start. This is why you are so cooperative with us after treatment," he says.

What is he saying?

We begin to understand. We need more treatment so we can figure out what they are trying to do. Plus, don't you want to feel better?

"Doctor, I really need more treatment. *Now.* I don't feel good at all. I need something to help....Please, Doc, You gotta help me. I just vomited, Doc. I feel like hell. Shit. Yeah, I feel like shit."

"Calm down, 971-22. We will put you

back on treatment shortly. Try to get a grip on yourself! We have to finish scanning you first to see the effects of deprivation after that you will be treated."

"How much longer is that? How long?" we scream.

Varius looks at us with disgust. He speaks in a harsh tone. "You aren't in any position to ask questions 122. You are an addict, a waste. You can serve humanity by being an experiment to help us cure a disease. You are nothing more than a lab rat. A bioprogram."

His words might upset us if we didn't feel so sick. "OK Doc, can we just have some drug?"

He takes a step closer, his demeanor seething with hate. It is the first emotion we have ever seen him display. "You are nothing. You are just a petri dish for my experiments. You exist to serve humanity now. If you die, there are many more to take your place, so shut up and stop making a racket and maybe I will make sure you don't die from withdrawal."

We look away and shut up like he says.

Regeneration

After many weeks, they say we are recovered. They implant a tracking system along with a timed-release system for the drug that counteracts the effects of Viprex™. We feel better now. We are normal and more on an even keel, but there is still a we, which we keep from our doctors. They say we are cured but still need to be observed, though with more freedom. They exchange our blue pajamas for two orange jumpsuits with 02-273-197-22 printed on the breast pocket.

A large sentry bioprogram with big muscles marches us to the Regeneration building marked "General Population," a large box-like structure with few windows high up on the walls in a large high ceilinged lime green room with 50 bunk beds in it and a few people hanging about, some plugged in to virtual at their bunks. It smells like disinfectant and a chubby young woman with blonde hair and dark skin is mopping the floor slowly, also in an orange jumpsuit but with a button down shirt over top. She nods at us as we enter. We nod back. She ignores the bioprogram.

"Please come this way 197-22. Your bunk number and lock number is 37B," says the biobot emotionlessly.

We follow. The biobot shows us to our locker and enables the retinal scan for our eyes. We put our clothes and toiletries in the locker and shut it. It locks automatically and it shows us to our bed and leaves us. We sit down and it creaks loudly.

A thin waisted v-shaped young man in denim street clothes looks up at the noise. His blue eyes seem cold, but he smiles at us under closely cropped light brown hair.

"They got you too, huh." he says familiarly in a slightly gravelly voice.

"Yeah."

"You cured now?"

"Yeah."

"Me too. I used to be on the streets, looking for violence," he almost sings the word violence in his gruff tone.

"Yeah?"

"Is that all you say? Yeah?"

"What are they gonna do to us now?" we ask.

"Do? Nothing. You hit the jackpot. Free living. Free drugs."

"Bullshit."

"No, it's true. You made it. That's more than I can say for those fuckers that are still in there with their fucking heads cut open."

"Yeah what happened to them. I thought that was gonna be me."

"Some people don't take to the new drugs well. Now they on cuckoo pill!" He says gleefully, his eyes shining.

He looks us up and down.

"You're kind of small. You any good in a fight?"

"I'm OK."

"Oh, you modest too," he laughs.

"Been around."

"Me too, me too…" He goes on. "They let us work out here. There are weights since they won't augment our DNA except in the ways they want to. I am working on that though."

"How so?"

He smiles, eyes gleaming. "I work the angles here. I can get things if you need them. I can trade you for your things once they give you a job."

He lifts up his feet and has brand new synthleather work boots. "These are Cats™ baby." He smiles proudly. "I can get you some."

"How come they don't make bioprograms do everything."

"They're teaching us responsibility. Don't worry, they have a job lined up for you. That's why they had you do tests and shit. What was your score?"

"Physical 81, cognitive 97."

"97? You smart. You're gonna get a job in

the labs if you're lucky. That's for smart people, brainiac."

He reads the number printed on our breast pocket.

"02-273-197-22, huh. That ain't gonna work. How's 22 for the 22 at the end?" he laughs. "That's a lucky number."

"How come you got street clothes?" We nod at his trim dark synthdenim jacket and pants.

"Cause I know what's gonna happen before it happens. I know when they're gonna do an inspection. I know when the good stuff is coming through. I know everything, I'm the Prophet. You need anything you can talk to me. I know everyone and I can get anything." He stands up, smiling, a little taller than us. "I'll get you out of that orange suit. Get some rest. They gonna put you to work tomorrow, 22."

On his way out he stops and talks to the girl mopping and we lay down, the cot/bunk creaking. Exhausted from our transition we fall asleep.

We are woken up by something grabbing the front of our jumpsuit. We open our eyes and huge hands clutch our orange clothing. Above the hands is a large feminine round face with dull brown eyes.

"What the fuck are you doing in my bunk?" says her deep voice.

We try to grab our assailant's hands and

twist them off but she is too strong.

"Ha ha ha. Mutant fucker." She booms as she grabs us out of the bunk and slams us to the ground. "Get. Out." The large woman booms. As if not worried about us at all , she turns her back and starts straightening up the bunk.

We stand back up and look around. The room is full of people who stirred from virtual or sleep because of the ruckus and every pair of eyes is looking to see what we will do next. We charge the giant and she spins with abnormal speed so we plant a kick in her stomach. She is waiting for us and claps a huge hand to our head. We fall to the ground again but we pop right back up and try to kick her again.

Again she claps an enormous paw to the side of our head and we are floored again.

"Stay down!" she booms.

We get to our knees and push ourselves up, feeling unsteady. She clenches her huge fists.

"Whoa, whoa. We can settle this." The Prophet seems to come out of nowhere and gets between us.

"Puffy here is too big to go on the top bunk."

"That's right," says Puffy. "You go on the top, little man," she says mockingly. Everyone laughs.

"Puffy, this is 22. 22, Puffy. Why don't you go on the top, 22. We'll make it up to you later."

The Prophet looks at us as if to say this

is the best you're gonna get. People start talking to each other and looking away. They know the show is over and we know we will just get beat even more badly if we fight the giant Puffy who is looking at us like she wants to twist our head off our body. Most of them just lay down and turn their VR back on.

"Respect, 22," says Puffy. We get the feeling that Puffy's respect is a one way street. Our head aches and we see a floater in our vision as we climb the ladder and pass out.

The Labs

The next day we wake early with a slight headache and see a package of blue synth denim clothes at the foot of our bunk. We slink out of the bunk while most people are still asleep including our new friends, hit the showers and put the denims on. We look in the steamy mirror and for the first time in a while we look clean and even kind of cool in the sleek blue denim. At the exit we are given our job assignment by the surly human guard for our building. He tells us we have been assigned to the gene sequencing and editing lab and to report there immediately. He says nothing about our lack of uniform.

The lab is located in a sub basement in Clinic Building G. The techs tell us to put on a white lab coat and invite us into the small austere lab. They show us how to edit and amplify DNA that will be used to inject into cells as medicines and/or modifications. The techs are not very friendly and they don't tell us what the edits will do, they just give us the instructions and tell us to do it.

"Can't bots do this?"

"They are too stupid," growls a grouchy black haired androgynous tech.

The other techs leave us alone to do our work and it is very quiet in the basement lab. Eerily so. For some reason we easily learn the protocols from the instruction screens and easily memorize the steps to make the medications we are charged with.

That is because we are helping us.

You're still here?

Never left. How do you think we got a 97 on cognitive?

I'm smart.

We are smarter together.

Guess we need each other.

We could make our own Viprex™.

Thought we were cured.

Remember how good it felt.

But we could get sent back to prison.

We will bide our time.

We go back to work,finish the day,are dismissed and go back to the dorm room. A large crowd of prisoners/patients are in a circle shouting and stomping. We join a few other people standing on a table to see what's going on as we can't see over the crowd. The crowd is in a big circle in the open part of the room. Inside the circle is Puffy and a smaller but more muscular female squaring up. The Prophet is on the sidelines and appears to be taking bets.

"Time for violence!" yells the Prophet gleefully in his gruff voice. "The bets are in."

"Fuck her up! Fuck her up!" The crowd yells rhythmically. We are not sure who they are talking about, Puffy or her adversary. The muscular female spins a heel kick to Puffy's head and Puffy, hands down, takes the kick and surges her oversized bulk forwards.

Muscles moves laterally, closes distance and lands a hook on the side of Puffy's head, then a right cross. This goes on for a while between the bull and the matador until eventually Puffy gets a hold of Muscles and falls on her, immobilizing and smashing her over and over again with elbows until she is pulled off her unconscious victim.

"Stay down!" she booms. This must be her catchphrase.

"Show's over! Puffy is still undefeated!" Barks the Prophet. "Same time next week."

The Prophet gives Puffy some money and then spots us and makes his way over to us smiling.

"22, how did the labs go?

"How did you know I got a job at the labs?"

"I know everything that goes on here. Plus I pulled some strings for you." He gestures at the clothes. "Got those for you too."

We don't say thanks because we know that we are going to have to pay for these "gifts." later on. Prophet smiles.

"Well don't get all sentimental on me. Let me know if you need anything."

Over the next few weeks, when we are not working, we watch the way our wing of the general population of the Regeneration clinic works. There is a pecking order and Prophet is at the top. He knows everyone and has a piece of everything in our wing. We watch as he gets the best food, clothes, women and even drugs. One day we watch and see he gets an autohypo from one of the other lab workers and pockets it. He looks around and sees we are watching and he smiles his wry smile and walks over to us.

"You want some of this?" he asks us.

"What is it?"

"You know what it is. *Real Viprex™.*"

"In the clinic? What if you get caught?"

"We can control that."

This is worth the risk

"How do you manage that?" we ask.

"Well well well, I finally found something you're interested in." The Prophet smiles mockingly. "But you gotta do something for me."

"What's that?"

"You gotta start making Viprex™ for me in the lab with my recipe when the other techs leave you alone."

"I don't know how."

"I'll take care of that."

He hands us an autohypo. We don't take it.

"Come on. Just take it. Not only is it Viprex™ but it is a bioprogram to put the recipe in your brain. Look at the engravings. You know those can't be faked."

He's right. Those machines won't dispense anything but Viprex™ bioprograms.

The Prophet smiles again. His blue eyes flash. "Come on 22. I'll take it with you and share my pass with you, no strings attached. You only have to make Viprex™ when you want to."

We take it. A pass around the Regen unit was worth it. He grabs two of his buddies, a surly femme named Skram and a tall guy named Jimmers. We all take the drug. It's been a while since we took it and the elation hits us hard and fast. The Prophet has a big smile on his face. "Let's go look around."

We explore the Regen unit and go to areas that used to be off limits. We go through access tunnels, alleys and other passages we have never seen before. We walk towards the edge of the hospital and we get to the bottom of the steep hills. The Prophet wants to climb one of the staircases but on the outside of the cracked up concrete. "Come on, bitches. When was the last time you had any fun."

The Prophet grabs a handhold and begins the climb. We all follow and it's pretty easy as there are service ladders most of the way up except at the top. The Prophet sees a way to get hand and foot holds in the crumbling concrete and pulls himself all the way up. Skram and Jimmers climb up and we hesitate, fearful of the rough looking wall. "Come on, I'll help you," encourages the Prophet.

Yes, climb. This is a way to more Viprex™. The recipe for Viprex™.

We climb and almost lose our footing but the Prophet reaches down and grabs our wrist with two hands. We grab his and he hauls us up.

"See, I got you." We push up to our feet and turn around.

"Check it out, only rich people get this view." Sprawled out below us is Clinic City, the buildings are lit up in the dimming light, mostly set in level terrain. Holocommercials are projected everywhere. At the river we can see the bright lights of the Pleasure Flats. Farther south we see the smoking fires of the mounds by the industrial district. Past that are the city walls. Northwest of the city, the sun sets over the lake, silhouetting the giant windmills towering over the red and pink gossamer waves.

"See, 22? How many people get to see the city like this? Only them." He gestures above and behind us at the mansions that sit on the crest of the hill. "People like us aren't supposed to be up here. But we can go where we please and do what we please." He smiles and everyone hits each others' fists, smiling and laughing.

He gets out the autohypo again and we take more. The scene becomes pixelated and we can swear we can see every single infinite dot of information individually. "You see that?" We say to the Prophet pointing out the setting sun's last edge turning green in the pixelated dusk.

"I've never seen anything like that before." He responds. All four of us are silenced by the beauty of the scene. We absentmindedly scratch the faint lingering darkness on our stomach.

We sit there transfixed by the scene, staring, almost in a trance.

The Prophet waves at the city. "Most people plugged into virtual right now. They wouldn't see this with their own eyes," says the Prophet.

"I don't usually plug in unless my doctors start telling me I have to."

The Prophet looks at us with his cool eyes. "Me neither. They gonna feed you lies in virtual." Jimmers and Skram agree. Prophet continues. "See there's us and there's them. They will go into virtual, live their fake lives and try to make it all perfect. But we are raw, we live real lives in the real world. We don't need that bullshit.

"But how do you get out of it, I mean with the doctors?" we ask.

"There's always a price, a way to pay someone and the doctors have their price too. They're just different for someone like me or you." He hands us the autohypo again set for 0.2 and we take it as do the others. All four of us stare at the stippled clouds in the sky forming shapes of Lurkers and mutants ebbing and flowing in an atmospheric battle in the moonlight.

After a while we break the silence: "Why do they call you Prophet?"

He smiles wryly. "Cause I know everything and everybody. I can tell what's gonna happen before it happens."

"Yeah right." we laugh.

"Aint it true?" The Prophet looks at his friends, his eyes shining.

Skram nods and Jimmers says, "Yeah, I seen it."

"I've got the second site. Like a mutant!" He sings the last 3 words.

"OK," we say sarcastically.

"It's true." He stares at us for a moment.

Ask him about the Viprex™.

"How do you get away with it? Dealing Viprex™ in a Regen facility."

The Prophet lets out a huge laugh as do his buddies.

"22, I thought you were smart," mocks Skram, her short green hair framing her disbelief.

"What the fuck's that sposed to mean?" We sneer.

"Nothing." The Prophet interrupts, giving Skram a look. "Everybody knows here that this facility isn't really to take care of people. This is an experimental facility. For some reason, they let you go to gen pop, but not before they did something to you in eval or treatment."

"Like what?"

"Don't know. Sometimes people get fucked up. The mental shits usually are kept back in the Regen unit where you started. They never will get out except to liquidation. We have a chance, people get let out. But I don't know what they did to you."

"I thought you were the Prophet."

"I got a few blind spots. Not many though," he smiles wryly. "Science is one of them."

"What they do to you guys?"

"Let us have some secrets," smiles Skram.

"I wonder what they did to me," we say.

Prophet looks at us for a few seconds. "Maybe we can find out, but it would cost a lot of something. Drugs, money. Your ass." They all laugh.

"How long have you guys been here?"

"3 years," growls Jimmers.

"2," Says Skram.

We look at the Prophet, he hesitates.

"How long?"

"Lucky 7, baby. I been here seven years. Long enough to run this bitch."

Everyone laughs. We feel good. Besides prostitutes, it is the first social interaction that we have had in years.

"So what do you think, 22? You in? We will give you a cut and you don't have to deal with customers, only production."

This is too good to pass up.

"I'm in." We say. They pat us on the back and we all bang fists again.

"You won't regret it." The Prophet says.

We look over the lights awakening in the darkening city, the cool air blows through us. After years of being alone, we might actually belong somewhere and it might be here with the Prophet and his people.

The lab is like a ghost town today and with our Viprex™ instructional bioprogram downloaded into our neural circuitry, we now have the knowledge not only to make Viprex™, but also how to use all of the equipment. It is easy to reprogram the sequencers and we know how everything works. It is the first time we have ever had expensive biotech inputted into us and it gives us a sense of purpose. After we get used to the rhythms and comings and goings of the lab workers, we know when we will have a free block of time to work. We hide the vials in our uniform and sneak them to our barracks where we give them to the Prophet.

It is clear that we have attained a status that we didn't have before, especially after being downgraded when we fought with Puffy. Puffy still eyes us with surly indignation but leaves us alone, a line drawn that she will not cross, at least while we are under protection of the Prophet's clique.

The clique is large, and we realize that it must go outside of the barracks, outside of the clinic as we are making thousands of doses of Viprex™.

All the more for us to skim.

The Prophet has a group of hangers on: Maniac, his muscle; Don, his shaven-headed-fast-talking gopher; and Burn, his hot-headed unguided missile, who would often get in fights for fun only to be put in solitary and then released quickly after a Prophet bribe. Though mostly male types, he also has Skram to do reconnaissance and many femmes in the coed dorm seem to vie for Prophet's attention. He and Jimmers seem very popular with the females in the dorm. We aren't sure of Jimmer's role but we think he is an old friend that Prophet keeps around because he is funny and they have a lot of inside jokes together.

This group lets us in and we feel like we belong to something for the first time. Viprex™ is readily available so there is no problem between us fighting for supply. We become good at programming the sequencers and quickly become the top producer. One day coming back to the dorm Burn is standing outside talking to

Don.

"There's a new arrival inside," squeaks a bald pasty Don, his eyebrows arching, "and she's pretty hot. Prophet's talking her up now."

He and Burn laugh.

"I wonder what else is gonna happen," smiles Burn. "If he doesn't want her, I'll take some of that." They laugh.

We walk into the dorm and see the Prophet in the common area talking to a girl with dirty blonde hair and a lithe muscular frame under her orange jumpsuit. The Prophet motions us over and she turns. It is Shaya. Recognition flickers across her face and then goes cold.

"22, meet Shaya," says Prophet.

"Nice to meet you," We say, playing it off.

"Good to meet you, 22," she smiles a toothy smile, her blue brown eyes shining.

"Did you come from Regen?"

"Yeah, I was in there for a while. You too?"

"Yeah, but I've been out for a while now." We smile back.

Prophet, ever shrewd, notices our smiles.

"Well, well, well, I've got important people to talk to. Why don't you show Shaya around and I'll talk to you later." He winks unsubtly.

"Sound's good," we say. "Follow me."

We lead Shaya out of the barracks and we can see the effect she has on people. They are all staring at her as the newest good-looking femme here. She even wears the orange jumpsuit of gen pop well.

We take her towards the mess hall. "You look good, how you been?"

She smiles at us. "Thanks, 22." She says "22" sarcastically in her quiet way and then laughs a little louder. "That's a funny name."

"Prophet came up with it."

"What's his deal?"

"He's been here a while."

"That's it? That's all you're gonna give me?"

"He runs this place."

"That's what he told me before you walked in. So he isn't full of shit. Do you work for him?"

"With him."

"OK. Is that why you don't wear orange?"

"Yeah." We walk by the mess hall. "So what happened to you? You look really healthy. Are you clean now?"

She smiles again. "I've been clean for a few months. They arrested me when they took you and gave me a choice-prison or Regen."

"Sounds familiar. They let a hybrid into Regen?"

"They need bodies here for their experiments. They didn't ask me if I minded." She says sarcastically. "What about you?"

"What up, 22?" some of Prophet's crew outside the mess hall approach us. We introduce them to Shaya. They hit on her and she smiles but otherwise ignores them.

"Wanna get out of here?" we ask.

"Yeah."

With a pass the Prophet gave us, we take her to the staircase that Prophet showed us when we first arrived.

"Can you climb?"

"Hell yeah," she smiles and jumps up and grabs a ledge one handed. She pulls herself up easily.

She follows us to the top and it seems that at any time she could overtake us, but she doesn't.

When we get to the top, the sun has already gone down. A crescent moon follows it, earthshine on the dark part of its face.

"You seem different," we say and she looks at us strangely. "I mean in a good way."

"Quit while you're ahead, dummy.You too though, you seem like they giving you respect." She gestures at our clothes.

"I work in the labs, most people don't get that job."

"Big shot," she grins.

We don't mention that the Prophet probably set it up. A cool wind picks up and she moves closer to us.

"So, 22," she teases us, her blue eyes clear and bright. "Did you miss me?"

We kiss her and she kisses us back. Her eyes focused on us, she lets her jumpsuit fall off revealing her perfectly proportioned body. We have sex under the darkening sky, the lights and holograms of the city swirling below.

When we are finished,we put our clothes on and climb back down. We take her to the barracks and her bunk is across the room from ours.

"Thanks for showing me around," she says sultrily.

From then on we spend a lot of time together. When not working our job, we take meals with her and walk around the Regen unit with her. Everyone can see we are together and some people give me dirty looks, though some congratulatorilly clap my back when I pass by.

One evening she spots us handing off Viprex™ to the Prophet.

"What's that? Viprex™?" Her eyes change, becoming almost predatory.

"Yeah. That's what I do in the lab. I make it."

"Do you still take it? I thought you cleaned up in Regen."

"I did but once I got access to it, I figured why not?"

"Can I get some?" Her eyes greedy.

"I thought you cleaned up in Regen."

"I did, but why not?"

Though we think better of it we give her an autohypo. "Yeah, sure."

We take some together and go find a place

to be alone. She is very affected by the Viprex™, and is sexually aggressive with us, which we like.

The next day we are in the front of the line in the cafeteria where other patients are serving us breakfast and Puffy cuts in front of us. "Get out of my way, I eat now." She uses her bulk to bounce us aside.

Everyone in the line including Shaya is watching us to see how we will react. We try to push in front of Puffy and Puffy swings at us, we duck underneath.

"Big dog eats first!" Puffy yells smashing the lunch counter. She grabs us with an enormous paw and flings us aside.

Shaya springs into action. With unnatural speed and power she spin sweeps Puffy's legs. While Puffy tumbles down to the ground, she is already in the air, bouncing her feet between Puffy's head and solar plexus till Puffy is out.

We turn towards her. "Thanks but I had that under control."

She smiles. "I know," she lies. "But I don't like this bitch, and I didn't want her fat ass eating all the food," she says more loudly than I have ever heard her speak, looking over the line behind us. Many people laugh, but some look suspicious. They begin to think that though she looks normal, Shaya may be mutant or military. Either way, we have both just lost trust with the others.

Later, when we come out of the basement

lab after our shift, Prophet is waiting with one of his quieter, muscular enforcers, Malaki.

"Well, well, well. I heard what happened today," says Prophet grimly. "Not that it's bad to be protected by a female."

He pauses. Malaki looks away for a second and then looks back at us coldly.

"Listen, I got no problem with mutants- I mean hybrids. But, some people here do."

"What are you saying?" We scowl.

"Like I said, *I* got no problem. But if Shaya goes around showing what she can do, people are gonna get pissed."

"Most of us didn't come from money. Except for Puffy and a few augments like Malaki here, we can't afford to have fancy genes. Puffy is so big only because her dad was a pro wrestler who paid to have a big kid but couldn't afford the bribe for a son." He laughs sarcastically. "So he took a chance and lost the coin flip!"

"Get to the point, Prophet."

Not used to being on the defense, the Prophet looks annoyed and starts getting irate. "I am doing damage control. I am mediating, something I hate doing. But because I like you guys," he says in a way that doesn't seem too affectionate, "I am trying to regulate the situation. Oh, she is probably just a good fighter. Oh, maybe her parents had money for athletic enhancements...but you gotta control your woman, I know the mutants, I mean hybrids are kind of wild."

"Like animals," Malaki adds, staring at us in the eyes.

"Shut up, Malaki," The Prophet grins, then to us. "But for both your sakes, you got to talk to her."

"Well she aint a hybrid. But even if she was, plenty of rich people do the same type of augmentation and everyone is cool with them. Shaya is just as human as you or me, and I will always have her back."

"I can see why," Malaki, nodding up and down and pursing his lips in a big kiss. "She don't look like a mutant."

"Stay away from her," we stare at Malaki and he stares back.

"Just playing." Malaki holds our gaze.

"I will talk to her and tell her to keep cool," we say to the Prophet.

"I already talked to Puffy and told her to stop trying to go out of her way to fuck with you. For some reason, she hates you, but I fixed it. Because I am your friend, man." The Prophet looks at us, his blue eyes clear and focused on ours. He claps our shoulder. "Take care of this, and we can all keep making money."

We go back to the barracks and go over to Shaya's bunk. She is laying down transfixed by a holoscreen she is holding.

"Hey Shaya."

"Hey babe." She doesn't look up.

"I gotta talk to you."

"What's up?" She flicks through the holograms.

"People are talking about us. About you."

"Oh yeah? What are they saying?" Still not looking up.

"They think you're a muta- I mean a hybrid.

She finally looks up. "Fuck them. I don't give a fuck, what they think." She says a little too loudly. "And if anyone has a problem with it, they can come get some."

"Quiet down," We whisper. "They'll kill you in your sleep."

"Let them fucking try." Her eyes are hard but she is quieter, speaking in her normal voice. "Give me some Viprex™."

We hand her a transdermal and she sprays it on her neck. In a few moments elation fills her eyes and she looks at us almost giddy, almost blind, her eyes disturbingly blank.

Before work the next day we leave her another dose. When we come back she isn't in her bunk.We take a nap. Later, we wake up and most people are in their bunks looking at holograms, but Shaya's bunk is still empty so we go to look for her. We don't find her on the grounds and when we get back, she still isn't in her bunk so we take a walk outside and we see her walking towards the dorms.

"Hey babe," she stumbles towards us, her shirt inside out and the hems showing.

Jealousy hits us like a brick and then anger.

"What the fuck? Why is your shirt inside out?"

She looks down and laughs, "Oh, shit. I must have put it on inside out this morning," she says, swaying almost drunkenly.

"Bullshit. Are you fucking someone else now?"

"No babe, only you. I want you." She comes towards us and we push her back.

"Get the fuck away from me," we say. She sways back almost falling. Why did we give her Viprex™? Now she's out of control. Her tolerance is nonexistent and she is taking doses like an addict.

We are on fire. "What did you do?"

"Why do you gotta be so mad?" Her words slurring. "You don't want me?"

"What, don't try to twist it." We walk away, rather than make a scene, but she follows us.

"Wait babe. Don't go. I don't want to lose you." She looks at us, suddenly more sober and hugs and kisses us. We don't kiss her back and she backs up a half step, still embracing us.

"You can trust me," she says, her brown-speckled blue eyes wide. "I care about you. It was an honest mistake, I just took too much Viprex™ and put it on inside out." She starts to rub our crotch. "Please?" She smiles and kisses us again. This time we don't resist even though we know she is lying.

In the lab the next day, we are making 1000 mL of Viprex™ for Prophet. We wonder why he needs so much. The other lab techs are nowhere to be found as usual and we feel the usual creeping feeling of dread that haunts us down here when we catch sight of a face in the lab's door window.

The drab wavelengths of the basement lights frame a dull mask free of any sort of emotion. We almost hide our vials and then realize this is not a person or even a bioprogram. This is our reflection.

When did we develop that crease in our forehead that makes us look like a bioprogram wearing a mask?

It is just cosmetic. Don't be so superficial.

That's not why it bothers us. Why are we wearing a mask?

That night, walking back to our Regen unit

near the main clinic building, we enter a service tunnel that we hadn't seen before. It is dimly lit with weak sourceless lights that turn on when we come near and dims when we pass. Whispers start and we are struck with an irrational fear and a tingle down our back. The lights are dimmer now, almost dark. This feels familiar to us.

In the darkness of the tunnel is a dark figure standing motionless, silhouetted by the flickering light behind it. We slow our gait, nervous but wanting to see who the shadow is.

"Hello? Who is that?" We call from 10 paces away.

The shadow is silent.

We take a step closer and in the flickering light suggest a shadowy ghost of Shaya's face with the iridescent eyes of a Lurker.

We stop, extremely unnerved. The shadow feels menacing and our skin starts to crawl.

"Shaya, is that you?" we call.

Faint whispers seem to say 22. We can't see her face again, shrouded in darkness.

"22," whispers Shaya, her eyes piercing the gloom. She comes towards us, the flesh of our stomach crawling in reaction. Her eyes are glazed, almost blind. Her face is paralyzed in the giddy stare of an idiot, almost as if she is neurologically impaired from an overdose of Viprex™ and she is moving, lurching like a lurker or a malfunctioning bioprogram.

"Come here, I want you." She grabs at us, mindlessly. "We're the same. We're the same," she keeps repeating.

Panicked, we back away towards another tunnel, a sulfuric smell emanating from it. The Shaya thing moves without feet in the flickering light. There and not there and then suddenly closer. We turn and run but we reach the edge of a precipice, blackness beneath. We snatch a look behind us. We don't see the distorted Shaya creature, but we hear her whispers. We climb to the edge and find a place where we can cross over, where we only have to jump a meager foot over the black bottomless chasm to reach another ledge.

Come on. Jump.

We'll make it.

Our palms are sweating. We are frozen by indecision. We can't bring ourself to climb back and face the malformation but our feet are rooted to the ground.

Sweating from every pore in our body, we start shaking. We can't hold on much longer. Shaya's voice pulsates loudly right behind us.

We jump with limbs that feel like they are made out of lead. We miss the edge and tumble down into the abyss.

We sit bolt upright in our bunk in a cold sweat, gasping for air, with whispers echoing in our head.

We get dressed and pass by Shaya's bunk.

She is snoring quietly. We go outside into the darkness for a walk to the old fenced-in bridge on the edge of the campus. We notice a hole in the fence that we haven't seen before.

Is that a new hole?

Haven't seen it before.

Let's see what's out there.

We crawl through the hole and make our way along a wooded hillside behind some hospital buildings to another deserted and crumbling bridge. Below us the dog killers are out. They would come out when a large number of pests escaped their quadrant by the warehouses and now they are infringing on the hospital grounds. Sometimes the dogs attack a human and it would be all over the news. "Time to send out Animal Control!" the news would advise, both a tool and whip for the masses.

Animal Control are bioprograms that are assigned to exterminate pests. When the strays become too numerous the flat-faced bioprograms drive the dogs into one area with sonics and slaughter them. You can't get too close to these scenes or the dogs might attack out of desperation. Across from the bridge we are at is a pedestrian walkway below with 20 drunks trying to get some kicks, all cheering and yelling, putting money on which dogs would survive the longest.

"I got spots," yells a drunk probably talking about a dalmatian mix.

"50K on yellow boy!"

"Bioprogram 5386 looks like a killer. 100K on his kill rate."

Below them cornered between some hospital buildings in an emptied out parking lot, a dozen bioprograms flank scores of strays and start letting loose into them with plastic bullets so as not to damage any buildings or pavement.

The animals yelp and scream but are torn apart by the volleys from the armored bioprograms. The crowd cheers when one of their strays makes it longer than others in their group or a bioprogram kills more than its fellows. The screams give way to whimpers and eventually the only sounds remaining are the drunks exchanging money and talking and arguing about what had just happened. The carnage produces puddles of blood, with furry appendages and parts floating in a soup of fluid. There is quiet whimpering from unseen survivors for a few moments before they expire.

The executioners show no reaction, as bioprograms are reportedly free of emotion, their faces flat and expressionless. They activate small floating orb automatons to spray chemicals on the soup. The black liquid left over is sprayed into the sewers with hoses. The killers file back to their autovans and disappear into the night. No evidence except wet pavement remains of the carnage. After the bettors exchange their money the walkways begin to empty, laughter fading into the night. Soon no one remains, the street deserted as if nothing has happened.

We are out of Regen. We could leave. We could escape.

We have Viprex™. Why would we leave?

Leaning against the railing of the crumbling bridge we can't catch our breath and begin to hyperventilate. We feel sick and go into a cold sweat. Tears well up in our eyes and we sob quietly, our arms cradling our head.

Things like this have never bothered us before. Dogs have tried to kill us numerous times.

Not sure if it was pity we were supposed to feel for the dogs, but if this was feeling, we liked it better when we didnt feel anything.

Calm down. We need to get ahold of ourself. We are fine.

Almost against our will, our breathing calms and we wipe our eyes. Feeling blah but better, we retrace our steps, we sneak back though the hole in the fence and go to the barracks. Before going to sleep we head for the bathroom to piss and hear some whimpering in the corner. Glancing over, we see the Prophet, his pants down having sex with Shaya from behind.

We back away, the sick feeling returning. We can't say anything but they spy us and stop.

"22, I can explain." The Prophet is pulling up his pants and Shaya is pulling on her underwear.

We slug Prophet in the face. He falls down

and we back away, looking at Shaya, feeling more horrified than we were in our nightmare. She returns our look unapologetically. We almost retch and back out through the entry.

We sprint by the now silent mess hall, run to the outdoor staircase and desperately climb to the top. Clawing our way and spending energy recklessly trying not to feel.

We stare at the cloudy sky and the lighted up city below. Why me? Impotent tears come to our eyes but stick there frustratingly unable to form. What have we become? Something is wrong with us and it bothers us that nothing bothers us. We are empty inside, feeling like someone has kicked us in the stomach, feeling a sickness born from betrayal by someone we thought we loved.

We see no beauty, no purpose in life at all. Those doctors didn't help us at all. We can't rejoin humanity, even virtually. There is no way. If remorse is normal, then we don't want to be normal. We have to get the Clinic City™ implant out and get out of this. We don't want to feel anything anymore.

Looking down at the darkened clinic we hear the echoes of rasping whispers floating up to our pearch. A cold feeling grips us and our stomach starts itching profusely. Looking down we see movement behind one of the bioprogram guards and a shadow comes alive to snatch the guard, dragging it back behind the barracks.

What are Lurkers doing here? They were by the mounds and now here after never being in cities. Maybe the waste from the dog killers attracted them.

A moment later the lifeless corpse of the bioprogram is flung from the corner and the dark gangly shadow hisses in anger.

Lurkers must not drain bioprograms. Another Lurker comes from behind the corner and another. They start to head towards the barracks.

Fuck fuck fuck. We can't let them get Shaya and the others.

Why not, Fuck that bitch. Fuck Prophet too.

I don't wanna become the heartless mask I saw in the basement.

We need to survive, and if we go down there, we are going to die.

We begin to climb down.

No.

We freeze.

What the fuck?

This isn't a choice.

We turn around and walk without choice. Shivering we realize we are not in control of our own body.

Don't take it so hard. We were always in control anyways.

Lurkers don't act like this and Regen isn't expecting this. We need to warn them and help them.

That can't happen.

We want to vomit.

We steal a glance down the stairs to see shadows enter into the building and we hear screams from inside. People begin flooding out of the exits to get ensnared by the shadows when they exit, writhing, screaming, praying.

The trapdoor opens by our feet and a security bioprogram pops its head out.

"What are you doing up here? Return below, immediately. You are not allowed to be here." It says tonelessly. We kick it in the face and it falls down the ladder it came up. We jump down after it and beat it joylessly until it goes limp. We grab its head and put it to the retinal scan by the top door, carrying it out to the street on top of the hill. It begins to wake back up but we manage to throw it over the guardrail.

"Alert...........Alert..................

Alert.............Alert!" The pitch of the bioprogram's cries lower as it falls down the 60 meters on top of one of the lurkers below. The lurker shrieks and looks up at us. The alarm goes off.

Another bioprogram stumbles through the door. We grab its large flashlight right out of its hand and smash it so it stumbles backwards against the fence. Some bioprogram guards start to come around the corner to my left. We sprint down the street the other way and another one tries to bar our way. We swing the flashlight at it and it hesitates. Maybe bioprograms have some form of self-preservation after all, or maybe they just have slow reactions.

We steal a glance below and see the lurkers draining people. Panicked patients exit the dorms and some try to sprint past them. Lurkers grab some of them, sucking them dry, their husks floating to the ground like dead leaves. Some people hit their knees and pray to their gods. We can almost hear them say "Lurkers be praised." But they drain their worshipers too.

The lurkers fade into the darkness and their whispers recede into the night. We climb back down and sneak back to the dorm so as not to be blamed for the bioprogram's destruction. When we get back inside the barracks, Shaya is bound to a chair and the Prophet is arguing with Malaki and Puffy.

Malaki is yelling at the Prophet, "This mutant bitch called those lurkers here and they killed Jimmers, Ruiz and Damon. Just drained them dry."

"No she didn't," says the Prophet calmly. "You guys need to let her go. She had nothing to do with this."

We stay at the back of the crowd. Shaya seems unshaken and unafraid, staring at her captors as if they can't hurt her.

"We should kill her and throw her body back to the sewers where she came from!" says Puffy in her slow low voice.

"No, no, no!" yells the Prophet. "She is useful to us."

"To you," Malaki says. "You screwing 22's girlfriend. Or should I say his pet" He laughs pervertedly and pets Shaya's hair like a dog. Shaya bites his hand and almost takes a finger off. He starts beating her face. We surge forward, tackle him to the ground and start elbowing him in the face. Unbelievably, we are beating the much larger man. Puffy pulls us off Malaki and the Prophet stands to the side.

"Let her go!" we yell trying to struggle out but Puffy has our arms wrapped up.

Malaki gets up wiping blood off his nose. "You fucking pussy. You snuck me." With Puffy holding us down he starts pounding on us and we go out.

Lying on the ground, we come to and push ourselves off the tiled floor. Our head is throbbing and our face hurts. Clotted blood clogs our nose and we are afraid to clear it. The barracks are dark and most people are sleeping. We sit up and test our body. We don't seem to be in too bad a shape and can move around OK. We look at Shaya's bunk; it is empty as is the Prophet's and Malaki's.

Tasting blood, we go to the bathroom and look in the mirror. Both our eyes are swollen and beginning to blacken and our face looks like a puffed up bloody mess. In the mirror we see some motion behind us and see the Prophet creeping.

"I tried to stop them, 22." He looks shaken but we are not sure if we believe him.

"What did they do?"

"They killed her. They killed her because she was mutant and they threw her in the street."

At first we feel empty but then our eyes get wet. We hold back tears.

"Get yourself together. You're next. I can't protect you anymore. You need to get out of here now. Malaki and Puffy blamed her for attracting lurkers and are framing you for her murder. They reported that you hate mutants and were so angry you killed her. The police are coming."

We need to get it together. We need to leave.

We leave the Prophet in the bathroom without a word and go down to our lab where we steal what drugs we can. We go back to the bridge where the dog killers were and find the hole in the fence.

We sprint towards the warehouses and hear sirens in the distance. The streetlights streak by in the night. We hop a small wall and jump into an old abandoned train yard, flashing lights speed by on the other side of the wall.

Let's get to the warehouses so we can hide.

High pitched sirens wail from far away. It

is happening too fast. We are getting closer to the warehouses and step up our pace. We sprint down an old dried up drainage ditch. We pass a black mirrored sentry bubble and we know we are done. We hear helicopters in the distance.

Get to the sewers. It is the only way to get out of here in one piece. They'll nail us for stealing those drugs, nothing worse than first degree felony theft and destruction of corporate property.

Murdering Shaya is worse.

Not to them. Keep moving!

The sirens are closer now. We see lights in the distance; they are gaining on us. The drainage ditch goes underground. A rusty old manhole from the days before automation is next to the drainage ditch. It is partially opened and we flip the cover up and off the rest of the way. The police autocars are almost on us. We scramble down the ladder.

Voices overhead. Lights fall on our face. We let go of the ladder and jump down the final five feet. Bullets whiz by our head.

"I missed! Gas the tunnel!" they say.

We run into the darkness. We can hear gas canisters explode behind me. We blow through the cloud not breathing with our eyes closed.

"Track his footsteps!"

"Send the bots!"

We hear them clambering down behind us and then the *tick tack* of the bots. We flick on our small light and make a quick right and then a left turn and head towards unknown tunnels. We see a mass of swarming brown feral creatures in our light and slow our pace, knowing what is coming next. Rats squeak around our feet. The bots are close behind us so we spring to the heart of the infinite hydra hoping to burst through with speed. The rats jump at our legs and torso biting at us and trying to bring us down with sheer numbers. We swipe at them with our hands and they keep coming with ravenous squeals, strange almost human cries. One bites at our face and we backhand it, smashing it against the wall.

We hear the cops yelling behind the bots through the pulsing mass of rats. We keep running and more shots whiz by us, some terminating in explosions of blood and fur. There is a ditch running along the far wall of the sewage chamber. We jump into the foul water and swim to the left hoping to pass to a chamber we somehow know lies behind the wall. We *feel* it.

Maybe the cops won't follow us past the rats into shit. Hopefully the bots will lose our scent. We swim for two minutes until our lungs are bursting and break the surface of the sewage. We are in a different chamber. It is quiet but it smells like hell. We swim to the edge of the pool and collapse on the edge, dry heaving. We roll over, staring at the ceiling of the rough hewn cavern coated in shit. We gather our breath to laugh but then we turn and retch instead.

We need to leave now. The bots might still be able to track us. Get up.

We push ourselves to our feet, looking around. A coating of shit surrounds us like a battered synthfish. Bending over, we again retch at the smell. Nothing comes out because nothing is left. An acidic taste and feeling of vomit stings our throat.

We gotta get out of here. The bots could track us.

Not through that shit. Where the fuck are we?

We are free and we need to move.

OK.

These old sewers are like death traps, and they are full of mutants. We have been in sewers a few times before but never this way, under the shit. We always go the other way if we see mutants.

We go through a tunnel using our small light. Gradually, the tunnels give way to smaller abandoned service ways. Strange calls and clicks echo through the tunnels and we become more cautious. We have a bad feeling that we might not make it out of here. For now we have to stay underground and on the move to avoid the police and their bots for at least a few hours, but we don't want to make it a permanent sojourn due to fatality.

We keep moving and the tunnels gradually become rougher and more crudely dug, looking more and more like the passageway to some dark, ancient and unholy crypt. We know there are mutants down here and we don't want to run into them. Stridulating noises begin and seem to increase and diminish in volume, pitch and rhythm when we move.

They are watching us.

The tunnels appear to dead end and we frantically wield our light back and forth, freaking out. Breathing raggedly, our heartbeat accelerates. We see a small hole we can crawl through, dried shit scraping off of us like snake skin against a rock. The noises cease and we pause for a second. What can we do? We can't go back to the rats and cops.

Strange whispers replace the insect-like noises as if trying to copy lurkers. Somehow, we know it is not lurkers. We can feel it.

Fuck it, go through.

We crawl through the hole and stand up. Light bursts into our eyes, blinding us momentarily. We automatically shield our eyes with our hands and try to make out the figures behind the light.

"What the fuck are you doing down here?" says one of the figures in a gravelly voice as if talking to an idiot.

Don't mention Shaya. A dead Nuclae might make them mad. Keep it simple.

"I was chased down here. I just want to pass through."

There is no answer. Our eyes aren't fully adjusted to the bright light but we begin to make out a half dozen bestial silhouettes behind the radiance. Large animal-like shapes stand on the fringes of the crowd. Insect-like heads float around us attached to dark armored bodies, partly lit by the backscatter from their light.

"*If* we let you pass, what can you do for us?" asks the gravelly voiced shadow after a pause, waving to himself and then to the menagerie of a dozen mutations with long serpentine arms.

A tremor runs through us. These are not hybrids that show themselves in the city above. As our eyes adjust, the edges of the large chamber suggest itself to us, roughly hewn. The leader leans in with reptilian eyes. "Well, human?" he whispers.

Offer them Viprex™.

"I have drugs. Lots of drugs. Let me pass through and I will give some of them to you," we quickly say. "Maybe we can come to some sort of agreement. There's another way out, right?"

We thought we didn't care much if we live or die but right now we don't want to die. As freaky as these things are, they seem more sane than Lurkers. Maybe they will make a deal.

We look around at them. A few have guns and knives, but many are not armed by conventional weapons. Instead, they have altered body parts-claws, fangs, eyes around their heads, extra appendages, alligator mouths at the end of their arms, beaks, horns and some even have spurs on their elbows and knees. We've seen hybrids with strange eyes or coloring but these big, dangerous, more heavily mutated types usually stay out of sight.

The more "human" mutants sometimes go to cities above but usually aren't accepted. They have a wildness about them. If one turns up dead in an alley, the police don't care. Most people fear and are revolted by them.

"We could just take your drugs and kill you," growls the leader in his strange coarse voice. His jointless arms bend like snakes but his hands seem normal. His snake eyes pierce ours.

For a tense moment the mutant's snake-arms are cocked and ready to strike when a ghastly sound echoes through the tunnel. A cacophonic sound that echoes like a recording of a scream playing backwards reverberates in our head and then resolves to whispers before it repeats. Our discoloration on our stomach begins to burn.

"Lurker," whispers a mutant raising a knife-like finger to his lips.

"Let's go!" whispers a big six-legged mutant also in a hushed tone.

We look up at snake-arms. "Lurker?" we ask, "What do we do?" His eyes large, his companions begin to bolt.

"Dying, I ain't," smiles snake-arms in a soft

voice as he lets our shirt go and fades away into the darkness.

Run!

The roar repeats, sounding closer now. Shivering, we run with the mutants, outpacing some of them thanks to Viprex™ addiction and adrenaline. We come to a fork and race to the left. The tunnel opens up and a cliff drops down to our right. The sound is even closer now, the whispering is becoming deafening. A scream from behind us and we steal a glance back. The husk of a mutant falls floating down into the chasm like a piece of paper. Something dark behind us reverse roars again. We aren't gonna beat whatever it is and we don't want to meet it.

We round a bend and look around and see some rough handholds leading up to a ledge.

In desperation, we clamber up it and pull ourselves up vaulting and rolling longways into the ledge cringing. We try to push our way into the rock. The whispers are so close they are in our head, paralyzing us with fear. Our abdomen is on fire. There is a smell of ozone in the air and the hairs on the back of our neck pulse with an electric fear. Frozen, we can't even lift our head over the ledge to see what demon stalks us. We hear another agonizing scream that is choked off, this time in front of us and a deafening whisper from farther up.

The extreme feeling of fear begins to ebb away with the fading whispers. The hot part of our stomach begins to cool. We feel the lurker fading away in the distance. Gathering ourself, we softly climb down. We hear more noises in the distance, make our way back to the fork and take the right side this time, hoping it will lead us out to the outside world away from this underground hell filled with monsters and demons.

We break away hard in the other direction, putting as much distance underground as we can between us and the mutants. We run through tunnels that become rougher and rougher with deep cave-ins descending off into the darkness. We slow down and tread more carefully as every step we take drops debris into the depths. We don't want to be next. The black down here seems to go on forever. We keep hearing strange noises and every broken rock formation is a monstrous being leering out of the darkness.

Our light gives out then and we start to panic, blinded. We are going to die. We have no way out and we could fall to our deaths at any moment.

Relax. Feel the vibrations with your body.

We stop. We take deep breaths and try to calm down.

We are OK right now. Everything around us is vibrating at its own frequency. We can feel it.

We open and close our eyes and it makes no difference. We still see darkness either way.

Breathe.

We calm our breathing and stay still. The strange noises die down almost like they were echoing our movements and mood. A magnetic resistance seems to be all around us. We push our hands together so they are almost touching and we feel the vibrations of the molecules in our hands.

Gradually, a picture of our hands becomes clear in our brain even though we can't see them visually. Next, our body begins to come into focus in our mind's eye. We breathe and relax and then slowly the walls around us seem to form out of the electromagnetic fog. We feel the objects around us with our entire body becoming a sense organ. We reach out and touch the wall of the tunnel that we are in and our hands feel what we already "see."

We can make our way now.

How can we do this?

It doesn't matter. We need to move now.

We start to move quickly down the tunnel with the tunnel making itself clear for about 20 meters in either direction, including behind us. But somehow, we have a memory of the tunnel we have already traversed and its path echoes in our memory

This must be how seers can see the world.

This is how we see the world. We learned how to do this from the dust of the lurker. The darkness taught us.

Is it from the lurker dust? It is amazing that we can feel this.

A gift from lurkers and us. We have learned to synthesize these lurker abilities.

And what should we do now with our newfound abilities?

If the mutants catch us and they don't want to trade for Viprex™ or whatever the drug we have is, they could possibly kill us.

But if the police catch us they will liquidate us after Sanitary, if they don't kill us outright.

Either way we are sunk.

We shudder.

Sanitary is the worst with its gang rapes and beatings.

That's why we are running. Don't stop. Maybe we can bargain with the mutants.

There must be a lot of holes in the sewer as we feel the pulse of a breeze flowing through the tunnels. It whispers to us and we speak back to it between our rough panting from the panicked pace we keep. We feel the chambers and tunnels immediately around us. We can almost see a map in our mind in the vast darkness of these tunnels, but we can't see for an infinite distance and we don't see a clear path back to the surface.

An emptiness fills us, our heart in our throat, as, for some reason, we visualize Shaya and Prophet. We flinch as we run almost blindly, fear and adrenaline pushing back against the jealousy and self pity we feel.

We don't need them. Focus on the now.

We see Shaya's corpse in our head laying in the street and the flinching becomes a sick feeling. An empty hole torn into by fear.

They are as meaningless as a speck of dust on an insect's back, floating in a vast chasm where foul creatures spread their wings and exhale their maggot filled untruths and mindless speculations. We don't need to focus on that. We need to focus on survival.

But we loved Shaya.

Love? Ha. We are different from her kind. From all kinds. We have no love, no compassion for any creature, idea or aesthetic. Love is for the weak, for the fools who believe in myths. We are untouched by their stories and acts and words, their mindless constructs. We cannot hold love, we cannot see it or taste it. We don't need it. We only need to survive and be free.

We realize that we will never have love.

Love is a lie.

We also realize that we are lost both spiritually and now physically. Really lost, we have no idea how to get out of here. Suddenly, we sense a processed kind of air, different from the stale air of the sewer in the direction we are going.

The gifts Viprex™ continues to bestow upon us.

As we continue on, the ground gets hard to

traverse. It opens up and we are not sure if we are in a tunnel or a broken crack descending to the bowels of the earth. Clicks and hissing noises fill the air around us as before. We catch glimpses of movement out of the corner of our eyes, actual light. Are our eyes playing tricks on us or have they found us again?

No point in turning back. Behind us was just as bad as the way forward. We hear a flutter of leathery wings behind us. We sense a big-winged demon that the lurker worshipers speak of behind us, ghosting us up above. Jacked by adrenaline, we swing around wildly trying to see the flashes of light we think we are seeing with our eyes. Our breathing loud and ragged, we turn back and go along the other wall.

We need to get control of ourselves.

We feel the tunnel getting narrower.

Keep going, we will be harder to flank in there. They will have to come at us one at a time.

It is then that we realize that in our panic we ignored the fact that there is no ceiling and that the "tunnel" opens up to a large cone shaped cavern above us. We are in the point at the bottom, the cavern widening up above.

This chamber is made to be a trap.

Something is hanging on the rough stone above us, jabbering incomprehensibly in some clicking alien rant. They creep down, spider-like, from the top and from the tunnels behind us. We can see some glowing a bioluminescent aura. Framed in this feeble light are silhouettes of demonic lab experiments leering at us with nightmare caricatures, even crazier than the last gang.

We are fucked.

We try to back out of the trap at the bottom of the narrow chasm awaiting the onslaught. We can sense them sticking to the walls of the tunnel far above and in the widening path in front of us like insects waiting for prey. We make out vague shapes and obscured features in the low light. Sharp teeth, eye shine, and antennae like tumorous growths. Cave creatures, snaking arms. Wings fluttering above. Small quadrupeds stalk us along the broken rocks to the side. Beings with exoskeletons on their torsos and heads for protection approach, scores of them. Rodent creatures start to pour from the cracks in the walls.

They pause. Snake arms is there again. He separates himself from their ranks and approaches us, looking surprised that we are still alive. The others hold their ground about a meter behind him. He looks us up and down with malicious but hypnotic reptilian eyes and then sniffs the air.

"Found you."

After a long pause he speaks again in his gravelly menacing voice: " Why are you down here, where you are not wanted?"

"The Police are chasing me."

"Why? And why bring them here where they will fuck with us?" he says in a very hard, almost whispered tone, enunciating the cuss words.

Chatter breaks out among the ranks of creatures. They might be arguing about whether or not to kill us. "Click click kill," they say. The reptilian eyes increase their intensity and their owner holds up a snake arm for silence. Everyone quiets down. "Tell us the truth. Your life depends on it."

"I stole some drugs from Clinic City. I lost the cops before I came down here."

"You lost them? I doubt it. If anything they let you go. What about the drugs? What are they? Show them to me."

We reach into our bag. Every eye snaps to attention. We can feel the tension in a way we never could before. "Slow down. Slowly."

We pull out one of the plastic containers and open it. 100 auto hypos filled with a blood-like fluid are within.

"Viprex?"

"Yes. but it does something else to me too." The eyes are visibly interested. We steal glances above, searching for the nightmarish climbers and we shiver a bit.

"What?" Piercing eyes.

"I don't know for sure, but I can sense things I couldn't before."

"Like what? Be truthful, we will know if

you are lying."

"I can sense things. Even if I close my eyes, I can still see some of you."

"The Clinic can't do that. They don't have the knowledge."

"Well, I could feel that lurker."

Snake arms gives us a strange look. "You did survive...Did you take this drug?"

"Yes." More chatter.

"So you are an addict?"

"Not anymore." We lie.

"You lie. You still have someone else in you."

How could they know about us?

"They were studying you?"

"Yeah."

"That's what we are going to do also. Don't try anything." He nods to the ghastly procession surrounding us, "They will kill you if you do. I may want to find out about your *human* drug but some of these are hard to control. I assume you were traced"

"Yeah, implant."

"Then one of our doctors will remove it and we will take your drugs."

"I could die with no replacement drugs."

"You will die for sure if you don't do what we say."

Regeneration II

They take our Viprex™ and quietly walk us through the tunnels. Eventually the tunnels become more regular. There is no light but like us they seem to be able to sense the walls around us. We can sense the phalanx of captors around us though they are almost totally silent. We can feel that we are deep underground. They take us through some armored doors to a large cavern about 20 meters high and lit in the visible spectrum. There is a dwelling-sized building next to the entrance.

We must be in a holding area.

They order us to strip and they spray us down with a hose to wash the shit and dirt off of us. Snake arms hands us some dark-colored clothes that we put on. Though rough to the touch they are surprisingly light and flexible. Snake arms and some of the others take us inside another nearby building to a three by two meter room that is dark with concrete walls and leaves us. There is one door made of material that looks like bone with slats in it for viewing, like a squared off ribcage. We try to peek through the slats but there is only darkness beyond.

It's a good sign that we are still alive. Otherwise, our future looks bleak. We kick at the boney door. It is solid as plasteel. We sit down against the far wall facing the door and wait. We need Viprex™. Our stomach is twisting in knots. We get on our hands and knees and vomit on the floor. We lean back against the wall, a cold sweat pouring from our body. We are very weak. We stare at the concrete ceiling and inhale the dank air. From time to time we hear clicking noises. But we wait, feeling sicker and sicker.

We feel like death and have given up hope when a bright greenish glow lights up behind the slats. The door opens and the pale snake-arms enters carrying a light followed by a dark-skinned female mutant. She is carrying a container of steaming liquid. We make no move and just stare at them from the ground. A strange look is on her face, somewhere between pity and disgust. "This little one escaped Clinic City, Sistid?" She looks at Snake arms.

"I think he's faster than he looks."

"He's a wreck." She kneels down warily and places the cup on the ground between us. "Take this drink, it is safe. It will help you." She stares at us with strange animal-like eyes for a moment before she rises. Her movements ripple with lithe power.

We pick it up and drink a few sips. We don't care if it is poison. We are ready to try anything for the pain at this point. The brew is warming, organic and almost pleasant. We wait for the effects.

We feel a bit better almost instantly. We start to drink it, greedily slurping it down. When we are finished we look up at them. Despite her eyes and black skin, she looks normal enough, attractive even.

"I understand who and what you are," she says, her voice fair and even. "Addiction to Viprex Neurophasia sometimes creeps into our people also. It is a selfish drug. It will leave nothing inside you for yourself. It will take your soul away and control you from the inside. Our people are given two choices. One is treatment."

"I have a choice?"

"The other used to be banishment. The people that were banished...well they were possessed."

She looks at us directly with a steady gaze. "The possessor within them saw a way to perpetuate its consciousness and the addicts became selfish and would betray us. Nuclae do not kill out of hand but death is the only other option."

We peer into her green cat-like eyes, then at snake arm's bright reptilian eyes and back at her.

"Don't keep me here. I don't know your secrets and I don't want to. I don't want to stay here with these....these....monsters! Why do you want me to stay here? You already have the Clinic's drug!"

"Shut up fool!" growls Sistid.

She remains calm. "Calm down, both of you. We wish to study you to see what your geneticists up above have accomplished with you. We can tell that your DNA has been altered. In the process we may be able to cure you of your addiction."

Don't trust them.

"My geneticists? Haha," we scorn.

"We can't trust someone like you," Sistid says, his arms waving toward us. "You drew unwanted attention to us when you came down here with the police in tow."

"You don't need my help to draw attention to you. Shit, you just walk down the street and people see you coming a fucking mile away!"

Get control. Breathe.

"That is why we stay in our own cities. We mean no harm," says the female, calmly, her expression reasoning. "We wish to exist just as you wish to do up above. Most of you stay away from our areas out of fear."

They both look at us. We are obviously the exception. Things seem very clear to us. "What is the treatment?" we ask.

"Genetic coding reversal accomplished with a retroactive RNA that codes for new DNA. This is applied at the base of your brain stem. The drink we gave you suppresses the effects of your parasite. This makes you calm enough for your treatment and protects me against any of its defense mechanisms. Believe me, we have experience with addicts." She takes a step back, her body muscular but lithe, her movements exact and confident. We see now that she has strange fingers that look like armored claws.

"How long does it take?"

"How long have you been addicted?"

"Two Years."

Try ten.

She gives us a hard look. "If you're telling the truth, we can apply it in a few weeks. Longer if not."

"I have one question," we say.

Her eyes shine in the dim, her face relaxed, waiting.

"Why, why would you want to help a human addict?"

"You intrigue us. Not only did you escape Clinic Cities net, but you also survived an encounter with a lurker. That is... unusual. Even for our kind."

As if we have a choice, after a moment we say: "I'll do it," She holds our gaze for a moment and then we look away.

"There are very few side effects and no physical pain due to our numbing tea. We make these drugs ourselves. We can take your DNA fingerprint to see if it is working. Once we apply the retroactive *you will never be able to take Viprex™ if you continue your doses*. You will know when you are becoming yourself again." She half smiles.

She really doesn't understand.

"What will happen if we take Viprex™

after the treatment?"

"At first nothing, but you will not survive even one shot of Viprex once the treatment is completed. I will administer your treatment. I am a doctor. My name is Alella Talon. This is Sistid Plastic, he will be assisting me for security purposes."

Strange names.

"Drink it. It will calm you," she smiles. "We will be back later with your first treatments."

Allela walks through the smooth tight tunnel flanked by rooms mined out by her genetic antecedents, the lights pulsing on when she approaches and off with her passing. The whole sewer is sealed with polymer armor not manufactured, but like most things, genetically synthesized by the Nuclae.

She turns, her muscular legs rippling in her black single suit and enters the door of a lighthouse-shaped building. A couple of Plastics hang inside the doorway. They look at her out of their reptilian eyes and smile the way many Nuclae do, with raised eyebrows as if to say I am your friend but what's up with you? Their serpentine arms undulate in the air, wagging unconsciously like a hunting cat's tail.

"I'm here for the head of security for this building, Sistid Plastic."

One of them gestures for her to go up the spiral stairs on the other side of the polymer door. Sistid waits at the top.

"How goes Alella?" Sistid asks in a gravelly voice, still smiling.

"Yes, that's I," she smiles back, showing white even teeth. "One comes quickly when summoned by the head of security."

Sistid laughs. "Follow me." he grins. "Though it is a Cancer who calls."

They go to a door in the wall of the lighthouse that leads to a tunnel.

"So, what facility *is* this? I have not been invited here before."

"A laboratory," he says simply as they walk together. After a hundred meters they come to a door made from dense synthesized bone carved with DNA motifs. Sistid opens the heavy door soundlessly,gestures for her to go inside and he follows. A burly bald white female Nuclae waits next to a metal stretcher with a shrouded corpse on it. The bald Nuclae regards her coolly under the bright light for a moment as if trying to get a read on her. Her white skin shines brightly in the light and her muscular frame is at ease under a white lab suit with an aura of command. This is a creature used to giving orders and being obeyed. She is a Cancer, one of the first strains of Nuclae and almost always in a position of power. This one is no different.

"Alella, I am Dr. Morora. Among your areas

of expertise, you have knowledge of genetic skin augmentation and we need your skills." Her voice is cool. She glances at the shroud and back to Alella. "You have to understand that you must not speak of anything you see in this room to anyone by Nuclae law."

"I understand Dr. Morora," she automatically echoes the cool tone of the elder Nuclae. "What do you need me to do?"

"Sistid," Morora gestures towards the stretcher with a muscular arm. Sistid pulls the shroud aside with a sinuous motion. The light is distorted around a ghostly corpse strapped firmly in place.

"What is that?" She asks, her green cat-like eyes puzzled.

"It's a body," says Sistid. "Feel it."

She comes forward, donning a glove on her clawed hand, and feels the distortion. There is something there. She traces the shape of a body, a head and what feels to be a face. She feels a pulse at the neck and pulls her hand away.

"What the hell is this?" She eyes Morora and the body. Morora flips on some instruments next to the stretcher that shows the shape of a human.

"BEC sensors show what we believe is a humanoid- genetically altered to be invisible or almost invisible. We need you to study this, figure out how they did it and see if you can replicate it."

"They?"

"We believe this is cyborg tech, infiltration. We are doing some tests to confirm this."

"Why do you think that?" She asks, her green eyes, questioning.

"That is need to know," says Morora. "And, no offense, you don't have the clearance. With all due respect, we know that you are one of the best and we need you to figure out how they did this quickly, plus we need you to keep it alive. Sistid will assist you. He has some physics knowledge in addition to security expertise. This thing cannot escape."

Normally calm, Alella feels that Morora is pointlessly withholding information. "I don't need security! I need information!"

"No need to be offended, Alella.," Morora says tersely. "This was decided by the council. It is a *command.*"

Alella feels her face get hot and is about to respond with words she knows she will later regret. Before she can speak, Sistid interrupts.

"Alella, here are your sequencers and coders." He holds up a small hand-held computer. "I believe that this individual is coded for some sort of synthetic material. It doesn't appear to be biological in origin"

"Sistid will assist you. Please have him contact us when you have finished your report. We need it right away." Morora stares at her for a moment to make sure she understands her place. Alella holds her gaze and Morora turns and leaves without a word. Alella grabs a sequencer out of Sistid's hand. "Give me that!" she says gruffly.

Sistid's eyes are twinkling but he chokes back his smile.

Do We Want A Cure

First, they slide our drink under the gate of our dark but dry cell. After we drink it, they come in again. They spray the back of our neck with some sort of computerized autohypo that Alella calls a sequencer. Sistid is always close at these times. He is staring at us now ready for action in case we try to attack her. We won't. Though we don't like them we won't because we know they can kill us.

They are polite to us and do not put us on like the doctors did in Clinic City. Still, though, they are using us the same way, for research.

We see how it is. Alella sometimes pretends to be concerned and asks us how we are doing, how we feel.

She is not to be trusted either.

Upstairs in the Regen unit we knew those who were like her: pretending to care, but we saw the true ways people were.

They think they're better than humans.

Looking down on us.

Betraying us.

"Drink your tea." she says.

We reach out our hand and sniff at the tea she gives us. The sniffing does no good anyways, but it makes us feel better.

It shows her we don't trust her.

"You alright?" she asks.

We look at our shoes and the hard ground. We look at the reclamation unit in the corner and then back at the ground. We remember old friends, overdosed and scattered corpses along the timeline of our life. Scattered along the wayside of time. They had their own interest at heart more than anyone else, definitely not ours. We were cast away like old pieces of garbage. There is no use for us anymore to anyone but us.

We need to fend for ourself.

We look up at Sistid and Alella, they regard us with a strange look. They are better than us? We sneer at them, but they don't have much reaction.

"We will leave you now. You need more treatment before we can talk to you," Alella says.

"Self-pity is for the weak," Sistid says coldly.

They back out and leave the room, shutting the slatted door securely behind them. We are alone in the semi-darkness. Our thoughts drift to times long past when we were a child. Times were so simple. We never knew what was ahead of us. Where were the instructions for life? Where were the warnings? Someone could have warned us that there are consequences for your actions. Someone should have warned us that once you choose a path, you suffer for it. Someone did, but we didn't believe them.

Alella is running in the darkness of a forest. A dark shadow flits above emitting infrasonic frequencies that propagate in waves around her, bursting any biotic material that they touch. Her brother Alell runs on one side of her and Vira, a hex, runs on the other side. They run towards the caves that are safe passage back to Subterra and out of reach of the Syrinx that are chasing them.

Jumping over fallen logs and weaving through the brush, they sprint in a zigzag pattern they learned as children to avoid Syrinx. The Syrinx sings its song and a waterlogged tree bursts into splinters above them.

The cave is 800 meters away. They know they will not make it but they keep running.

Vira slows, bleeding from one of her legs. Looking up, they don't see the Syrinx. They catch their breath under an oak.

Alell looks at Vira's leg and frowns.

"Sisters, get ready to run. I am going to pull that thing away from the caves."

"No, you won't make it," cries Alella, grabbing Alell's arm.

"I can make it. I am faster than either of you now that Vira is injured."

"We can make it together," Vira's words ring hollow even to her.

"Give me time to draw it off. I will meet you guys back at the caves. Don't worry about me. Dying I ain't."

Before they can disagree, he takes off. The Syrinx's shadow instantly eclipses him and gives chase. They wait a few moments and run in the other direction. Alell is out of sight, but the sisters sense the infrasonic Syrinx screams crashing through the forest. Gasping for air, they make it to the cave and wait safely in the mouth, looking for Alell tensely, almost in a panic.

Finally they see him sprinting towards the cave mouth, coming closer and closer until he is a hundred meters away. He zig zags. A wave blasts next to him bringing up a cloud of distorted dust. He loses his balance and regains it, sprinting even faster towards the cave mouth.

Vira and Alella grab each other's hands. He is going to make it!

He does a series of sprinting maneuvers and the wave of the Syrinx narrowly misses him. He is 50 meters away when a screaming wave comes even closer. He dodges to his left.

The Syrinx screams a wave directly at Alell and suddenly Alella is sitting bolt upright in her bed in the dark room, sweating and breathing hard, the scream echoing in her head. She calms herself, gets up and looks in the mirror at her dark features. The dream feels like reality to her and it takes her a few minutes to get back to her normal stoic self.

She takes a shower and looks at her naked form in her mirror. A few battle scars decorate her abdomen and muscular legs. She pulls on a black single suit onto her legs and over her body, black fabric on her dark skin. She leaves her apartment and walks alone, worming her way through the dark tunnels. She reads heat signatures of the few Nuclae passing her in the dark and they nod to each other. Most of her people have this ability. Her ancestors made themselves thus to help them obtain employment. Now, most Talons keep this alteration not only to honor their ancestors but also because it increases their rate of survival both below and above.

She passes by others in the dark caverns greeting many familiar faces. Some have lights and some don't as night is simulated at this time. As above, so below.

Strange how she feels more comfortable with light even though she doesn't technically need it. It makes her feel safer. That must be ancestral instinct from back when humans didn't edit their DNA.

Walking in the dark, her thoughts drift to

the strange almost invisible being and then to the addict. She doesn't trust the new addict. She pities him. Her people will not kill the innocent, but she doubts his innocence. Her people would defend what was theirs no matter what the cost.

They had built their cities underground to stay away from outsiders. Different Nuclae cities throughout the world were separate cells that coexisted but did not absolutely need each other to survive. Many were underground and they were always hidden. Communication could be blocked by the humans above when it suited the Corporate Government's purposes, so each Nuclae city existed autonomously, fending for themselves. To travel between settlements required exiting through tunnels into forests that were forbidden to the human population above. Technically, trespassing the forests was also forbidden to the true humans, the Nuclae, by the Corporate Government.

She passes several Hexapeds and they nod their armored vaguely human heads at her. Hexapeds and Talons have a natural affinity for each other that was born of the mines years ago. Hexes use their shovel-like front appendages for construction and mining and Talons would do the finer work or the climbing work. Both genetic lines are also among some of the Nuclae's fiercest fighters. But Hexes are the toughest of all hybrids. Tougher than almost every other living being, except for maybe the lurkers. Lurkers are a mystery, an enigma, simultaneously in many places and nowhere at once or never.

Hexapeds are created in the womb, their stem cells altered before normal human tissues can form. They are human in mind only, the only remnants of humanity in their appearance was in their faces. They usually will only copulate with their own. However, their mutations are not at the level of their gametes and their progeny are fully malleable in their DNA. Any recombinant can be formed. Usually, they choose to give birth to other Hexes, just as most other subspecies of the Nuclae choose to perpetuate their own.

Alella's close friend Vira is a Hex. She is one of the fastest runners in the colony and her kicks can crush rocks. They often spar together and it is all Alella can do to keep up with Vira who often seems unbeatable even when pulling her punches. They have been bonded since they were young.

Alella enters a side tunnel into a cleanly hewn stairway. She takes it down four levels to a walkway. From this vantage she can see the great cavern that her people, the Talons, had worked with the Hexes to carve out the ground deep under Clinic City into a vast underground city of their own; a lesser twin to the great corporate behemoth above. A great shiny globe-like building looms above her, luminescent in the semi dark of projected morning. It is partially embedded in the great wall of the cavern with several other smaller globes nearby. Covered walkways connect the buildings. Soon to be glowing with the deep yellows and reds of the artificial sunlight of morning, is her city, Subterra.

She enters a walkway and takes a rare lift to Vira's floor. A corridor spirals away from the elevator chamber from the center of the building. She follows it to near the exterior of the globe. She presses the buzzer..

Vira opens the door. She is standing on four of her legs in a semi erect position, her forelimb on the door handle. "Sister," she smiles. "You're late. Come in."

Alella enters and Vira gives her a brief hug. "I got caught up last night with a human addict they just captured. We are treating him," Alella conversates. "So I woke up a little late."

They walk to the center of the large unfurnished room. Vira looks puzzled. "Treating a *human* addict? Unusual."

"Head of security,Sistid Plastic, assigned me to him. And now a Cancer has given me another job."

"What job is that?"

"That is all I can say." Alella smiles mysteriously.

"Big shot, working with the Cancers," Vira mocks knowingly, smiling back. "A human in Subterra? Very unusual."

"Let's start." Alella sneers and charges Vira with a flying kick.

Vira absorbs the blow to her armored neck and takes a step back, collapsing defensively onto all six feet. "Not bad, Alella. For a Talon!" She smiles again and, surging forward, she thrusts her shovel-like front appendages in a series of blows that Alella narrowly dodges. Vira stands back on her 4 hind legs to swing her forelimbs at Alella who gets underneath Vira's forelimbs and launches a hard kick at Vira's softer underbelly. Vira is stunned momentarily but she spins with the hard force of the blow and shovels right into and through Alella's thigh, flooring her and attacking with more blows.

Alella rolls out of the way of Vira's repeated downstrikes and retreats back in a crab walk, launching upkicks from awkward positions. Vira pins her down to the floor, one shovel-like appendage for her ankles and one for her neck, her legs pinned together like a trussed bird.

"You lose," says Vira.

She lets Alella get up.

"Again?" Vira asks.

"Alright."

They fight for an hour, Vira usually getting the best of her. Her armored body's size and strength are too much for Alella who only sometimes gets the jump on Vira because of her speed.

Like most of her people, Alella loves to

fight, especially with Vira. If she can keep up with Vira, she can beat almost anyone else.

When they are done they sit on the combat mats and drink water to cool down and talk. The water always tastes good, purified by synthetics. At these times Alella thinks that there is nothing better than cold water and Vira's company. They can talk about anything. They give each other advice, talk about history, politics, love, biology, art and music. They argue. They can talk about anything together, kindred sister spirits.

"There's something about the human addict that bothers me." Alella says as they rest.

"What is it?" asks Vira.

"There is something wrong with him."

Vira raises her eyebrows. "Well he is addicted to Viprex."

"He seems so soulless. He acts as if he has no compassion and not just for us Nuclae, but even his fellow humans. I believe that he could kill and feel no remorse about it at all."

"Many humans are like that. But, how do you know what he is thinking? And isn't he so possessed by his alter ego that he is not really in control of himself?"

"I don't buy that," Alella says in a hard tone. "He is still responsible for his actions."

"You speak of compassion, maybe you should have some for him even if he does not for you. You will be on a higher plane and can observe him and not prejudge him like most of his people do to him and to us. You will be in a stronger position if you come in with the least amount of preconceptions."

Alella looks at Vira and smiles "Where did you come up with that bullshit?"

Vira smiles but doesn't back down: "It's true. The less you assume, the more you will be able to see him for who he really is. You won't be surprised when he does something... unexpected"

"Like what, do more Viprex?"

"Maybe not. He could surprise you."

" He doesn't trust us. He looks at us as freaks."

"That's OK," Vira says. "We do alter our phenome in extreme ways."

"So do the humans!" her face wrinkles up in disgust. 'Especially the addict."

"Yeah, but not to such visual extremes. Humans are visual creatures, often limited by this sense. Also, I think that the addict is probably ostracized from *all* groups. Have compassion for him."

"No, he is hypocritical. Humans are all so hypocritical"

"Do you know all humans? They might not all hate us. Some of them must know that though separatism harms us, it harms them also. Some of them must not be controlled by the software of their governments."

"The stereotypes harm us more," says

Alella. "We live on less; we have to sneak between our cities. Our people can't work together. They always fight."

"They lose out on much of our medical information. Their Corporate Government allows them only a trickle of what their wealthy enjoy. Our more egalitarian ways allow us all to be treated more equally. Also, our kinship runs much deeper than theirs."

"But we have to hide underground!" Alella snaps, eyes flashing.

"We survive and we are stronger for it and when it matters, we always pull together. Someday we will all come together and make them face reality."

"You have way too much faith in a dream."

"No," says Vira, staring Alella in the eyes. "You have too little."

Get the Cure

So dark is the sky tonight. Outside the window lurks a hazy darkness obscuring the lights of the city, oppressive in its totality. From this viewpoint he could see the lights of the city all the way to the city walls, where the blackness starts.

Varius, staring off intently into the void, as if it could give him the answers to his problems, suddenly becomes aware of his reflection in the window staring back at him. Even in his conventionally handsome face, there are faint lines around his eyes and his mouth, light creases in his forehead born from years and years of concentration. In the dim light, his eye sockets look like two caves that shadow a practiced look of compassion that he now still feels only faintly.

Nearing 110 years, time is finally starting to catch up with him. Every time death has come knocking he has staved it off. He has replaced most of his organs, some more than once. He has beat cancer several times. He even survived an autocar accident. But he knows that he is running out of time. Retirement has not crossed his mind. His experimentation on Viprex™ addicts is unlocking new doors in genetic experimentation.

Genetic cures to Viprex™ addiction are not his main concern. Varius's research goes beyond that. The addicts are his lab rats, his guinea pigs. He does experimentation to determine if the process of aging can be stopped permanently, even reversed. Varius does not want to die. He has so much he can still offer this world, so much he still wants to see: space exploration of the outer planets and other star systems, The International Union™ becoming the strongest government on earth. He wants to meet his grandchildren's grandchildren's grandchildren. He loves life and he knows immortality is almost in his grasp.

He believes that the mutants now hold the key to it. He has lost a key subject to the mutants below Clinic City, a human subject, the inmate 02-273-197-22.

After further analysis of the subject, he has realized that somehow inmate 02-273-197-22's mutations seemed to change over time depending on the situation. This suggests that something maybe sentient was consciously controlling his mutations. Data has shown that this may be a way to control immortality based on some of the vector's cell samples. However, cell degradation would result if coding interpretation was attempted on samples. Varius needed 02-273-197-22 alive.

Somehow, his AI implant, one of the best in production, missed that 02-273-297-22 was the most important test subject to ever come through Clinic City. This would have to be addressed as well.

The mutants, gifted in genetic code, would discover the humans secret. Varius had convinced President Hunter to send Corporate Military to go into the city below and get this subject.

President Hunter has finally given him the go ahead, partially because Genation™, one of the multinational corporations, has been able to reverse engineer Synthetic Oxygen Bioprograms, making the mutants somewhat expendable as this is their main export. Hunter is old as well. Varius knows that Hunter wants to avoid death's scythe as much as he does. He knows that Hunter will support his plan to try to ferret out the addict from the mutants. Varius will become one of the most powerful men in the world and he will be around to enjoy that power for a long time. It all rests on recovering his vector now.

He lets out a deep breath and stares at the heavens above the city. There is an abyss of total blackness floating up above him. He knows he could become equal to the infinite void as long as he has more *time*. Soon, time will no longer be a concern.

◆ ◆ ◆

The next day, when we wake, an androgynous gray hairless person is standing in our cell with a blank expression on its flat face wearing only dark trunks.

"Who are you?" we ask. "A bioprogram nurse or something?"

It ignores us.

"I'm talking to you! Who are you?"

It still does not move. Is that a flicker of disdain across its face?

We get closer to it. "What the fuck?"

It is still like a corpse.

"Are you even alive?" We put our hand out to feel its cool skin. It punches us in the face and returns to a defensive position. We back up, our face stung.

"What was that for? I was just trying to see if you were real."

No response. No expression. Just hands up and the figure in a fighting stance, eyes straight ahead.

We size it up and wait. It still doesn't move. We approach slowly, hands up defensively. It again jabs at us, landing and following up with a kick to our leg, just hard enough to sting.

Yelling, we charge forward and try to punch it in the head. It side steps off to our left and jabs us in the right cheek, following up with a body shot and a leg kick.

We back up and it freezes in fighting stance.

We feint towards its head but punch it in the body. We actually land! It closes distance and throws us down to the ground, standing at the ready but not attacking.

We hear laughter outside our cell. It is Sistid, laughing uncontrollably. Eventually he stops, wiping tears from his reptilian eyes. "Haha Addict. Do you like *our* bioprogram? It is a fighting model set to the lowest setting. I see it put you down." He starts laughing again.

We charge forward and it claps us with a leg kick and circles out. We charge it again and it jabs us twice in the face, Sistid laughing all the while. We feint again and land another punch but it knees us in the solar plexus and we fall to the ground clutching our body, gasping for air, not able to breath for a few seconds.

"Haha addict. You can't even beat the setting that our children face. This is a Nuclae bioprogram, not a shitty one we sell to humans. I know humans are weak, but I thought that a street druggy would be tougher than this. At least keep your hands up."

With something to prove, we attack again and fight the thing until we are exhausted, our face and body aching but not injured. We sleep well.

For some reason Sistid keeps the sparring bioprogram in our cell. We spend all the next day trying to beat it but it punches, kicks, elbows and knees us in always unexpected combinations. Sistid and Alella sometimes watch us and give us advice on our technique, which we ignore until they leave, sweating profusely.

We fight the bioprogram every day after our treatments. We imagine old enemies and old friends and beat them. We imagine the dealers. We imagine the addicts who chased us and beat us and tried to take our Viprex™. We imagine the dogs that chased us. We imagine the Prophet and Shaya. We imagine Varius and his crew. We imagine the police.

Our body grows stronger and our movements become quicker again despite the influence of Viprex™ fading from our system. We start to land more strikes on the bioprogram. We spend our hate every day this way.

Strapped in a stretcher, the specter remains silent under the bright lights of Subterra's prison medical facility carved out of the bedrock beneath Clinic City. Alella can tell by the specter's breathing that it, or rather he, is conscious. She knows he is a male by his karyotype which she has now analyzed. There is dried blood on the stretcher underneath the distortion. She has also learned that his brain, though organic, is part bioprogram. This invisible soldier is possibly organic tech.

"I can find out a lot about you even if you won't speak," Alella says to the shimmering subdued ghost.

"Why even bother talking to this filth?" growls Sistid who stands close behind her watching.

"Why filth, Sistid?"

Sistid doesn't say anything.

"Well, I will tell you what I know. He is a human male. He has sustained trauma to many of his organs and skeleton. He has altered DNA that codes for organically synthesized skin. Unlike active camouflage that is employed by Nuclae there is also a technological aspect to his camouflage, I believe this skin can bend electromagnetic rays."

"Why do you think that?"

"Look at the blood pattern underneath him. It is warped. A chameleon would try to copy its surroundings and not appear a distortion."

"He can't be Nuclae," says Sistid with a measure of disgust.

Alella eyes him for a moment. Why the hate? *What does he know that he isn't telling her?*

"I think you're right. The recombinant DNA is in clusters not commonly used by us. I believe this is an altered human, or something I have not seen before."

"This scum is Corporate Government," hisses Sistid like a true snake, his eyes narrow and his arms look ready to lash out at the ghost.

"I believe he is Corporate Military by some of the coding I saw."

"What's the fucking difference?!" says Sistid harshly.

"True," she agrees. "They are two heads of the same beast."

"They are all the same. They are our enemy!" he is almost yelling at her and edges closer to the specter.

Alella puts her arm between him and the ghost and gently pushes back. "Calm down, Sistid. We need it intact so we can study it and find weaknesses, by the code."

Sistid takes a step back and exhales slowly. His shoulders drop.

"What is your story, ghost? Huh?" she says rhetorically.

In response she can almost see the outline of the specter's head turn and focus on her.

"You are not invisible. You have heat leakage and I can see the edges of you. I can see where some of your wounds are and I'm gonna keep you alive whether you want it or not."

"Alella, this one has killed-" he chokes off the last words realizing he is not authorized to tell her. But he obviously wants her to know.

She understands. "We are not savages," she says quietly, half to Sistid but also to remind herself. She proceeds to wash and dress the ghost's wounds albeit roughly.

Alella and Sistid come to our cell, their faces serious. Sistid lets Alella in and waits outside. Alella gives us a cup and watches while we gulp the serum down all at once, grimacing at its sharp taste.

"Do all humans consume like you?"

"How?"

"Greedily. Thoughtlessly. Ungratefully."

She pauses for a moment.

"What's wrong with you?" we ask, annoyed. She has never insulted us before.

"Selfishly." She adds quietly, her eyes accusing.

We feel like throwing the cup at her but it would just make this situation worse.

She disrespects us.

Our arms seem to move on their own accord and Alella looks at us knowingly.

"I sense violence in you, addict. Natural for your people."

We breathe and gradually see her from our eyes again. She seems calmer as well and takes a sterile, medical tone.

"You haven't been sleeping very much lately. Why?"

"Could you sleep if you were coming off Viprex™? I am afraid to sleep down here. I don't trust you."

"Look who's talking," she says almost angrily again. "We should trust you? Viprex is still too strong in you for us to trust you."

"Whatever, I don't need you."

"That's funny," she sneers. "You would either have been caught, or you would have died in the tunnels if we hadn't taken you in. It is more than any human has ever done for one of us.

"You had your reasons. And besides, that was extenuating circumstances."

"Still though, we did save your life. The humans were trying to catch you. Why?"

"I don't know, I killed a bioprogram. Maybe that's why."

"The biomechanical beasts they sent for

you are still near where you entered the sewers," Sistid says in his coarse voice from outside our cell.

"The bioprograms? How come they haven't tracked me here?"

"Oh addict, we have our ways." Sistid says from outside our cell.

"The samples that we took from you are still being processed by our scientists. Until then, Sistid and I are in charge of studying and treating you."

"But why do you help me, why not just study me and then get rid of me?"

"It is the Code of the Nuclae."

"What does that mean?"

"It is what we call ourselves. We are not mutants or even hybrids as you call us."

"I know that, but what is the Code of the Nuclae."

"This is our code. Our rules. Our Central Dogma. This is how we survive. It is our binding contract together. Central Dogma Chapter 5 verse 5: Share with my brothers, sisters and be free of want" Her eyes have the look of a true believer.

"But I am not one of you."

"And what are you?" she asks, almost mockingly.

"I am human."

"As human as I am."

"But you are a mut- I mean Nuclae."

She pauses. "You seem familiar with our name."

"I was friends with a Nuclae before, for my part."

"Well, we are not mutants. A mutation suggests an error in DNA. My people have *purposely* altered the DNA in our genome. *We have no errors.*"

"So, you are not human anymore."

"You humans alter your DNA to fit your purposes, too. *All* of you. Are you not human anymore?"

"We are not the same."

"We are not. We are much more skilled at it and we are not cybernetic. This is not allowed for my people as it is for yours. It is forbidden. So in a way, we are still more human than you."

"I am not cybernetic and my brain is not computer augmented. I can't afford it."

"No? But haven't you had instructions downloaded into your brain like a bioprogram when you were in school? Also, cybernetics are common among your military, your police, your rich and many of your criminal classes."

We hear the truth of what she says but we don't acknowledge it. "Why can you not add cybernetics but you alter your DNA?"

"We can accomplish more with bio circuitry than your cybernetics ever could." She says proudly.

"Bio circuitry?"

"What you do with metalloids and electronics, we accomplish with organic materials. We do what we want to do with our physical forms. The difference is we have free will. I am not sure anyone up above does, not even your leaders."

"I don't understand, you want to be mutants, or as you say Nuclae?"

"I told you we are not mutants. Anyways, it is not a matter of want. It is a matter of necessity."

"How so?"

"Every Nuclae child knows our history. Some generations ago, around year zero, when humans shaded the stratosphere with particulates, scientists needed to make a choice. People were getting priced out of work by automation and a primitive bioprogram. Some scientists worked for the Corporate Military and made a lot of money, but other citizen scientists began to experiment with ways to alter their own DNA. The studies included drastically altered DNA tests on human fetuses. Religious groups lobbied their political constituents and got the tests banned as "unwholesome." Many of these scientists who weren't imprisoned went underground to continue their research. They also taught students rather than plug them in like your people do. That is why so many of you are easy to control."

"Not me," we say. "I haven't been hooked

up to that shit since I ran away from school as a kid."

Alella raises her eyebrows but continues, almost reciting, "These scientists tended to fund their research by altering the DNA of people that could not get a job because of automation and overpopulation. They altered their DNA in ways to make them more employable. Miners had their eyes adjusted to see in the dark and their body parts adjusted to take the place of tools. Divers had gills grown so that they could breathe underwater. Many other alterations were created to combat automation. Corporations paid our ancestors bottom dollar but at least they had work."

"Some of the early experiments would have Frankenstein results with the subjects persecuted unfairly and sometimes killed by angry mobs after being blamed for murder, rape or anything else that people needed scapegoats for. There was a huge backlash against the people who received what was termed "forced mutations" or mutants. Hypocritically, at the same time the government was using AI to change DNA to make super soldiers, to treat diseases, and even to enact cosmetic changes, the people who flouted the rules with illegal mutations were driven more and more to the fringe. There were now three types of people, unaltered, legally altered and illegally altered."

"To escape persecution the illegally altered

fled to the newly abandoned sewers that were no longer needed due to advances in environmental technology to curb pollution. Many humans fled inside to their virtual world and never came out again. Antibiotic resistant diseases wiped out a large part of your population, especially the unaltered ones, but our scientists acted quickly and saved most of our people."

"Our scientist learned how to grow food that didn't need visible light for photosynthesis, but rather used underground energy sources for a 'slow photosynthesis.' Naturally, these rogue scientists and workers formed mining and seafaring communities together. They sold both mined and genetic products to the humans above to keep the governments off their back and for supplies they couldn't make themselves. As they mined deeper into the ground, their knowledge grew, and eventually their skills altering DNA made flesh, senses, and all matter so malleable in their hands that your governments formed covert operations to steal the technology while performing counterintelligence and media blitzes against them. According to corporate media and thus popular opinion, their self-reinvention reached nightmare proportions. Holopictures of 'mutants', smuggled to the surface, struck horror in the hearts of your people."

She continues, her eyes now focused far away, on another time, "Our knowledge of genetics became standard information that was taught to every Nuclae child in school lessons *in classrooms (unlike human virtual learning which is far inferior)!* Our numbers grew and our alterations were becoming more and more potent, physically, intellectually, economically and even defensively. Our minds have similar processing power to human-augmented AI brains. This made your governments above more and more wary, but we were strong enough and in good enough defensive positions so that the governments left us alone as long as we occasionally furnished technical information on genetic alteration. We would throw you some old code that we considered obsolete but you cherished, especially if it was cosmetic."

"Not me," we disagree. Alella focuses on us and screws up her lips for a moment but continues the herstory lesson.

"Of special concern to the world governments was the fact that past pollution and the darkness from their atmospheric dust to stop warming was killing much of the world's forests and farms that produced food and oxygen. The atmosphere was feeling the effects. The Nuclae had used their knowledge of genetics to produce "Synthetic Oxygen Factories" to save the atmosphere, basically synthetic green organisms that use photosynthesis to produce O_2 missing due to human-caused deforestation. The government scientists couldn't figure out how they had created these tough organisms that could filter toxins out and survive almost anywhere, as the code was and is too sophisticated for your scientists. One of the Nuclae's main exports are SOFs. We are also a big exporter of synthetic food and ores. Even our factory process is based on the expression of DNA."

"I am a Talon. Traditionally we are mining stock but I chose to become a genetic doctor to care for all Nuclae because of Chapter 5 Verse 5."

"Over the years we Nuclae have formed some general groups, though some are more individual. All Nuclae are hardworking, but Talons tend to be especially so and we are modest and not too extreme in the visual expressions of our alterations. As a doctor, my knowledge of the code and the Central Dogma, *our* bible, is very deep."

"Even though I bucked convention, I am proud of my heritage as a Talon. We are a climbing strain of the Nuclae and one of the first successful adaptations of the Nuclae-synthesized polymorphisms to compete with increasing corporate automation. Our strain are direct descendants of the miners that had their DNA altered to see in the dark and climb any surface so that they could outcompete mechanization for mining jobs before we were forced below."

Around the same time as the Talons

formed, also came the Hexapeds (six legged fellow miners), and the Plastics (bendable arms and legs) like Sistid."

Sistid glares at us, but remains quiet, letting Alella tell their story.

"Blades (so skinny that they were almost flat to fit in tight spaces), Nightcrawlers (workers with night vision), Webfoots (gilled sea floor manganese miners), Deoxies (No-Breathers for sea and space exploration) and the hairless Cancers (traditionally scientists and doctors) along with many others who did not fit into categories. Our names describe our adaptations and many are crossbreeds. A number of Nuclae decide to get further alterations later in life."

"Your government keeps us around because of the black market products we can provide: no-brain servant bioprograms, no-brain reclamation bioprograms, security bioprograms, allomone sex bioprograms, pet bioprograms, organic inanimate O_2 factories more productive than plants, synthetic food along with many other useful things. The human government scientists have not been able to figure out from studying our products how to make them as well as we can. They still buy things en masse and inform the population that this is their product. If word got out that the Nuclae provided so many of the world's necessary products I am not sure what would happen, but chaos would ensue. I know that "Buy human" is a popular slogan up above."

She firmly believes what she is saying but it goes against everything we have ever been taught. We still have questions.

"How come we have not been able to reverse engineer your products?"

Alella's eyes narrow and she clenches her lips. We have never seen hostility on her face before but we realize that it must be deeply rooted in her and the rest of the Nuclae.

Sistid and Alella exchange looks and then she speaks again, quietly.

"When I visit the city above, I hate how they look at me, how they talk about me in hushed voices and most of all how they talk to me. Your people threaten me and the others like me for no reason except for jealousy and ignorance. We know this eventual backlash towards us could be a kiss of death for our people and there are already rumors of attacks on some of the smaller Nuclae settlements all over the world."

"That's not what I learned. When they plug us in for sleep school as a kid, everyone learns that the mutants, I mean Nuclae, hate humans and that is why lurkers evolved to protect us, even if they sometimes kill humans by accident."

"That story is a lie. Most of us don't hate humans, though the same can't be said about you. Lurkers are surely human weapons meant to terrorize the Nuclae, but also used to control the human population."

"What? No way, lurkers are mutants just like you."

Alella laughs. "I feel sorry for humans. Your people believe without question or you question the wrong things. That is why we don't include cybernetics, they are too easily controlled. They plug you in and fill you up with bullshit."

"I haven't seen anything to tell me different. You look kind of different than lurkers but you are also the same in a way." We are unsure of our words. This time we are quiet for a moment before we speak and actually think about what Alella is telling us.

"Why are you telling me all of this? Your history," we ask quietly.

Alella regards us for a moment, weighing something in her head.

"Addict, just remember one day. Maybe there will be no more Nuclae, maybe your people will wipe us out. Just remember that we did not kill you when we could have. Maybe you can change your people's ideas about us."

"Me? A loser Viprex™ addict?" We laugh for a bit, at the irony.

Sistid walks to the door and looks through it at us.

"Addict, remember the lurker. It killed my friend Cas."

"You can't control those things? Or fight them?"

"No, we try to run, they are hard to kill. But, addict, I find it strange that the lurker didn't find you."

"I'm good at hiding."

Sistid sneers at us, annoyed as usual and opens the door to the cell.

"The Nuclae believe data points the way to the truth," Alella continues, "and I do find it strange that a self proclaimed 'loser Viprex addict' survived so long in the tunnels with lurkers around when so many humans and Nuclae usually die at their hands within seconds. But we will need more data before we can figure you out. I have a feeling there is more to you than we can see with just our senses."

Alella turns away from us and powers through the open doorway and Sistid slams the door. We scratch our stomach, the slam echoing in our head as we hear them walking away.

TRANSLATION

trans·la·tion

/trans'lāSH(ə)n,tranz 'lāSH(ə)n/

the process of translating words or text from one language into another.

- a written or spoken rendering of the meaning of a word, speech, book, or other text, in another language.

- the conversion of something from one form or medium into another.

(BIOLOGY) the process by which a sequence of nucleotide triplets in a messenger RNA molecule gives rise to a specific sequence of amino acids during synthesis of a polypeptide or protein.

"It is time for us to go back up to the surface and take control in a way that will benefit *our* species," says Malthus to the assembled. "We have been in hiding for years and years and the other recombinants only hold us back. They are so content with this underground life. My colleagues and friends, it is now time for us to rise above this banishment. We have been underground long enough. The time is now for us to go above and take the thrones that we deserve."

A murmur spreads around the table in the dark, hot meeting hall where Malthus and 15 other nearly identical hairless Cancers all sit around a table discussing their plans for the future like they have been doing for countless years.

"We have always been in control anyways. With our knowledge of the Central Dogma and the Code no one is our master and few suspect what we really are."

"Yes, but we must proceed with extreme caution," says Morora. Her white skin gleams under the artificial lights, an adaptation well-suited to cave-dwelling species. . "We must not turn the rest of the recombinants against us. They are very numerous and it could be our undoing if we did. We should take small steps at first and test the reaction before we proceed."

Some of the others nod in assent. Though they look similar, Malthus knows that all their personalities have survived the years in some form, though mutated with age. "I know what your concern is, the Nuclae will not like us to provoke a fight with the humans because now we have an uneasy peace that they do not wish to shatter."

Many heads nod in assent, among them Morora's.

"However," he continues, "a fight can do one thing for us. After the smoke clears, the Subterra recombinants could be made extinct and we could rise above and blend into humanity in positions of power. Our appearances are much more malleable than they suspect. It would also remove the problem that they expect to receive a profit from *our* work on the code. They would never have been able to survive without *our* knowledge."

Malthus can see he is starting to win them over. They all have been together for years and their conformity and anonymity has been a great boon to them all. They really are together forever.

Morora speaks, "We can begin to stir up resentments among the different groups of the recombinants against the humans. This will lead to an eventual military investigation of them. Perhaps we can let the human addict out into Subterra. Reports say he is somewhat of a loose cannon, and he could stir up resentment against humans as well."

Malthus looks at her approvingly. "Good idea. The humans are also sending raiding parties into some of our outlying settlements." He has always been able to count on her straight-to-the-point attitude and words. Now he can see that the others are realizing the path to being the most powerful creatures in history. They had increased their brain capacity and processing power, armored their body structure and greatly increased their strength with muscles attached to bone keels for extra leverage. They consider themselves superior to every being on the planet, but they hide this even from the other Nuclae.

Ulana, who was normally one of the quietest Cancers, speaks up, "We don't have to be in outright control, though. What is wrong with subtle control? We can slip into positions of power without eliminating the other Nuclae. They could be useful to us. Chapter 2 Verse 6 says, 'a tool is never to be thrown away, unless it causes danger to other Nuclae.'" She sits back and eyes Malthus directly, waiting for an answer.

"*We,* Cancers, developed the code and now

it has become very malleable in other Nuclae's hands. They have used what we, the true Nuclae, have worked so hard for and would be a danger to our power. Plus, once they realize that we plan to leave, they could see us as a danger to them," responds Malthus. "Our secret is not safe with them."

"They would not turn against us," Ulana disagrees.

"How can you be so sure?" asks Malthus. "They fight each other over nothing. Their intellect is almost as short as their patience!"

"Not anymore, some of the younger Nuclae are becoming great scientists and doctors, like us," counters Ulana.

"A few, not enough to matter. Even among the most advanced Nuclae, under the surface you can see that the potential for factionalization and violence is still there. They are a danger to us. By doing nothing, you could turn everything against us. Remember when the press coined the headlines 'a cancer upon us all' speaking of recombinant scientists and what we do. I don't know if you pay attention to what goes on up there, but they still hate us. This is a way to excise what they consider an abomination and disassociate the recombinants from us. It would be that much easier to do some cosmetic alterations to ourselves and take over."

He gauges the reactions of his colleagues. Most of them seem to agree with what he says.

Ulana and a few others are frowning. He makes a note of who.

"We are stronger together. We need each other," levels Ulana.

She and the other opponents to his vision would have to be dealt with one way or another.

"No, they are a burden," Malthus says firmly. "One that no longer needs to be borne."

Subterra

As Subterra, the Nuclae city, is a self-contained security vacuum, Sisitid is ordered to begin to let the addict out under loose supervision to see how he interacts in their environment. Though puzzled by the order, Sistid is sure the addict cannot escape.

They watch the addict go through the crowded streets of the underground city and generally keep to himself, knowing that somewhere in the crowd, he is being watched. He begins to doubt if he wants to escape anymore.

The city seems warmed to a vibrant state in the artificial sunlike hues. The more he goes through the streets the more he begins to see similarities between many different Nuclae. Alella has explained to him that there are different groups that reflect the different jobs each group designed themselves for when the original colonies formed. These jobs were reflected in their appearances. Alella came from mining stock, explaining her eyes and hands.

The people in the city don't seem to even notice him. Sometimes from afar he sees them gazing at him but when he gets up close they look past him or around him. Never at him. So he keeps to himself and sits on a wall and watches the goings on: the mutant children playing games in the streets, the vendors selling or trading their wares. He begins to realize that despite their appearances, these people are very similar to humans. The main differences are that they actually interact with each other in person instead of just in virtual and the total lack of corporate interests.

He begins to explore out of the center and in the surrounding areas. He goes into bars and watches their strange rhythmic musical styles and has a drink of their alcohol. Sometimes, mutants would approach him and engage in curious small talk about the city above, though most keep their distance and avert their eyes. He isn't sure if this is because he is a human or because they might be able to sense that he is an addict.

Alella warns him not to go near the shipping areas. The Nuclae sell their products to the International Union and they are taken from here up to the service on Hexes. Ignoring her, he goes anyway, the crush of the workers here is tinged with an odor of sweaty violence and when he realizes he should get out he is too deep into the crowd of angry mutants.

"Murderer," a tall plastic says next to him. With a big scar across his face. "I keep this scar to remind me what your people did to me!" The plastic shouts and pushes at him with a whip-like movement that slams him back against other Nuclae. He gathers himself and tries to exit but the other Nuclae block him.

"Where you going boy?" says a razor thin mutant. He tries to push his way through and receives a blow to his head from behind. He puts his arms up to protect himself and they hit him. A tall female plastic gets between him and his assailants and wordlessly pushes him to the edge of the crowd and he flees. He slips back to the safer areas of the city shaken up and bruised. After Alella's herstory lesson, he doesn't wonder why they hit him.

He still doesn't care too much about himself. He thinks that he lives for himself, but rather, he lives for all the things he has become and in changing has lost his sense of self. He is an outsider, above and below. In his mind, they treat him just like the humans above do.

They look at us as less than them.

They keep him in their city. He doesn't want to be here. He has tried to be friendly and it has gotten him nothing. Not learning from the incident at the shipping area, he walks around with a chip on his shoulder but doesn't go near the shipping area again. In crowds of Nuclae he begins to rudely shoulder his way through aggressively, ready to run if they become too agitated.

He explores the club district of the city. There are a few venues as Alella told him that the population of this city is currently about 3,000. He finds their music to be very emotional with violence just below the surface. They play instruments that are similar to computerized instruments like the humans above, except that he is told their circuits are similar to nervous systems in animals.

He finds this electronic music intriguing but by far his favorite are the bands that play acoustic and electric instruments from ancient times. The beats swirl into a harsh cacophony of rhythmic pulsing with emotional wails over it. The bass lines are repetitive and set up a trance-like state in many Nuclae. He looks over the crowds of not more than a hundred bodies and sees the people either sway to the more somber rhythms or gesticulate wildly to the heavier beats. For the more aggressive songs, some dancers simulate fights with each other, but mostly pull their punches and kicks.

The songs are hewn from the environment, deep tunnels echoing different paths open to the song. Sadness, anger and frustration seem to be expressed by the music. The lyrics are often about Nuclae history or social problems. When he can understand their strange slang in their multifaceted voices, it often resonates with him as he can relate to being an ostracized outsider.

At a club one night a singer in particular gets his attention. He has gone to about 2 or 3 shows and they usually have 2 or 3 "bands" at each show. A band could consist of one person to many. Instruments could be modern or ancient or non existent as some bands are acapella with beats being played with strange organs that could only exist for the Nuclae.

A band comes on stage. The singer has an abnormally large chest and a long neck with an extremely exaggerated larynx. As far as he can tell, this hybrid is a one of a kind original and not one of the main subgroups of the Nuclae. When this strange bright-eyed creature starts singing, several frequencies echo loudly through the club at once, as if the vocalist has more than one voice box. He can sing 2 or 3 different lines simultaneously with harmonies that layer upon each other and resonate with ghostly echoes in the room. The Nuclae watching seem transfixed by the singer's tones and messages.

The singer speaks in several registers at once, almost in his singing voice: "Let us sing with the Lurkers." A cheer goes up from the audience.

The music starts and it is slow and violently powerful with booming drums and powerful strings contrasted with echoing vocals.

They walk in darkness
They walk alone
They walk where god walks
They didn't have to beg

Out there's a shadow
A distorted eye
I see a future
Where none will die

Being alive's a dead weight
It pulls you down for years
I walk where god walks
I didn't have to beg
I didn't beg

It brings back the memories of the time in the sewers that he was almost killed by the lurkers. He shivers, but the music strikes him as powerful and wild at the same time. The Nuclae dance their simulated fights and he moves with the music as well, closer to the back of the club.

After the show is over he sees Alella, a Hex and a smaller blonde female hybrid sitting in the back by the bar. Alella waves him over. He goes over to them and says hello.

"Ah, human," the large six legged creature with the human face smiles at him. "Alella tells me about you. My name is Vira." Alella orders him a Nuclae beer.

"I'm Cris," says the blonde, smiling at him pleasantly. "We don't get humans down here." She laughs, almost a snort.

"Nice to meet you both. You guys like the show?"

They turn towards him and regard him for a moment and then look at each other and smile. "Nuclae? Yeah, we love them. Very emotional," Cris says, still smiling. "Do *you* like it?"

"Yeah, I think it has a lot of feeling. But I thought that your people are the Nuclae?"

"They picked that name for their band as well. Is there a band up above in your world called Human Being or Cyborg?" Cris laughs.

He smiles. "Probably. There are a million bands up above. Mostly AI members though, or a combo of humans and AI, not using these ancient instruments that your people play. I think it sounds cool." He pauses, then: "Do you guys worship lurkers or something? Alella, I thought you said that they are made by humans."

"I don't know that for sure. It is a theory of some Nuclae. We actually do not know the lurker's origin," Allela admits.

"Not trying to be rude, but why do you have songs that seem to praise them? There are humans up above that worship lurkers."

"It isn't praise," says Vira, adjusting her bulk in the large Hex sized booth, dwarfing the small Cris next to her. "The lurkers have been here as long as any Nuclae can remember. It is like humanity's respect for an awesome force like nature," she says sarcastically and crushes her beer in one sip.

"Very funny," he laughs. "Not sure how much humanity respects nature after year zero."

"That's debatable, but anyways it is a healthy respect for a force of nature," Cris says firmly, using Vira's language.

"Yeah except I'm pretty sure they are not natural," he disagrees. "Don't think that when they used to have lions, tigers and bears that there were lurkers too. And the way they seem to distort the air around them is very strange."

They look at him strangely and he realizes that most people, human or Nuclae, don't usually live to tell eyewitness accounts of lurkers.

"Anyways, that last song was amazing. I wish they had music like that up in Clinic City."

"It probably wouldn't be too popular up there," says Alella. "I think that most people's taste is pretty much dictated by their programming. And your music up above is corporately dictated and technologically based. Very computer driven and a lot of it is written by AI to be pleasing and not to challenge the corporations."

"First of all it's not *my* society," he sneers. "But there is some good music in Clinic City. Or there was in the past when I used to pay attention to those things."

"Good music comes from the heart," says Vira. "If you can actively reflect what you have inside then you can make good music. It doesn't matter the medium as long as it expresses emotion to the hearer. Even you could make music, human."

"I wouldn't know how."

"We could teach you," laughs Vira, the idea obviously pleasing her. "Imagine a human playing Nuclae music. You could be a crossover sensation, human teenagers always like music that their parents don't approve of." They all smile again.

"You would be a star!" Cris laughs and smiles at him, her gray eyes shining.

"Well, I like the music, anyways. You guys have it pretty good down here: good music, decent food that doesn't taste too synthetic, biological machines that do the work of mechanical machines up above. I am surprised that the International Union™ hasn't more directly tried to court the Nuclae as an entity that they could do business with."

For the first time he sees displeasure creep across Vira's strange feminine pseudo human face and one of her limbs smacks the table loudly. "That would make sense on a humanitarian level. Unfortunately, your Corporate Government doesn't wish to trade fairly with a nation that it does not control the profit margin with. "

Alella speaks up also: " They would never recognize the separate Nuclae cities as one entity. Technologically and numerically we would become a large power in the world. They prefer it this way, with us underground and separate, secretly supplying many of their product needs. In exchange, we receive some processed materials that we do not have the facilities to create, some of your entertainment, transportation for our underground roadways and usually power; though we don't trust that the power wouldn't be turned off in a second if there was a falling out between our two groups."

"What would you do if it did?"

"Don't worry about that. We don't need your corporation's power to survive. It is just cost effective."

"You know, I am starting to get annoyed that it keeps being "you' and "us." It's not my power," he says.

"Yes, you're right. You are kind of between groups right now," says Alella thoughtfully, her eyes shadowed in the darkness of the club.

"Maybe there is hope for humans and Nuclae after all, human." Vira says.

"You could be the mediator," smiles Cris.

"I am a nobody. You would need rich people on your side."

"Have more faith in yourself," says Vira smiling.

"That's not it, I am just realistic. People

above only listen to people with money and corporations. How come there is not a Nuclae corporation?" asks the addict.

"It is not allowed," says Alella. "We all have jobs and if no one wants to do a job, it gets assigned."

"By who?"

"Councils elected for this purpose."

"But you have money."

"Our money is not the same as yours," Cris almost sings, slightly superiorly. "We have a cap."

"A cap? What's that? Like a limit?"

"Yep," smiles Cris in the semi darkness of the club. "We don't allow anybody to have too much."

"Why?"

"It is called redistribution," says Vira. "By limiting the amount of money the richest of us can make, we give the money to people that need it more. Money for us is just a marker to keep track of work. Though many Nuclae don't have much, we all have what we need. There is still some inequality, but not to the extent that you have up above."

"Redistribution? Huh, I like that. We should do that up above too. It would make things more fair-"

"Why do you think your government villainizes us so." Alella interrupts. "This concept would ruin the corporate power structure you humans have and your leaders would never allow it. This is one of the reasons we are kept contained and only the most human of us are let up above."

He begins to see, it wasn't the genetic augmentation that his government feared. That was just an excuse to keep the Nuclae political structure isolated from the human population. It was too egalitarian.

The next band starts tuning up their primitive electromagnetic instruments. Cris tells him they are called Dox Breath and they are fronted by a screeching female and the drummer is a quad with 4 arms. He takes a sip of his beer and listens again to rhythms and sounds alien and exciting to his ears.

The leaves in the gardens never change, always in their arrays of darkness with highlights of red, orange and yellow. Alella has told him that photosynthesis results from heat energy funneled from the rest of Subterra to create frequencies that the genetically altered varieties could use to produce their food.

The addict finds the gardens the most fascinating place in Subterra, albeit on the periphery. The Nuclae have picnics and parties in the gardens. It is their gathering place to party and relax. The gardens are safe for all, Alella tells him, because there is some sort of unspoken agreement that they will not defile them with violence towards each other. Since they are a major food source for the Nuclae, utmost care is taken to make sure that nothing goes wrong and many quads patrol the rows of trees and other plants.

He often goes to the gardens and just sits down under an apple tree and relaxes. Sometimes he goes to the tropical gardens where it is warmer and sits under the banana trees and watches the laborers. The plastics and the four-armed beings that pick fruit are extremely quick at their jobs and watching them is surreal. Up above in Clinic City most food is factory made. Only the very rich can afford fresh produce.

When they pass by closely he averts his eyes and pretends that he is not concerned with them at all, though he is fascinated. The level of complexity and organization in their society dumbfounds him. So many different jobs, and everyone does their part, contradicting the stereotype of the mutants as lawless malcontents. The beauty of their civilization is their cooperation in the work environment, despite what he has interpreted as chaos in their city. It is an organized chaos.

Sometimes, however, it is a bit disturbing to see how they relate to each other in normal pedestrian life, where they are quick to anger and violence between their different strains, which are really only based on the plasticity of their mutations. However, fights are quickly broken up by Nuclae and often seem to only be for show of status.

The shadowy high caverns of the arbors are eerie to his human eyes. Seeing the silhouettes of Plastics, some Hexes and the Four-arms going back and forth like the insects they engineered to pollinate their plants is a strange sight. In the garden, a four armed Plastic approaches him and speaks in their raspy way: "Why do you come down here?"

"It's relaxing," says the addict.

"You're getting in the way of our workers," accuses the grayish Plastic, some of its hands pointing accusingly at him.

"No I don't. I always keep to myself and move out of the way if I have to."

"I am getting complaints about you. We don't want you down here."

"Why, I never mess with anyone."

The multi-arm's eyes squint and it raises its voice: "This is our garden, not yours! Get out of here, *borg bitch*." More mutants start coming from behind the trees and plants and stand at varying distances in the garden netherworld, their eyeshine menacing in the near dark. The sight is intimidating and otherworldly. They look like evil spirits in a dark garden.

He begins to retreat towards the exit. When he is almost out of the cavern, they all start laughing and wooping, victorious barking sounds emanating from their lips.

Pheremone Tracking

1000 Pawn™ 3rd generation mechanical bioprograms are injected with a DNA sample from the subject. They use pheromone tracking and will not stop until they locate their quarry. These bioprograms are flesh muscles attached to a metal skeleton with synthesized brains controlling movement and assorted weapons systems. They can be programmed for search, surveillance and/or extermination. Their weapons are varied but most consist of firearms mounted onto their "heads," which also contain sensors for wide spectrums of information. Quadrupedal, they can move faster than most humans and can move over any surface no matter how uneven. They are also very hard to destroy.

500 shadow agents are also deployed to Clinic City to support the bioprograms and carry out the extraction. The Pawn military bioprograms will wait for orders at locations surrounding the search area as the bioprograms are dispersed into the city's obsolete sewer system at different locations. This is a large number of corporate military to disperse and it is very expensive. Considering the gravity of the situation, it is deemed necessary. The golem-like bioprograms creep out of the RPWs canine-like and into the sewers all the same size with the

same gate, fading into the darkness followed by shadows.

Alella invites the addict over to her apartment along with Sistid, Vira and Cris for a real Nuclae meal. She asks the addict what he wants to eat and he says he'd like to try typical Nuclae food.

Sistid picks him up at his cell and does not engage in small talk with him. He guides him through Subterra's lighted tunnels of daylight. They pass groups of different strains of Nuclae along the way. They always acknowledge Sistid but almost never the addict.

"Are you a big shot or something?" asks the addict as they walk.

Sistid ignores the question. "This way, addict."

"Everyone greets you, but you just nod back."

"I am head of security for Subterra. Everyone knows who I am and they respect me and my position."

"You are a big shot."

"Nuclae recognize that I got where I am by hard work, intelligence and grit; something a drug addict wouldn't understand."

"There's the real Sistid," smiles the addict.

"Hurry up, we are running late. Do all

humans walk this slow?"

They get to Alella's and ring the buzzer. Alella comes to the door and is wearing a dark dress, the color of the leaves in the garden. The addict realizes that she is beautiful for the first time.

"Welcome, human, to *my* home." Alella holds the door open for him and Sistid and he enters an oval chamber, carved out of the bedrock roughly 6 meters by 4. It is lit by frequencies that remind him of late afternoon sun. There is a table and some chairs that seem to be made of the bone material that the Nuclae synthesize from DNA. On the wall are some pictures of various Nuclae as well as art and a large mirror. A small kitchenette is on the far wall and Cris and Vira are preparing something on the counter that smells of garlic. Quiet Nuclae music plays from invisible speakers with a relaxing instrumental rhythm.

"Hey Sisitd. Hi human," They laugh and smile genuinely at him.

"Hello Vira, Hi Cris." He smiles back. "Your place is beautiful, Alella. This would cost a fortune in Clinic City."

"Thanks. This is a typical apartment for a single person."

"You don't have to share it? I guess you are a doctor so you must get the best stuff."

"Maybe that's how it is up above, addict," Sistid sneers. "But down here all Nuclae have access to something like this as long as they work."

The addict thinks of Shaya. "What if they refuse to work?"

"Well they don't get something this nice," smiles Alella. "Do you want a drink? You seemed to like the Nuclae beer so we got you some."

"Thanks." He pops the cap off with an opener and takes a swig. Cris comes over with a garlicky flatbread and some dip.

"Here you go, human."

He dips the steaming bread into the bowl and takes a bite. He can't believe how much flavor is in the dip made from some sort of protein. There is also cut up fruit and grapes.

"I've seen food like this in commercials for high end restaurants but I have never tasted anything like this. It is delicious."

"Thanks," smiles Vira. "Here is the main course." She brings a large wok to the table sizzling with a spicy aroma.

They sit down at the table and serve a spicy garlic synthesized protein stir fry with real gai lan to the addict. Rich in flavor, and again, one of the best things that the addict has ever eaten. While they eat, they tell him about how they manufacture pretty much everything by protein synthesis, from food, to textiles, to furniture. They are proud of their city, of their science and their people and they let him know. He asks questions but mostly they talk and tell him about their city and their culture.

"But what about other cities? Do you visit other Nuclae cities."

"Your people try to prevent it," Sistid frowns at him. "We have some communication but it can be jammed, and you know humans or Nuclae are not allowed to travel between cities without visas. Nuclae are very rarely granted visas by your government."

"But you must have other ways. I have been through your tunnels and they go on forever."

"It is true, there are other ways to go, but they are guarded."

"By lurkers?" asks the addict.

The Nuclae look at each other.

"Have you never tried to leave Clinic City on foot?" asks Vira.

"Never, it is forbidden. Plus, I wouldn't know where to get Viprex in the wild. Why? What is out there?"

"Other things besides lurkers lurk in the wild. Traps your people have manufactured."

"Like what."

"Enough, addict!" Sistid raises his voice. "Do human guests usually insult their hosts?"

Unsure what he has done to offend, the addict looks around at the Nuclae who are quiet. The music plays quietly in the background, bittersweet, melancholy yet joyful at the same time.

The next day, the addict is abruptly moved to a higher security wing of the facility by a large guard of Cancers. Alella and Sistid come to his cell that morning and are surprised to see it empty. They go straight to Dr Morora and meet her in the hall outside of her office about to rush off somewhere.

"Where is the addict, Morora?" asks Alella.

"He has been moved to high security. This is beyond you. I am taking over his treatment as of now."

"What? He was starting to respond to us. Sistid and I were making real progress with him." She is incredulous. "I synthesized his karyotype and I am analyzing it now."

"Not anymore. His DNA has been fully analyzed by *us* and there are decisions that need to be made. Please turn in any samples you have of the addicts."

Alella bristles. "What decisions? He still needs our help."

"We will provide him with his treatment. This research must be conducted by more experienced hands than yours. Besides, you have been playing doctor so much, you have been neglecting your skin research."

"But I sent you my full report a week after you assigned me the shadow. And I neutralized his camouflage. Then, I was also assigned to the addict. I am making progress with him."

Sistid speaks, his face showing real displeasure. "Dr. Morora, Alella is doing both jobs you assigned her. She knows code as well as anyone in the city. The addict was under our charge; we should have been consulted before you took him away. We could have advised you on our observations and the safety of all concerned."

"For his safety, I care very little. Only so that we may study his mutations does he need to be alive. As for your observations, I have read both of your reports, Alella. Though thorough, the council views it with some displeasure. You both seem to have developed some sort of rapport with the human. That will not do. He is an experiment, nothing more. He is unimportant besides that."

Alella loses it. "But we know what is going on with this subject! We don't have to stop treating him just because we are studying him. One moment we are treating him as a patient and now suddenly he is a lab rat? Chapter 5 verse 9 says we shall not cause unnecessary harm. You're as bad as a hum-"

"Alella!" Sistid interrupts her and grabs her arm haltingly before she can say anything else.

Morora regards her with a steeled glare and speaks after a pause. "I would watch your words, young woman. You are lucky to be practicing the code at all, being a *Talon*," she spits the word. "The council has decided, and that decision is final. I would not stand in the way of a council action if I were you. It could have dramatic repercussions. For *both* of you."

Alella stares at her for a moment and seems about to burst into violence but she turns on her heel and powers away. Sistid looked at Morora and speaks in his gravelly voice. "Morora, what you do is not right. I don't like the addict but he does need our help. I wanted to have him killed at first, also, but he isn't evil. He has made progress in his addiction and he could be a key to relations with the humans."

"Sistid, I appreciate your candor, but the decision is final. We need to totally control the addict's actions and environment for our tests. This means no outside interference. We will advise you of the results periodically if we deem necessary but you are both off this assignment as of now."

Sistid turns with his strange and serpentine movements and starts to depart. He turns back around and looks again at the Cancer. "I hope you are right Morora. I really do. Because that is a life and in that is a code just as precious as is all code."

Morora rolls her eyes. "Don't you quote the code to me too, Sistid," she says, waving him away.

He turns and strides away, his legs

forming circular movements as he walks.

Morora turns around and starts back to the lab where the addict is. Her mind is on the tests she needs to oversee. Sistid's words are already forgotten.

The humans build bioprograms from mutant corpses in the city morgue and alter their DNA to function with the CPUs from the stock bioprograms. Though it disturbs him to be involved in the fabrication of the Clinic City Nuclae bioterrorism attack, Varius knows it is necessary, but he hadn't planned on getting his hands dirty doing this part of it.

Corporate Military had insisted, saying the less people involved in their clandestine op the better. He said to make sure the event took place in a part of town where "no good people will get hurt." When pressed, they told Varius to "make sure that mostly poor people died."

The mutant puppets detonate their "disease bomb" after a standoff in Clinic Square with the police on a public assistance day so it is extra crowded with rabble. People fall ill immediately and it spreads quickly. Hospitals control the innoculations but many people die if not treated immediately. Calling it the "terrorist mutant virus," the press stokes the rage against the hybrid bioterrorists who are clearly seen on sentry systems throughout Clinic Square. A political and public outcry goes out to attack the Nuclae, a perfectly natural gut reaction. Corporate Government orders strikes against the "mutants" as a preventative measure to stem the tide of any further bio attacks.

Ulana arranges to meet Alella in the gardens. She hopes to be inconspicuous in there and she doesn't want to be seen speaking to Alella because it will put both of them at risk. They meet in the grape arbors because they are enclosed with enough cover to not be recognized but it is also thin enough to see if one is being watched.

Alella is not aware of who it is she is meeting nor why. She had found a message slipped under the door of her apartment saying: "Addict equals danger. Meet at Sublevel 4 Garden 17 northeast quadrant tomorrow at 1900 hours. Make sure you are not followed, a friend."

To Alella, it seems like a set up. She doesn't understand why anyone would want to set her up as she is generally agreeable to all in the city but she feels paranoid about it. She speaks to Vira and Cris and they arrange to be on Sublevel 4 at 1900. This makes her feel better.

She enters the garden; the only visible light shines from luminous plants kept there for light to work by. Because of this her heat sensors are not functioning at a high level. Her sensitive olfactory nerves smell something in the air. Many scents, she is not alone.

She pauses, why would anyone want to set her up? Surely not Morora? Over so little a disagreement as the addict. No, she is safe. Maybe someone wants to tell her something and doesn't feel comfortable telling her in public. Still something doesn't sit well with her.

Her eyes pierce the gloom and she continues on to Sub Garden 17. She sees a figure waiting near one of the large yellow fruit trees. She starts towards it. The figure is bulky and bald. *A Cancer?* She thinks. She approaches and she recognizes a doctor from the Genetic Programs Council. Ulana is her name.

Ulana looks around suspiciously. "I have to make this quick, Alella. I have something very important to tell you about the addict you were taking care of."

Alella eyes her. She has always thought that Ulana was one of the more decent people on the council, at least as far as politicians go, but she seems jumpy. Alella can smell her sweat. From her pheromone mixture, she can tell that Ulana is scared.

"Are we alone here? It doesn't feel right in here."

Ulana grabs her hand and looks into her eyes. "The addict lives and is in Morora's care," she says out loud while she starts tracing signals into her hand that many Nuclae scientists are taught to use to avoid Sonars, the flying modified odonata insects that are the ears of the Nuclae, so that genetic secrets can less easily be stolen from each clan.

Pay attention carefully. We are probably being spied on right now. I had a disagreement in council with Malthus and the others. They are planning to betray the Nuclae and turn us all against each other. This has been an idea of theirs for a long time but that addict is the catalyst. We think he can consciously alter his own DNA just by thinking about it.

What? That is impossible, even for us.

We think that it may be a result of his possessor and the experiments they did up in Clinic City as well as interactions he may have had with lurkers.

Lurkers?

He seems to have some characteristics of lurkers but we haven't been able to test this yet.

So the humans want him back? Why did they let him go?

I think they didn't know what they had till after he escaped, aided by the lurkers. We believe the possessor can code itself, maybe even for immortality.

Why is it such a big deal to the Cancers if the humans develop immortality? They are overpopulated enough already and won't be able to support exponential growth with no death.

Alella, this may be hard for you to see, but this is the biggest secret of the Cancers. We are immortal. All of us, all true Cancers. We were the original scientists that started the Nuclae colonies underground because of persecution. We never died.

Alella's face shows disbelief and then recovers.

That is against the code.

We have a slightly different version.

According to Nuclae code, that is a sin. Also, it doesn't answer the question why the Cancers want the addict?

The Cancers want to make sure that no one, especially you and Sistid, will trade the addict to the humans for peace. They want to make sure there is violence committed so that at the same time they will slip into human communities. With what we have learned from the addict we will be able to dopplegang into their society and introduce immortality for a profit before the humans can develop it. This profit would not be redistributed as it would down here.

We all look very similar for a reason. Plus occasionally we would change our appearances and pheromones to hide our identities but it would take a coder and some time. With the information we can get from the addict, we can now just become "human" by willing it. Can you imagine a being consciously in full control of their code? The possibilities are endless, as well as the repercussions.

Ulana continues. *They want to be in full control of immortality and they want to be accepted above. They want to start a war against the humans and then slip out after they weaken the rest of the Nuclae.*

Weaken? How?

By letting the humans kill many Nuclae and then turning the survivors against humanity. There will be a war.

Alella felt like someone had kicked her in the stomach. *But what about the code, the Central Dogma? We all work together. I was taught code by many Cancers. They are decent, hard working.*

Some are, Alella, why do you think I am trying to help you now. I will probably be killed soon for it. I care about our people and our knowledge and so do some of the others. We are all Nuclae. I know you have the respect of many of our people. They will listen to you and even follow you. They know you are not prejudiced against the other strains and that you help all equally. I trust you and know that you will do the right thing. That is why I am talking to you. You must start pulling people together and tell the truth to them. Prepare them for what is going to happen.

Human and mechanical attackers will be underground soon. They want the addict and they are sending troops in here to get him. Malthus will use this to turn the others against the humans to start a war and the Cancers mean to disappear into humanity. They see the Nuclae as a future problem that is best reduced or even eradicated now and they are going to start with Subterra. The humans are playing the same game, they attacked their own people as well and declared war against the Nuclae today blaming us, playing right into the Cancer's hands.

Alella senses movement behind her. *We are not alone in here,* she signs.

Get out of here fast. You are marked. I am sorry to burden you but I always thought that you were one of the strongest, most honest doctors we have ever trained. Plus, you are tough as a Hex. Find your people and get the addict and escape with as many Nuclae as you can save. Get the addict to Mutaria and their scientists and get the truth out to the rest of the Nuclae.

Mutaria? Why?

Their scientist will follow the code and make decisions about the addict that we are too corrupted to make. No more time to talk. You must go. Get out of here now.

Ulana releases her hand and Alella stumbles back unbalanced by the weight she now has to bear. As she regains her balance, her eyes meet Ulana's for a moment and then she spins around; she has to get to Vira, Cris, Sistid and the others and tell them... but tell them what? Maybe if they can get the addict and release him to the humans they may call off the attack.

She runs towards the exit, looking

carefully around for any spies. She sees a small quad dart off into the undergrowth and knows she is being watched. She hits the door and is in a tunnel leading to the general population area of Level 4. Vira isn't far. She heads towards a more populated area where Vira and the others have arranged to meet. They would be safer together.

She looks behind her and sees no one. Her mind starts to race with possibilities. Somehow, she knows that what Ulana has said to her is true. She starts to grow angry.

Those bastards, the Council, how could they betray their own. But it makes sense. And the poor, pitiful addict, caught in the middle. He would have to be saved, and then traded right away to the humans to avert a war. She feels sorry for him but some things come before the welfare of one addict, despite the fact that she actually has started to like him in spite of himself.

But, if humans get ahold of the addict they would be more powerful than the Nuclae, they could become a lurker Nuclae hybrid. That would be more formidable than their best fighters.

She could kill the addict. No, that is against the code, against the very core of her being. Revulsion wells up inside of her at the thought. She may have to desert her people and take the addict to Mutaria.

He is locked in a dimly-lit clear-walled cell made from transparent material by the strange bald hybrids. They are very cold to him. Strange that he misses Alella and her friends, even the grouch, Sistid. He is scared he doesn't know what these strange mutants are going to do to him.

They pull him out of the cell and take him to the lab room where they strap him down to do tests, the bald hybrids speak about him as if he isn't even there. He is an experiment again, just like above in Clinic City, except now the experimenters look scary. He hears them talking about him consciously mutating on a cellular level or something like that and asks them what they mean. They don't even look at him and continue to speak to each other.

"Hey, I'm fucking talking to you!" he yells at them. One of them says coolly that if he doesn't stop yelling they will make sure he can't talk at all. He stops, and they continue their blood and sensory tests with something that looks like a hand held robomedic. When they are finished he is cuffed and unstrapped from the examining table and is led back to his new cell down the hall.

He looks for a way to get free but three of the large bald hybrids flank him and no openings present themselves. They release his plascuffs only when he is in the cell. He has a very bad feeling about them. Even Varius's staff was more agreeable than these pale, cold, muscular beings.

Across the hall from his cell is another cell with transparent walls and doors just like his. Inside is one of the strangest sights that the addict has ever seen. Sitting on a cot is a humanoid-shaped stain. The air itself seems to be stained with a person made of gray smoke, almost like a living shadow.

The addict can't take his eyes off the ghost. Is it a mutant? It must be.

Not sure if the clear walls are soundproof the addict says loudly: "Are you a lurker?"

The ghost doesn't answer.

"What did you do to get locked up in here?"

The ghost's head seems to turn imperceptibly. Where there should be eyes there are holes like two pits in the smoke. The smoke says nothing, its "eyes" watch the addict.

The addict suppresses a shiver. "Not the talkative type?" He says just to say something and then looks away. From time to time he looks back and sometimes the ghost will be watching him or laying down on the cot. It always appears to have its "head" turned towards him.

The bald mutants don't pay him much mind. They bring him and his fellow prisoner some tasteless gruel and water. Out of the corner of his eyes, he can see the smoke making food disappear out of the air, another strange sight in a day of them.

When lights darken for night, he hears a

commotion outside his cell in the form of yelling and loud thumps. The door bursts off its hinges and clanks to the floor followed by a six-legged Nuclae. It is Vira. She smashes through the clear plastic of his cell and then turns and does the same to the smoke's cell. She knocks the smoke to the ground hard and turns back to the addict.

"No time to explain. Jump on my back."

He can see Alella, Sistid and some others in the hall fighting the strange bald doctors. He rushes outside. Alella dropkicks a large bald guard in the stomach and plants her hand. Her feet never touching the ground, she inverts her body and lands a spinning head kick to another Cancer. Sistid is whipping his body around and getting inside the Cancer's defenses with ease, wrapping them up and cracking them with constrictor-like arms. They fight like circus acrobats in circus freak bodies, flipping over each other and narrowly dodging blows from the bigger but slower Cancers. They are winning for now but more and more hybrids are pouring out of the far entrance. Another Hexaped comes in and grabs the gray ghost. The addict is floundering, unsure how to contribute.

Alella spins around, her eyes wild, "Get on Vira's back, now! No time to explain."

This spurs him into action and he does as he is told. Vira starts running her six legs almost instantly, going impossibly fast. He holds on to her shoulders that almost seem to be made into handles. He looks behind and is amazed that Alella, the Hex with the stunned smoke man in its forelegs/hands, and the others, are keeping somewhat close followed by their pursuers who are striking at Alella's people from behind.

"Hold on!" says Vira. "We will meet up with them later. We are going through the tunnels and will circle back to the city. Now we are going to really get moving."

Her pace increases and they slip into a dark portion of the tunnel. He can't believe that any being with legs can keep the pace she is keeping for so long. They are going as fast as an autocar on the skyway. They whip by windows with their strange autumn colors behind. They whip by other hybrids that turn to look at this strange pair, a parody of a horse race.

They come to the tunnels and darkness engulfs him again. He cannot see where the path is leading, but he can still somewhat feel the tunnel around him, his latent ability muted. Vira threads her way through the abyss with a speed that is beginning to scare him. His adrenaline is so high that his heart beat sounds like a motor in his ears.

"How do you like the ride?" she yells in the darkness over her shoulders.

"Holy shit! Didn't know you could move this fast!"

"Six legs, addict. They probably have lost us by now but they will get something to trace our scent. Are you OK?"

"Yeah. Those bald people are cold ones. What were they gonna do to me?"

"Probably just study you for the rest of your life, which either could be a very long time or cut off prematurely."

"Why do you say that?"

"Those bald doctors, they are called Cancers. They believe that you can control your own protein synthesis."

"What does that mean?"

"You ran from a human hospital where they were treating an addiction to Viprex, right?"

"Yeah."

They maneuver around a series of corners and almost run into some Nuclae children. She nimbly avoids them and continues. "The doctors there might have done experiments on you to alter your possessor and to be able to control your DNA and make it malleable to its will. We believe your possessor has altered your DNA so that you can live forever. The Cancers want to keep this knowledge only for themselves."

"What?.......That.........That doesn't make any sense." The addict is confused. "Wouldn't I know if that was going on?"

"I don't know, but we have to figure out what to do about this. Corporate Military is looking for you also. This could spell a lot of trouble for Subterra."

He says nothing.

"I don't know you, addict. From what Alella says you are ok, but we have to make hard decisions about you.

"I see."

"Cheer up. The Cancers probably would have killed you and liquidated your corpse after they finished with you so that no one would ever find out the secret your DNA contained. Even if we do send you back to the humans, at least they won't kill you."

"Yeah, I'll just be a lab rat for Varius. Maybe I would be better off dead."

"I am sorry, but we might not have a choice in this." Her pace slackens a bit. He could jump off and try to get away in the dark tunnels. She will catch him though, and he has few illusions about being able to beat her in any kind of physical contest.

He speaks more softly: "I understand. Now it makes more sense. Why would you guys fight your own kind just to rescue one human addict?"

"That is true, although Alella was getting into trouble just by protesting for your release into her custody."

"Why would she do something like that?"

"She and Sistid have developed a liking for you and they didn't understand at first why access to you was denied."

He smiles in the dark. His first real friends in years are mutants. That is fitting. In a way, he is a hybrid also, though not by the same methods. "So you have to give me back to avoid conflict with the outside?"

"It is more complicated than that but I will let Alella explain to you when we meet up with her. We believe that the Cancers are immortal also and they want to protect this as their sole power."

"Why don't they want other people to live forever if they can?"

"I think that they wanted this to be a currency to trade for more power. Or maybe they want your powers for themselves so that they can become something more."

"Oh, so they were going to betray you, that is why you stole me from them."

"You are smarter than you look."

He laughs.

They moved fast in the tunnels, wind whipping their faces.

"You're sure Alella and Sistid are safe?"

"Them? I spar with Alella all the time. She is one of the toughest Nuclae in our city and she is with thirty of the toughest fighters we have. I fear very little for her, though your concern for them is touching," She mocks.

He laughs out loud, more to get rid of nervous energy than from humor.

She laughs too for a moment in solidarity and then they continue along in silence for a while, following the twists and turns of the rough hewn tunnels. He begins to sweat and realizes then, that the Cancers hadn't given him his daily treatment. They continue on for a few minutes and he starts to shiver between the sweat and the wind from their progress.

"Are you alright?"

"I feel sick."

"You need your treatment. We didn't have time to prepare it for you in the rush. Alella will treat you soon. We will meet them shortly at the edge of Subterra, by the entertainment district where we saw the bands play. They are not far behind. Try to relax till then."

Massacre

The Pawn™ bioprograms creep in the darkness; they have picked up 971-22's fresh pheromone trail in the tunnels below the warehouses and meander in stealth mode after it. One set falls back near the surface and transmits their findings to central command from a crack in the interfering earth above. Reinforcement bioprograms are deployed along with the ghost-like shadow troops. The bioprograms move quicker than the humans and several dozen of them follow to the coordinates left by the first wave that waits near the target for reinforcements.The trail is getting stronger and the agents are not far behind the set of bioprograms guiding them. They know that they are getting close to the city below the city. It is a sight few humans have seen. They use their near invisibility to take out guards and enter through a maintenance shaft. The scent of the addict grows stronger as the small canid bots creep into the bar district on the edge of subterra which is popular with the Nuclae, and very busy.

The shadow battalion catches up to the bioprograms outside a cavern crowded with Nuclae near the edge of Subterra that doubles as one of the city parks near the bar district. They can hear firing of the bioprograms' guns inside along with screams and the screech of twisting metal. The shadows rush inside and are greeted by carnage and destruction. The Nuclae are fighting the bioprograms and many are dead. They are dispersed around the chamber in order to make themselves more difficult targets behind trees and rock formations that children usually climb and play on.

Bioprograms are being torn to shreds by the Nuclae who fight like whirlwinds, destroying bioprograms with torque generated by spinning and crushing strokes born of training and enhanced speed and agility compared to the average above ground human. Hexapeds smash against bioprograms, which uselessly fire their light caliber guns at the Hexapeds' armored hides. Talons, Razors, Plastics and others fight behind the Hexes using them as a phalanx and then swarm out from behind them to mob the bioprograms. The Nuclae are beating them.

Flanking the scene, the military shadows begin their projectile attack on the mostly unarmed Nuclae and the tide quickly turns. Nuclae are being slain by the shadows. The remaining bioprograms also target any bystanders as secondary targets. Nuclae children and seniors are caught in the fire and most are killed and injured as they are evacuated.

Unbelievably, the shadow troops see another shadow that is almost visible, strangely gray and even more unbelievably, *this shadow is fighting bioprograms.* One of their own is a traitor, and it is next to their primary target, the addict who is surrounded by a fierce pocket of mutants.

The shadows stop shooting and charge the addict. Vira yells an alarm as the Nuclae can almost see the shadows' outlines with their enhanced senses. Alella's small group of Nuclae grab the addict and slip down a side passageway; the lone gray specter still fighting the bioprograms hesitates.

With the addict out of the mix, some of the bioprograms target and shoot at the gray shadow. He turns quickly and follows the addict's company. The bioprograms and the shadows are momentarily beaten back by the increasing number of Nuclae in the bar district and cannot give chase without losing many of their number. In retreating, they begin a counter attack while the bioprograms immediately start investigating other tunnels trying to find another path to the addict.

Stronger On Our Territory

Sistid, a bitter taste in his mouth from watching the attack and being forced to retreat without defending his people, leads the way into the tunnels that, as a security agent for the Nuclae, he knows better than most. He is followed by Alella, the addict, Vira, Coleth (a seer) and about 20 other Nuclae. For the moment, it is quiet but they are not safe. They know the bioprograms will track the addict and then more of the human shadow soldiers will be close behind.

He feels a personal sense of failure. As head of security, he should have somehow prevented the attack, but he didn't know, had no way of knowing. Nonetheless, he is angry that so many of his people had to die, and for what?

They move silently alert to every noise. All Nuclae know that it is dangerous to venture far from their cities and into the old underground tunnels that their ancestors carved. But they have no choice as they are being chased by humans, Cancers and even some of their own kind. Even worse, they are entering an area known to contain lurkers.

Sistid shudders. All Nuclae fear the lurkers. They are unpredictable and almost indestructible. They often seem to come out of nowhere as if they could appear from thin air, especially underground. Winding through the tunnels, he peers around a corner motioning for the others to stop. There is a large chamber up ahead with cliffs falling off to the side where the tunnelers would often throw debris. It looks clear but even the seers among the Nuclae have been killed by lurkers in the past. None of the whispers that often presage a lurker attack are audible, though it smells of an electric odor that is synonymous with lurkers. It is also just a characteristic of the lurker's territory, which Sistid knows they are in.

Sistid gathers Alella and the others, the addict is kept away by a couple of the bigger Nuclae. "This tunnel leads to the mountains. Towards Mutaria. There are other side tunnels that lead to other Nuclae cities, but the Cancers probably expect that we are going to try to contact other Nuclae," he says in a whisper. They know that all routes are dangerous.

"They may not expect that we would go as far as Mutaria. However, that is one of our options as it is the most powerful Nuclae city in this region. We also can try to bargain with the humans." Alella glances back at the addict and adds quietly. "It is unfortunate, but the fate of our people may depend on us being able to make a deal trading the addict for peace."

"Why should we make a deal with the humans? They just slaughtered our people, those lurker fuckers." Cris says a little too loudly, pain written on her face.

Sistid immediately shushes her. "Quiet! Or the lurkers you speak of will find us," he whispers angrily.

"I don't trust the humans, but if the Cancers are willing to betray us as sacrifices then it may be our only move," Alella says quietly.

"I don't know," says Vira thoughtfully. "I think it is too late for peace. So many of our people were slaughtered. The humans are not taking prisoners."

Alella weighs this for a moment. "You're right. They are not. Logic says that the Cancers will try to kill the addict and destroy his remains, rather than let the humans get a hold of him. If we can get him to Mutaria's labs, we can synthesize the addict's mutations and decide who to release it to. That could prevent a full scale war."

"Mutaria lies outside Clinic City's walls and far across the mountain forests," says Sistid. "We will be hard to track through there and we can lead the humans away from Subterra, saving what's left of our people."

"It will give us time to decide how to warn the other Nuclae. Sistid is right, if we stay down here the humans will keep on sending bioprograms and shadow troops and more of our people will be slaughtered," reasons Alella. "At least we can lead the trackers away from our people and put some space between us and them."

Cris angrily whispers again a bit too loudly. "We should just kill the Cancers-"

"Something's behind us!" interrupts Coleth in a harsh whisper.

"Lurker?" asks Sistid, adrenaline pumping through his body, his arms freezing in place.

"I don't think so, it's pushing frequencies, and a lurker usually doesn't."

Sistid relaxes and signals for them to fan out. They put the addict near the back of their formation and hide behind some mining debris in the chamber. Sistid is aware that their rear is exposed and he knows that lurkers could attack from the direction of the cliff but they could attack from any direction so they chance it. The addict is in the dark, his sensory augmentation dimmed by his withdrawal from Viprex™ but all the Nuclae see a shadowy figure appear around the corner. They train their guns on it.

The shadowy figure puts its hands up and approaches slowly. Two Nuclae that had been watching the entranceway sneak up on it from behind and grab both its arms roughly. It does not resist.

They bring it over to Alella. It is the gray painted shadow the Cancers had been holding.

"Let's kill him!" Cris whispers loudly and starts towards the shadow. Other Nuclae are visibly angry as well.

"Wait!" Alella commands. "Hear him out. Talk, ghost."

"I am a traitor to the shadow battalion. The bioprograms tried to kill me during the attack because I wasn't transmitting the correct code since you changed my skin. Once I defended myself, shadow battalion attacked and I killed some of my own soldiers. Now they want to kill me because they saw me fighting for you. I got no choice but to run and why not run together. I can help you." The ghost's quiet voice is masculine and hoarse from disuse.

"How?" Alella asks harshly. "How can we even trust you? We know nothing about you."

"I know the methods of the shadows. I know their strategies. I will be able to see them before you can."

"Pff, I doubt it, dick bag." mocks Cris.

The shadow ignores her and looks back at Alella, knowing her to be their leader. "I know that many Nuclae can sense us better than humans who only see in the 300-700 nanometer spectrum, but we are still dangerous. I can help you because I know how they think, how they attack and what strategies they use. If we go above ground, I can help jam spy satellites."

"That still doesn't answer the question of *why* the hell should we trust you?" Alella says roughly and looks hard at the shadow.

"I have nowhere to go. My people want to kill me."

"So why join with us?" asks Vira. "Why not just run."

The shadow again seems to look at Alella. "You patched me up. You could have just done your studies as your superiors commanded but you chose to take care of me. I owe you."

Based on all their facial expressions, the Nuclae don't seem to be buying it.

"Plus," the shadow says ironically, "what fun is being alone? I got nowhere else to go."

"Bind his arms and hold him near the addict," Alella commands. "But watch him, and don't let him get too close to the addict either."

They powwow for a few minutes, and against some of the Nuclae's wishes, decide to take the shadow with them as he may prove useful as a tool or as a bargaining chip if nothing else. They settle on the tunnels to the mountains as they are unpopulated. Once concealed in the tunnels, they can regroup and decide how to proceed with the addict. They will need more water and supplies and the mountains might be their only hope to attain these things.

The shadow speaks then, "Alella, get your people out of here. They are coming."

"Quiet, Ghost. Coleth, talk to me."

Coleth looks almost human except for his eyes, which have huge pupils as if to process more information. His ears are large to pick up more frequencies.

"We got problems." Coleth says. "He's

right. There are bioprograms coming through that side tunnel." He points to a small tunnel that empties out into the chamber. "I think there may be humans behind them as well."

"Trust me, there are, and there's gonna be a shitload of them." says the shadow quietly.

"OK. Let's get out of here. Sistid, lead the way."

"Follow me. I know this territory better than anyone." Sistid whispers. Except for the addict and the shadow, the others can smell a tinge of nervous pheromone coming from Sistid.

They follow the tunnels, moving quickly and silently. But the bioprograms are gaining. They will have to make a stand or get shot in the back.

They find a large area in an acre square chamber where big chunks have collapsed from the high ceiling and formed a maze of debris that can be used as cover. Some parts of the chamber are dimly lit by old mine lighting that the Nuclae designed to take power from low wavelengths and only light up when something approached. This will be a good place to ambush their pursuers. They hide in places around the maze in a way that the addict is most protected, farthest away from the entrance, and closest to the exit.

Some telltale noises from the entrance faintly signal the bioprogram's arrival. A quadrupedal fleshbot appears and scampers over the collapsed edge into the chamber. Another follows and another. Soon there are eight bioprograms in the chamber fanning out over the rubble and heading for the location of the addict, almost as if they know where he is. The Nuclae attack. Bullets ricochet off of rocks but not flesh. The Nuclae are too fast and too smart for the bioprograms. They wait until they are right next to them and then destroy them quickly.

Some of the autolights go on in an area of the chamber where there is no motion. The Nuclae realize that shadows are in the chamber too. The bioprograms are just a diversion. The lights blink on closer and closer to the addict and the traitor. Though almost invisible, the Nuclae eyes can see the radiation leaking around their edges and attack. A shadow falls. And another. A Nuclae falls as well. Dozens of shadows seem to come from nowhere and their tech starts interfering with the Nuclae's vision, so that it is unclear to even Coleth how many are in the chamber with them. "I can't get a read! They are everywhere!"

A distortion grabs the addict. The addict yells and flails at the shade. While the yell echoes in the chamber the gray shadow, with hands bound, spins a reverse roundhouse to the distortion's head, floors it, and stomps hard. The distortion lies motionless.

Whispers start to permeate the dark hot air of the chamber followed by a faint smell of electricity. Hairs begin to stick up on the back of everyone's neck, human and mutant. An unnatural fear grips them all. The addict's stomach starts to itch and his scalp tingles.

"Lurkers!" hisses Sistid.

The shadows hesitate, then halfheartedly renew their attack on the addict, but their intensity is not the same. They sense it too.

"Follow me!" Sistid yells, fighting off the shadows and retreating towards the exit. *Towards the whispers.*

The addict and the gray shadow are roughly pushed forward along the narrow path of the cliff edge. They are followed by the other Nuclae with Vira bringing up the rear and using her armored bulk to smash attacking shadows and block projectiles.

"Are you sure you know what you're doing, Sistid?!" yells Alella.

"Trust me!" he barks over his shoulder running forward. "I hope I know what I'm doing," he says under his breath.

The whispers become deafening and it is all Sistid and the others can do to run forward as the cliffside path opens up to a larger area strewn with debris. Two paths lie ahead: one leads to the mouth of a cave-like formation and the other path goes past the cave. Sistid makes for the cave followed by the rest of the Nuclae. The whispers are getting louder and the smell of electricity is even stronger. Everyone's mouths seem to dry up and their saliva thickens.

The shadows trailing the Nuclae hesitate again but the Nuclae rush forward. Faint red light comes from the cave that projects outsized shadows on the sides of the cave walls in ways that dodn't seem possible. Shadows seem to be where light should be and light is where shadows are.

Unnerved, the Nuclae enter the cave. Phosphorescent pictograms decorate the rough hewn wall. They shift in ways that aren't possible on a 2 dimensional surface and seem to rotate the surrounding walls like a carnival tunnel. The Nuclae experience vertigo and whispers become roars.

The pictograms against the back wall are particularly dark and seem to squirm in the red light. They become pulsating silhouettes that rear up out of the back of the cave and come towards the Nuclae, screaming deafening whispers of rage that their territory has been invaded. The monstrous silhouettes become three dimensional and spring forward.

"Run!" screams Sistid who is already leading the charge out of the cave. Cris, caught near the back of the formation next to the addict, feels the lurkers on her back. She pushes the addict forward and makes it to the cave mouth with Coleth next to her. Suddenly, Coleth is snatched from her side screaming. Fleeing, she glances back and he is being sucked dry. His husk falls from the cliff, see-sawing back and forth in the still air to disappear into the darkness.

The shadows are approaching the entrance, a mass of distortions that look to be thirty to forty strong and stretched back to the wide part of the cliff edge outside the cave mouth.

Led by Sistid and Vira, the Nuclae come storming out of the cave mouth and catch the shadows off guard driving a wedge into them and getting as far from the cave as possible. They push their way through the phalanx of shadows, taking casualties. The shadows encircle them and a deafening whisper fills the air louder than any scream, sucking the air from all ears, human and Nuclae. A shadow flies through the air. And then another.

Lurkers have broken through the circle of shadows and fling the shadows around like dolls. The lurkers roar their whispered screams, seeming to delight in the carnage, seeming to have no problem locating the almost invisible bodies of the shadows. Shadows versus undefined, the shadows fire their projectiles and their sonics uselessly at the lurkers.

With the addict and the gray ghost at the nucleus of their party, the remaining Nuclae keep running. They know the lurkers are almost unbeatable and they aren't going to stand around and see who survives. The way to the mountains is blocked by lurkers and dead shadows so they retreat the way they came, back towards the Cancers and hostile Nuclae.

Glancing back, they see the lurkers seem to be toying with the shadows and they start appearing at different places around them like a movie missing a frame, they drain the shadows' energy and their husks fall to the floor. The shadows break ranks and try to follow the Nuclae.

Running for their lives they get picked off one by one.

Dead Weight

The gray assassin, Alella, Vira, Sistid, Cris and the addict are all that remain of the original company. They are in an access tunnel close to their city. With their sensory Nuclae, Coleth, dead, they stand a greater chance of being surprised. They take a few minutes to drink and wolf down the small amount of rations they have left. Alella gives the addict his tea and frowns to herself as she knows she will only be able to continue his treatment when and if they reach Mutaria. The death of many of their people, including children, is starting to fester within her and the other Nuclae as well and it shows dismally on their faces.

"We're screwed," says the addict to Alella, losing all hope. "We got nowhere to go."

"Of course you already have given up, addict," mocks Sistid, his arms dancing in anger and fresh rage.

The addict seems unaware of the Nuclae's suffering. Thoughtlessly, he keeps on. "You just got lucky with the lurkers. We should all be dead now."

"No, I had a plan and it worked." Sistid whispers hoarsely, still raw from the death of so many of his people. "But now the tunnel to the mountains is cut off by angry lurkers."

"Haha! A plan? I call that blind luck. Where are you gonna lead us now, snake, Clinic City?"

Sistid gets inches from the addict's face. "Maybe if there were some drugs there you would have done something besides just getting your ass saved. You're dead weight, junk! Many Nuclae died because of you, a worthless piece of shit!"

The addict motions to strike Sistid but Alella and the others, including the gray Ghost, break them apart.

Sistid looks at the Ghost intensely. "Even the ghost is more useful than you, at least he fought against-"

"Hush, Sistid! You need to calm down." Alella says. "We need to come up with something fast."

They stare angrily at each other, Plastic and human, but say nothing.

"Maybe the addict has an idea. Sistid,

where does this access tunnel lead?" Alella tries to refocus Sistid.

"The city-gene district," he says, still staring at the addict. "But that is suicide, especially with a Hex."

"It might be our only choice. It is late at night now, and we need to get out of these tunnels."

"I might have a solution," says the Ghost. All eyes turn to him. "Before I joined the Corporate Military I was a member of a tech gang near the gene district. We may be able to find a place to hide if they are still there."

"A tech gang?" Alella sneers. "Again, why should we trust you?"

"At any time I could have fought against you, but I didn't. I fought for you and I saved the addict."

Sistid turns back to the addict "You are dead weight. You are cursed," Arms flailing at the addict but not striking. The addict puts his hands up defensively.

"No, he is the only bargaining chip we have," Alella gets between them again and pushes Sistid back firmly.

"It's true," says the ghost. "For some reason you are important to someone very high up. That many Shadow Troops is a huge investment and could only have come from the top levels of Corporate Government™. Why are they chasing you?"

"Mind your business, ghost." says Alella. "You are not asking the questions here."

His face still vague and hard to read, the ghost backs off a step.

"If I had an editor, I could alter his DNA and make him harder to track. It could buy us some time," says Alella.

"Well, we are by the gene district. If there is equipment to alter DNA, you'll be able to find it there," says the addict with new hope.

"He's right," says the assassin. "These are non-medical facilities so there is less regulation as well. We can buy time."

Alella convinces the others that this desperate move is their only move. Until they can figure out a way to convince and warn the other Nuclae that the Cancers are traitors, they need time. Leading the way, Sistid takes them to the surface without running into any ghosts, Cancers, Nuclae or lurkers.

Coming out of a rough tunnel in the wastelands near the mounds, they cut the assassin's bonds. "We will kill you if you try to escape," they warn.

"I need you and you need me," says the painted ghost quietly.

"He can't move faster than me," smiles Vira.

The addict leads them through back alleys until they reach the edge of the Gene District without running into anyone at all. Some all night places are open, displaying their services in neon lights in the windows and holograms outside. The ghost and Vira stay back in the alley, as they are the most conspicuous now that the ghost looks like painted air.

Sistid puts on a hat pulled low and all three Nuclae insert contacts to hide their eyes. Alella pulls on gloves to hide her almost mechanical fingers.

The addict leads them to a place near the alley called the Cosmetic Genetic specializing in improving one's looks or changing them altogether. The business also has a hologram that crudely advertises temporary gender reassignment.

"This place will work," says Alella. "We need to secure all people inside and get to the lab so I can figure out how to work their gene machines."

The glass doors slide open and they enter. Only one gene artist is on duty surrounded by a cot and some sequencers. She is a lavender woman with a face that says you won't push me around. Her eyes lock the four strangers in her gaze as soon as they walk in. Her hands are not visible.

"What you want tonight?" She says tersely.

The addict speaks: "Can you make me taller? I want to be taller tonight and I have a lot of money."

The artist laughs. "Honey, height takes a long time to take effect. I can do other things tonight but that takes some serious cell growth." Her face gets serious. "And, no offense, but you don't look like you have a lot of money."

"What software drives your mutations?" asks Alella, trying to change the subject but sounding slightly alien in her Nuclae dialect.

The artist focuses her silver eyes on Alella and they harden into a metallic sheen. Alella and Cris start towards her as she pulls out a projectile weapon from underneath the cot and fires, hitting Cris in the shoulder before Alella knocks her to the floor so hard that she goes out. Immediately, Alella kicks her weapon away and Sistid secures it.

Alella crouches next to where Cris has fallen to her haunches and instantly puts pressure on the wound. She gets a small medkit out of her bag and squirts something into Cris' wound that foams up and solidifies. Though in pain, Cris's bleeding is stopped. Alella helps her to the cot and lays her down, dressing her wound. Sistid checks the back rooms and the addict secures the front door. He turns off most of the lights so the place looks closed.

"There's no one else back there," Sistid growls.

Cris pushes Alella away. "I'll be alright. Tend to the addict."

"Hush, child."

The artist starts to stir.

"Sistid, secure the gene artist." Alella says as she starts familiarizing herself with the sequencers and synthesizers. The artist stirs and sits up on the floor next to the cot. Sistid trusses her roughly.

"Fucking mutants," she spits vehemently. "I knew it as soon as you walked in."

"Quiet," Alella says. "You shot my friend. You are lucky we let you live. Give me access to this editor."

She stares at Alella and holds her gaze for a moment before telling her the access code. "You won't figure out my synthesizers. This is the latest technology, not some homemade editors from down in the sewers."

"Sistid, if she speaks again, break something." Alella holds the new synthesizer in her gloved hands.

Sistid smiles evilly. "On her body, or in the shop."

"I'll let you decide." The artist shuts her genetically altered purple lips for the moment.

Alella quickly draws blood from Cris and starts playing with the DNA synthesizer. The synthesizer is not so different from the ones she grew up using and she quickly figures out how to program for tissue repair. She reinjects the altered blood near to the wound.

The artist has been watching her and is nonplussed by how quickly Alella has figured out her synthesizer. She had spent hours reading the manual just to understand simple programs. Embarrassed, she curses under her breath but is not foolish enough to tempt the wrath of the Nuclae.

To further compound the artist's humiliation, Alella instantly makes some adjustments and draws some blood from the addict. She reads the sequencer and hits buttons, changing the addict's genetic fingerprint enough so that he will be undetectable to the bioprograms' sensors at least for a little while. Between Cris and the addict the whole process takes her about 30 minutes. She looks at the artist gloatingly. "Now, what should we do with you?"

The artist whitens her lavender a bit. To her credit, it is the first time she has shown fear. The mutants scare her. She thought they were just big dumb monsters but the girl with the gloves on figured out the tech instantly and had easily knocked her out and disarmed her.

"Let's kill this bitch!" says a recovering Cris, back to form.

"I have a better idea," says Alella snottily. "Sistid, hold her down."

Sistid's serpentine arms whip down to the artist and hold her in place. Alella draws her blood and starts programming.

"Please. What are you going to do?"

"Nothing you don't deserve. Don't worry.

We won't kill you even though my friend wants to. You are just going to sleep for a while."

The artist looks relieved.

"Oh and you might wake up with some features you didn't have before."

"You bitch-"

"Shut up," Sistid shakes her.

She shuts up. A smiling Alella leans over her and draws blood into the sequencer. After a few minutes of programming, Alella injects her with new instructions and a sedative. As she passes out Alella laughs cruelly, her mean side exposed to the addict for the first time.

They exit the darkened Cosmetic Genetic, the streets nearly empty. As they walk back to the alley the addict asks Alella what she has done to the gene artist.

"Just a few improvements. Her hair will be invisible, coding I learned thanks to the ghost. Her eyes will be good old regular brown."

"That's all? That's not too bad. You were cackling like a witch. Kinda scary."

"That's not all."

"What else?" says the addict, intrigued as much as the addict could be.

"She will smell like urine," she smiles. "And it is a genetic riddle I doubt she will solve anytime soon."

Cris and Sistid laugh. Even the addict smiles. They turn the corner to the alley and there is a group of three humans with antique shotguns pointed at them. Vira and the Ghost are nowhere to be found.

Hunters

The Prophet, having secured release after most of the people at Regen were massacred, holds court at the Reality Bar™ drinking whisky. Vapors swirl around the lights creating a haze dappled by androgynous hanger-ons around him. Their faces are caked with heavy make-up, concealing both their true features and making any assumption of gender impossible.

"You all don't know who I am."

"Yes we do, you are the sexiest guy in here." says one of the girls, or was she a boy?

"No, you loser, that's not what I'm talking about. I'm talking about where I come from. I come from money," he drawls loudly.

"I thought you said you were from the streets," says Rolo, a big guy with a high voice that the Prophet keeps around in case he has to fight.

"I grew up in the streets and that's why I am a mean motherfucker, but I ain't trash like you are. I ain't scums."

"Fuck you, Prophet," says Rolo in his high voice. "You think you're better than me."

"Not you, Rolo, you're *special,*" the Prophet says with a toothy grin. "But all these other fucks are scums!" he yells. Laughter echoes.

The femme who has been trying to get his attention all night makes eyes at the Prophet. "Prophet, do you want to come up to my apartment? I live across the street."

"You think I have time to fornicate with you? You think I even want to? Rolo, take care of my fluffers. I have someone important coming to meet me. Not scums like you."

She is offended but this is the Prophet's place. Plus, she still wants his feather in her cap. She comes closer and leans into him for a kiss but he slaps her face.

"Get away from me you jezebel. I have doctors coming to visit me. A doctor. What do you have? Drug addicts? Bioprograms?" More laughter.

At that moment, Varius walks into the bar, a distasteful look on his face.

"Ah, Doctor. See everybody, I am sophisticated. A *doctor* is visiting me. Who's coming to see you scum, your Viprex™ dealers?" Insults and yells rain down on the Prophet who laughs them off.

"See Doc, these ignorant scums wouldn't know class if it hit them in the face. GET A WHISKEY FOR THE DOCTOR! Top shelf only! You don't mind if I call you Doc, do ya?"

Varius's laugh is a bit forced. "No of course not, Prophet. We have a long...association." A drink is brought for Varius. He doesn't reach for it.

"First name basis with a doctor. Rolo isn't even on a first name basis with his allomone doll!" More hoots and laughter from the Prophet's entourage. He grabs his whiskey and turns towards Varius with a grin. "So, what do you need, Doc?" he says more quietly.

"I need your magic. Only you can do this for me, Prophet."

The Prophet smiles. "Oh yeah? I guess it's hard to find good people these days."

"Do you know that addict nicknamed 22 that you spent time with at Regen?"

"Yeah, the one who loved his dead whore?" the Prophet says loudly. More laughter.

Varius continues in a voice for the Prophet's ears only. "Well, he got away."

"I remember. So what, I can give you a thousand more addicts like him."

"This job is only for this addict."

The Prophet speaks quietly then, in bargaining mode. "Let me get this straight. You need me to find this drugged out waste but you are occluding information about why you're looking for him."

"There is 300 million in it for you."

"Let me tell you something," the Prophet sneers. "I am a free agent. I don't *owe* you anything. I don't *need* your money. I own this town. I know everybody and everything that's going on."

"Prophet, I know you know this area better than anyone. I know you know everybody and you control the flow of Viprex™."

Varius knows that since being released from Regen, the Prophet has built up an even more extensive network with sources from Regen. Despite his difficult and unpredictable personality, the Prophet is a valuable ally. Plus he knows the addict so he needs the Prophet in particular. "I need you to use *all* of your people for this one. High alert. I can raise your rate."

The Prophet is quiet, twisting his straw in his drink and staring Varius in the eyes.

"Corporate Government has jobbers reprogrammed with pictures of the addict in their heads, programmed to detain the addict.

This makes the Prophet even more mad. "No, no, no. Call them off. Now. This needs to be an exclusive contract. I don't owe you shit. I'm gonna walk away now and go talk to my scums."

"What if I told you that if you help us, we can help you to cheat death."

"You're bluffing, it's not gonna change my mind."

"The addict can change his DNA so he won't die."

"Oh yes he can, a couple bullets will fix him. Or maybe he could get lost in a dog cleanup."

"No, he can be killed, but his cells don't

age. He may be able to live forever. We need him alive."

The Prophet instantly sobers and looks at Varius in a rare speechless moment to digest the full gravity of what he has heard.

"If you help me find him alive and keep your mouth shut I might be able to make these alterations on you if you wish."

The Prophet sizes Varius up for a moment, then he speaks. "You want to live forever on this worthless planet where humanity is destroying itself? I can't say that I do." He pauses gauging Varius for a moment, always working the angles.

Finally, he speaks quietly and more friendly than before. "Well Doc, for a billion, you got yourself an exclusive deal and I want the option of immortality for me and whoever I want it for after you get your lab rat."

Varius doesn't hesitate. "You have a deal if you can work with people of my choice," Varius, not phased by the Prophet totally changing his tune, "but if you tell anyone else about the addict's mutation, the deal is off and I can't guarantee your safety."

The Prophet looks down at Varius's outstretched hand for a moment and then reaches out his own hand and shakes. "For a billion, I'll work with the devil."

Varius smiles in response.

The Prophet rallies his people. They are more suited for the city than Corporate

Military™. When the Prophet puts out word of a 100 million reward, there are hundreds of people that are instantly on the prowl throughout Clinic City.

All Your Fucking Buildings

"Oh yeah. We're gonna get some money!" says a big human to Alella's right.

"Your ugly hologram is all over the web, bitch," says one of the gangsters wearing a pinstripe Yankers™ baseball hat and pointing an ancient shotgun at the addict. "Big money for you," he says in a deep stupid voice.

"No mention of these fuckers though. We can just waste them and take this mother fucker for the cash!" says the big one on the right.

The third one speaks. He has blue skin with orange hair and eyes which is the latest in cosmetic synthesis, especially in the more hip parts of town. "I dunno. These two are pretty hot." He says looking at Cris and Alella. Their eyes wander to Sistid with his strange bone structure and disjointed arms. "Are you a fucking mutant?"

They all swing their guns towards Sistid who stands relaxed.

"Should we kill him?" they seem unsure what to do.

"The fuck you will!" says Cris surging

forward. Alella grabs her and wraps her up as the gunman pumps his shotgun at her.

"Settle down," says Alella, "you don't have to hurt us." She puts her gloved hands up, palms open.

Seeing her long pointed fingers under the gloves, the big one approaches her and lowers his gun at her torso. "Oh shit, you a mutant too aren't you?"

He tries to push her against the wall but she resists. He holds the gun to her neck, his eyes wild. "I will blow a hole right through you." He grabs her and throws her hard against the wall. This time, she lets herself be thrown and bounces off the wall, relaxed and ready to strike.

Before she can act, his gun seems to be pushed up in the air by gray smoke and his head twists with a snapping sound. At the same time Vira crashes into the other two as they fire shots at her armored hide. She decapitates one and crumples the other with the shotgun against the wall. All three are dead, killed almost instantly.

"Now we are even, Alella." says Ghost, his gray body shifting from transparent to more opaque behind the corpse with a shotgun. "But that noise is going to draw attention. Those 3 were surely programmed to look for the addict. There are probably more. Many more."

"They came suddenly," says Vira, unharmed. "We retreated rather than fight and draw attention. We waited until we had to act."

"You did the right thing, Vira. Now we have to go. Ghost, you need to take us to your friends. Now."

"This should be interesting," mutters the Ghost. "I know some old ways with no cameras." They flee the alley, zigzagging through backways. It will be getting light soon and people will definitely notice a six legged humanoid among the buildings of Clinic City.

The buildings become smaller and smaller as the Ghost leads them northeast towards the warehouses. They eventually come to an ancient brick building with doors set in concrete arches. Some of the bricks are decayed into cankers making the wall look eerily diseased.

"Stay here for a minute," says Ghost to the others. He suddenly is not a shadow anymore and is instead a man with natural looking brown skin, closely cropped hair, and a muscular frame wearing black close-fitting military issue. The Nuclae look surprised but say nothing. They stay back about 3 meters as he walks towards the door in the arch and knocks loudly.

"Yo, it's Fitty fit. Open this door, man," says the Ghost.

"You're not bad-looking," says Cris, smiling at him.

"The door opens. "Fitty is that you?" a scratchy tenor voice from a skinny dark figure.

"Yeah, Rat. I need your help. I got nowhere

else to go."

"Hey I got your back, but are those *mutants* with you? What the fuck, is this one a bug?" he laughs nervously.

"Listen Rat, we need to get off the street ASAP."

"No, it's OK. Thug saw you from the cameras and said to let you in. All of you."

"Thanks, man." The former shadow grasps Rat's hand and gives him an embrace as he walks into the fortified front office. Ten hard-looking humans are waiting inside, guns at their waists. Clad in synthetic leather they stand about random circuitry and metal pieces that are strewn everywhere on every table, on the floor, even on shelves.

A large light brown man with cold eyes enters and looks at the former ghost eye to eye. "Well, well, well, what do we have here? Fitty Fit, I can't believe it's you. I haven't seen you since you disappeared, right when we needed you for the Independence job."

"Thug, I was incarcerated. I had one choice, join the Corporation Military or rot in a cell. Give me some credit, man."

"We needed you, man; and you weren't there. Job went bad. They got a couple of us. They got Carmichael."

"Look, I'm sorry that happened." The ghost is very serious. "If I could have done something, I would have." He stares Thug in the eyes.

"You still-"

"What the fuck are you doing with these mutants?" Rat cuts in. "You look like a bug, no offense." He smiles, but Vira has no reaction on her face. "What's their story?"

"Rat, Thug, I was left for dead on a military mission and these people helped me out."

"People? Hahaha!" Rat mocks. Thug and the others laugh out loud.

"You can laugh but they stick up for each other just like we *used* to." He stares at Thug. "You would be lucky to have them at your back."

The hard eyes of the tech gang seemed to bore into their former charter and the Nuclae. The Nuclae try to appear non-threatening as they ready themselves, subtly, for battle: a shift in stance for Alella, a slight shuffle forward by Sistid, none of which is missed by the gang. The tension grows as Thug takes a step towards them.

Thug laughs again. "Fitty fit, my brother, we are just fucking with you." He smiles. "You and your friends can stay here for the day, but you have to leave when it gets dark. This dude is too hot!" He slaps the addict on the back. Rat and the rest of them laugh. Ghost starts laughing. The Nuclae and the addict stand stoically but relax their stance a bit.

"We had you going Fitty Fit." They all

embrace him and exchange greetings. Ghost introduces the Nuclae to Thug. Sugarbear, a girl techie brings out water and snacks and embraces the Ghost.

"I missed you," she says and kisses his cheek.

Thug looks hard at them. "Don't think you're gonna get your old girl back. She's mine now." He bursts into laughter again. "What the fuck you been doing? You a sol-jah now? What the fuck can you do?"

With his new moniker, Fitty Fit disappears except for a trace of smoke-like distortion thanks to Alella's coding. Thug grabs his neck as a loud slap fills the room.

"What the fuck!?" He jabs at the air and Fitty Fit reappears behind him.

"You motherfucker!" But Thug is smiling. He grabs Fitty Fit and gives him a rough bear hug. "I missed you man," says Thug, adding a rough head pat.

"Alright, alright," says Ghost smiling, trying to disengage.

Alcohol and drugs begin to appear in the techies hands along with their devices and they offer it to their guests. No one has Viprex™ as that is a loner's drug.

The warehouse is huge and has different labs and rooms to hang in. The Nuclae retreat to the back of the warehouse where they were told that there are sleeping pads. They watch the tech's party from across the main room of the huge warehouse.

The gang drinks, wrestles, and a fight breaks out. They make out with their girls who have shown up. Eventually,Thug comes over to talk to the Nuclae, but he is clearly addressing himself to Alella and Cris, they being the attractive females in the group. And Thug is clearly attracted.

"You know what we do here?" Thug asks them.

"What?" says Cris cockily.

"We make magic." he brags.

The Nuclae wait expressionless in their way.

"We can make any tech we want. You want a motion tracker? We can make it. You want an android? Strength increasing exoskeletons? We can make that too. We are artists and visionaries."

"Can you design something that will make you talk less?" Cris smiles good naturedly.

Thug laughs again, enjoying the comeback by the blond with the elfin good looks.

"We're not so different." She says, "We can do the same things you can do, it's just that our circuits are organic."

"No, it is not the same, pixie. We create something pure. Alella, you change the DNA of your people?" Directly addressing the Nuclae leader.

"Yes." She says.

"So you are not humans anymore. You've altered yourselves to the point where there is a fundamental difference."

"How so?" Alella perks up.

"We were created how we were supposed to be created, yeah we put some tech in our bodies but humans have evolved with technology. We evolved to be the apex predator. Humanity will always be on top because we won't let any other species rise above us, even if we have to exterminate them with that superior technology."

"So you would exterminate us?" Alella says cooly.

"That's not what I'm saying. I am saying that you can't improve on the original. The prototype. Sure, you can add some motherfuckin' bells and whistles but I will always be an alpha, baby." Thug flexes his muscular arms.

"Look at all your technology. You are weak without it, cyborg." Sistid sneers from where he sits on the floor.

Rat speaks reasonably. "Hey, we aren't so different. We both code to improve our abilities. You know, do things we couldn't otherwise do. What you do with codons, we do with code."

"We can sense everything your instruments can and more." Alella says. "Vira, how many hearts are beating in this warehouse."

"I count 25. 21 humanoids, four canine."

"Shit, she could have counted when she came in." Thug questions. "You are a she, right?" He turns towards the hexaped.

"I'm female."

"Shit, that's some exotic pussy." Thug says, the techies laugh.

Vira rises up to her back legs full size and stares down at Thug, who is big for a human.

"Shit, you're big but we are apex," repeats Thug, working at the cut he is trying to create among the Nuclae.

"We are apex," Cris stares at the techies. "We have everything we need right here." Her leg snaps an impossibly angled kick behind her back, impossible to do for any being except a plastic. She holds it with perfect balance for a few seconds before she lowers it.

Thug bursts out laughing. "I can't argue with that!" He exclaims, swigging his tequila. The others laugh too, except for the addict who is in another world.

After the party winds down and some of the techs sex each other in the recesses of the old building, the Nuclae huddle among themselves with the addict. Alella is angry at herself that she let her group be antagonized into giving up information about their abilities. *The best*

abilities are mutations that we can hide from our foes. Central Dogma, chapter 4, verse 3. The book of strategy.

Eventually Ghost comes back in his new visible form. Alella looks at the Ghost levelly. "Can we trust your friends?"

"I think so, they hate the law. From what I gather about the price on Thug's head, a man could buy half the city with it so he keeps somewhat of a low profile. But we should be ready in case they double cross us and we should leave at nightfall."

"I thought they were your friends," Alella snaps.

"What option did we have? Day was coming. Mutants in Clinic City in daylight? I don't think so, girl. This was the play we had to make. The only play."

"I'm not gonna sleep today, I'll tell you that." says Alella.

Ghost wrinkles up his face and walks away.

They set up nap rotations to make sure one of them is always awake and as the day wears on they all realize how tired they are and they drift into sleep, even Alella, for a few disturbed hours, exhausted but waking every few minutes on an old sleeping pad.

She awakens to the addict shaking her roughly by the shoulder.

"Wake up, Alella. It's getting dark soon."

"What time is it?"

"1500," says the addict tonelessly.

She gives the addict a look and he looks down at the ground seeming to find interest in the old cement floor. Rubbing the sleep from her eyes, she shakes all the Nuclae in turn, quietly waking them.

"Did you sleep?" Cris asks the addict.

"Kinda," says the addict. "We got a problem." He gestures to the empty sleeping place where the Ghost had been. "Missing Ghost."

Requiem

The cold gray afternoon is electric. Every holoscreen in the business district shows news edits of the horrors that the human traitor addict and Nuclae terrorists have committed and posts the reward money. The ghost walks among the crowded streets, invisible now because of a hat pulled over his head. He doesn't show his face to the cameras in case the corporate military are looking for him as well, which he expects they are. He goes down a synthetically treed thoroughfare with Sycamaples™ and giant Yewcottons™ that leads to a huge silver-glassed building and goes inside the huge perfectly-balanced automatic glass doors.

A silvery robot sits behind a golden desk. The hall is empty otherwise.

"Good   afternoon   sir,   welcome   to

Riverview Cemetery™," it says unobtrusively in friendly metallic tones. "Can I help you?"

"Flowers for marker 16-1409." the Ghost says, transmitting a counterfeit cred signal to the bioprogram.

"What kind, we have-"

"A dozen roses, mixed red, pink and white."

"Thank you sir. 16-1409 is overdue for payment and contents could be liquidated as soon as the first of next month."

"What the fuck?" Corporate Military™ must have stopped his pay. The cheap motherfuckers.

"I'm sorry sir."

"OK, charge this account indefinitely."

"Yes sir, Elevator 4 is ready. And thank you for doing business with Riverview Cemetery™"

The ghost grabs his flowers and goes to the elevator to level 16. He sees an old man with wet eyes when the door opens and averts his eyes, ashamed because he feels like the old man deserves some privacy with his grief.

He walks down the hall and turns left until he gets to grave 16-1409. The name Marshall Williams is carved out of the synthstone marker at head level. He puts the fake roses in the water ring.

"Miss you boy. Sorry I haven't been here in a while."

He stays for a few minutes and then has

a mini panic. This is stupid. They might be watching this site.

But I needed to do this, and now I got her grave squared away for good. His eyes are wet but he sheds no tears.

He touches the cold stone again, closes his eyes and imagines her voice for a moment. Rubbing his eyes dry, he turns,strides back to the elevator, takes it down to the lobby, and goes out the door. It is getting dark outside and he walks back to the tech building. He comes around the corner of Clair Avenue onto 55th and he sees shadows around the dark building. He quickly ducks back around the corner and deliberates.

Shit, how did they find them? Thug? But he has a price on his head, he wouldn't want the government down here in his business. Ghost feels responsible for Alella and her people. They trusted him. He vouched for the techs.

Ghost, in almost invisible combat mode, cuts down an alley keeping to the sides in the darkness. He dispatches a couple of his former fellow shades at predictable locations behind the tech building and lets himself in the back after quickly cracking the code. He knows all of Rat's tricks. He sneaks into the large room where Alella is talking to Thug. He stays invisible and edges closer. So far there are no signs of the shades.

"I don't know where he went," says Thug. "But I don't have a problem with you and your lady friend staying here another day if you want to wait for him." Thug smiles charmingly: "As long as you have a drink with me."

"I need to stay with my people," Alella says.

"Of course, which is why I brought this." Smiling, he brings a flask and cups out of his jacket. "Please, if your friends would join us." He is looking at Cris.

"Cris, come here." Thug's smile cracks even harder across his dark face showing white teeth. He pours three cups.

"We make these cups here. They chill anything we put in them instantly to whatever temp we desire. I have these set to 0 degrees celsius for the alcohol to be cold but not frozen."

"Lovely," says Cris, smiling.

"Another thing that our *artisans* create. You ladies would like it here if you just gave it a chance."

"So now we have an invitation? I thought we had to be out tomorrow." Alella does her best to smile at Thug.

He looks at her for a moment. "You are so damn beautiful. You both are. Are all mutants this damn sexy?"

"Friendly is good, but let's not get too friendly," Cris says grinning. Alella is thankful that Cris is there as she is better in these situations than Alella is.

Thug's head jerks forward and he collapses almost slowly, as if being lowered. The ghost's smokey outline was lowering him slowly to the ground.

"Ghost? What the hell?" Alella hisses, puzzled. The others gather round, semi defensively.

"Corporate Military™ is outside. I snuck in the back. We need to get out of here now."

"Well, well well. Looks like the cats are trying to escape the rat."

Rat and a few others are at the back entrance of the room. "There's nowhere to go. Shadows like you are coming in the front now. You don't think we have cameras everywhere?"

Thug was starting to get to his feet rubbing his head. Without turning, Cris nonchalantly ax kicks him in the head and he falls down again. The Nuclae and the Ghost separate and Vira leads a charge towards the techs who start blasting shots at her. Her head down, her armored head and hide hold the bullets off and they attack the techs scattering them like bowling pins. Shadows start filtering in the front end of the warehouse followed by a man with a familiar face to the addict.

"I need you junk and now I got you." The cold blue eyes of the Prophet burrow into the addict's from across the warehouse. The Prophet raises a sonic gun and starts shooting at the Nuclae. The addict pushes Cris out of the way and is grazed by a sound blast that does no real damage. The Prophet keeps shooting as he and the shadows start charging forward.

"Come back here, junk! You ain't gonna live forever!" yells the Prophet surging forward.

"Follow me!" barks Ghost. Alella roughly grabs the addict's arm and they follow Ghost out to a room in the back of the building where he lifts up a trap door to a tunnel below. "Ghost, where does this go?" asks Sistid.

"Doesn't matter, we got to go down. Now!" Sistid nods to the dark shadows and techs behind them, gaining quickly. They jump down into the duct, Sistid first and then Vira picks up the addict and tosses him down to Sistid who catches him and sets him on his feet. The rest of the Nuclae all jump down.

"This way," growls Sistid. "We need to leave Clinic City now!"

They charge down a long easterly tunnel with eight shadows a hundred meters behind them. The tunnel starts to twist. Cris and Vira look at each other and start to slow down.

"We'll hold them off," Vira says

Alella looks at them hard. "No, we will do it together. This is a good place to make a stand and I don't think they have bioprograms this time. They space themselves out with the addict at the back of their group around the corner waiting silently. The shadows know they are ahead but don't know exactly where they are.

A minute later the shadows come in slow and cautiously, almost in unison. One appears next to Vira and she shovels right through it, smashing it against the sewer wall. Another appears next to Alella, but she senses it and ducks under, back flipping into a heel kick and caving in its face. Blood gushes out of nowhere. Vira takes fire destroying another one, but she rushes a group of four and smashes them together, allowing Sistid and Ghost to mop up after her. One grabs the addict but Cris rapid whip jabs it multiple times and it crumples like used plastic wrap. She spits on it after, a fire in her eyes, and turns to the addict. "Where's your friend? The one that was shooting at us?"

"The Prophet? He usually isn't a front line type of guy. I am surprised he was at the tech's warehouse at all. There must be something big in it for him."

"Yeah, you guys were all over holovision and then suddenly you weren't; but the price on your head is ridiculous," says Ghost. Let's keep moving, there will be more."

"Where did you go?" asks Alella, eyes focused on the Ghost.

"Personal business. No, I didn't snitch."

"How do we know that?" yells Sistid from the front.

"Why the hell would I warn you and then be running with you now?"

Sistid says nothing and leads the way further east. They go quietly and without incident for the better part of the night. They reach another old sewage cistern and decide to rest for a few minutes.

"This is the end of the tunnel system. We are going to have to leave the city now," Sistid whispers in his gravelly voice.

The other's eyes are wide with trepidation and dread. Humans and Nuclae do not usually leave cities on foot. Since year zero, lurkers and other creations owned what was left of the unhealthily forested hills surrounding the walls of Clinic City and much of the world.

"There is nothing to be done about it," Alella says. "We have to get to Mutaria and warn the Nuclae there of what is happening in Clinic City. We have to analyze you further, addict. I am sorry, but you are a huge piece of the puzzle if the Nuclae are to survive."

"So, am I your prisoner?"

"Do you want to go to your friend, this Prophet?"

"I will stick with you guys. I guess I owe you guys thanks for saving me from him and the treatment facilities at Clinic City." He smiles at Cris and their eyes meet. Something passes between them and it isn't lost on the others, including Alella.

"We will break camp now."

"That was camp?" mocks Ghost.

Alella smiles. "We need to move in light. Lurkers are mostly nocturnal so we will be able to cover more ground in daytime. If we keep away from roads, we should be safe from air patrols and satellites as long as we keep to the forests."

"Hopefully they still have enough leaves to shield us from aircraft," says Vira.

"We also have this," interjects the ghost, showing a small black plastic multi antenna'd dial. "Frequency jammer. I stole it from the techies. It can jam anything from x-ray to radio."

"It better work," says Alella. " And it better not be a tracker," she warns but has no choice but to trust Ghost. "Let's go."

They clamber up a rusting old service ladder and they are at the top of a hill in old forest a mile outside the city walls. It is dawn and the cool morning wind carries the sound of crows cawing to the south along with a fruity aroma of fungus. Sloughed out ruins of old dwellings have been overgrown with ground cover, bushes and trees. Though many are unhealthy, the trees still have brownish green leaves and tower over the ruins. Even many of the oaks, usually resilient, have sloughed bark like snakeskin and many trees have fallen and are being eaten by bugs and fungi. There are still enough healthy trees with foliage for coverage.

Even the addict is moved by the beauty and tranquility of the natural world. Even a sickly forest gives him and the others feelings they are not familiar with. Silence descends on the group, half out of necessity and half out of awe, and they make their way quietly down a hill and across a dry stream bed and back up a hill to a stand of dusty pines with reddish wood showing through piecemeal bark dotted with insects. As the sun briefly shows itself at the horizon, blue jays screech their arrival and flitter furtively out of sight. A dried deer carcass rots under the pines and a buzzard flies off when they approach.

Sistid holds a finger up to his mouth for silence and they creep forward. Tingles of whispers tickle up their spines and they silently increase their pace, putting as much distance as they can between them and the carcass. The tingling ebbs and they continue on a game trail trying to stay under trees. They hear a helicopter in the distance, and they all crouch under some hemlocks and wait for it to fly over, Ghost playing with the dials of his jammer. Directly overhead, the rotor wash is deafening but then it recedes. They wait a minute until the forest background noises return and then Sistid signals them to move again.

Heading east toward the sun, now hidden behind an overcast soup of pollution and water vapor, they start over wooded hills. All Nuclae know basic species, and trees are no exception. Ghost knows some from survival school in the military. The addict is ignorant of species nomenclature but even he notices the differences between pines, sycamores, oaks, maples and tulips: survivors from year zero when scientists and governments tried to stop global warming. From time to time, they see a faraway deer spooked by their presence despite their almost silent progress.

Following game trails, they make their way through the woodland maze. Up hills, down into stream valleys, walking along layers of shale millions of years old.

The addict feels a life force he has never felt before in the city. The power of it humbles him. Even in decrepitude, the forest resonates in him in a way that makes him feel small yet part of a cycle of life and death. It gives him strength in a way he has never experienced. The whole party feels it to varying degrees as well and though they are on high alert, the environs begin to give them peace and vitality.

They continue on until after dusk and find another stand of ragged pines to camp under in the clear cold starlight. Without a fire, they sit in a circle. Sistid produces a flask that is passed around and they begin to speak names and memories of the Nuclae dead, of brothers and sisters lost in the fighting. The flask is passed to the ghost and the addict and even they drink. The Nuclae sing and cry for them, harmonizing in quiet melancholy voices, clapping the rhythm with their hands against their bodies.

Ain't nothing safe in this world
So hold her closer
Ain't nothing worse in this world
Than growing colder
It's a long way darling, if
that's the way you go
It's a new moon, starling, way out there

    The ghost and the addict sit respectfully quiet, feeling very much like outsiders. They take turns as sentries while the others eventually sleep uncomfortably and cold, all huddled together in the dark, the wind howling through the trees and eating away at their body heat.

    The addict tosses and turns, sometimes waking the other, speaking in his sleep. They rise slightly before dawn, shivering and hungry. They drink some water, but there is nothing to eat. They hike all day until the sun is back on the descent into clouds gathering in the west. Hunger is a constant reality. The last time they ate was at the tech gangs.

    "What time is it?" asks Alella.

    "15:45, two hours to sunset," says Ghost.

    "We need to find food," Alella says. "What we had was left with your old gang, Ghost. We can cover more ground if we pair up and meet back here at dark or sooner if you find something." Alella grabs the ghost, Sistid goes with Vira and Cris goes with the addict.

The addict and Cris walk in silence for a while as the gloom pushes out the light, their breaths fogging the air. They go up a switchback and they cross an overgrown field where some dusty old corn is growing. They open a few ears, but it is all rotted out.

They throw down the rotten ears and the addict says: "I think that this used to be a farm, from when they could grow stuff outside back before zero."

She says nothing, her eyes questing towards a sem- burned blackened wooden structure a few hundred meters away on the edge of the field.

"Maybe some of the other crops dropped seed and reproduced like that rotten corn back there," he suggests. "Maybe something more dark tolerant."

She nods quietly and they look around for a few minutes, getting closer to the burnt barn.

"I am sorry your people were hurt," he says.

"You mean murdered?" she meets his eyes and stares him down. He looks at her again.

"I never wanted this to happen. If I knew that this would happen I wouldn't have come to the Nuclae."

She hasn't averted her eyes. The colors of planet earth still stare at him. "A debt is owed, a debt is paid" she speaks, as if reciting.

He has no answer and is not even sure what she means as they start walking, finding nothing at the abandoned farm. They follow a creek until they creep to a river where they see a big gray blue bird with a large beak standing on the shore a good distance away. They crouch down. The bird seems to be hunting for small fish in a pool lined by ancient plastic bottles that have collected along this still edge. The bird hasn't seemed to notice them in the gray drizzly morning.

Cris reaches down and grabs a fist sized rock and hefts it a couple times in her hand. She sizes up the bird for a second and starting from a crouching position she flexes her whole body and lets her rubbery arm go like a whip. The rock shoots out of her hand at a 45 degree angle, sails the 150 meters, and strikes the bird dead center in the head. It falls, convulsing and then is still.

The addict looks at her disbelievingly, his eyes wide. "Holy shit. I didn't think that was humanly possible."

"It's not, for your kind," she says confidently and stands up. He follows her to the bird, its head is crushed in, its eyes staring lifelessly at the sky.

"I had to kill it, so you can carry it back to camp."

"No problem," he says, happy to be of use. The bird is large but lighter than it looks. He drapes the bird over his shoulder and they walk back up along the creek.

After a few minutes, he speaks to her. "Sometimes I wish I had been born a Nuclae."

This appears to amuse Cris and she smiles somewhat sarcastically. "Oh and why?"

Glad to see a smile on her face, he continues, unaddictlike. "You can do incredible things. Even genetically engineered ball players can't throw the way you do. And the way you fight. You guys could probably beat a lurker one on one."

"Vira could," she says with mock confidence.

"Also you stick together. Humans never stick up for each other like you guys do."

"The techs seemed to."

"Not really, they betrayed Ghost."

She thinks this over. "Yeah, but he had become an outsider to both his old groups. Kinda like you." She moves at a faster pace.

He shuts up then, and looks at Cris from behind as she walks up a hill, her shapely figure and round bottom punctuates the twilit sky beyond her. She is as tall as he is and her short blond hair bobs up and down as she walks.

She turns her head and her one eye that her blond bangs does not cover catches him staring. "Taking a hologram?"

He reddens and catches up to her walking shoulder to shoulder. They pass by the blackened barn in the darkening evening. The wind is picking up again and it starts whispering its hollow song through the barn and the trees.

He suddenly realizes the whispering is not the wind as he feels the tingling in his head, on his skin, and a familiar itch on his stomach.

"Lurkers," he whispers to Cris.

In the doorless frame of the barn lurks a dark figure that begins to flow towards them.

"Run!" Cris whispers and roughly shoves him the other way. "Get back to the others."

He hesitates and she pushes him again, this time with much more strength than she looks capable of. "Go, asshole!"

He takes off running. As he glances back, he sees that the lurker is coming for him in the darkness. Cris is ready and she already has another rock cocked and launched, pegging the lurker in the face. The rock almost seems to go through the lurker as if the shadowy form is made of gelatin. It lets out an insane reverse scream, changes its course, and comes for her. She flips laterally, flicking a backhanded uppercut that momentarily stuns the charging lurker. It misses her but then seems to flow to a new location to her left. She sprints in the opposite direction towards the tree line with the lurker a few steps behind.

The addict runs for his life, blindly clutching the heron. In the directionless night he loses his way, his breathing ragged. Confused, he starts darting aimlessly back and forth like an injured animal. Cris was already doubling back around with the lurker following when she sees him and gives him a dirty look. In desperation, he throws the bird at the lurker and it catches and pauses, perhaps momentarily placated by the small carcass.

Cris and the addict sprint up and down several hills and a switchback as fast as they can before they trip over each other and collapse in a heap staring up at the sky, whispers seeming far away in the dark. Cris starts laughing and before long it infects the addict. They laugh for a while and when the giddiness subsides he stands up, helping her to her feet. Glancing over their shoulders in the darkness they walk back up to the camp spot, Cris looks over at the addict.

"Maybe I was wrong about you, are you stupid or brave?"

He says nothing and she grins.

"A little of both probably," he answers honestly.

He smiles uncomfortably.

"I don't even know your name."

He doesn't say anything for a moment. "People sometimes call me 22."

"Did you make that up yourself to be cool?" she mocks.

"No, it's the last 2 digits of my corporate number. It is common for us lab rats to call each other by the last few digits or so."

She doesn't say anything for a second and then she looks at him and smiles almost warmly. "Okay, 22." She says in a low mocking voice. "Hardened criminal. A wanted man."

They laugh and rib each other warmly. For a moment they both forget their troubles and are still laughing when they get back to the campsite. The others look at them somewhat puzzled at their good spirits, especially the addict's, who they have not ever seen laugh. Smoke is rising from some glowing coals and there is cooked meat on rocks next to a low fire hidden by large stones.

"What's so funny?" asks Sistid, clearly annoyed.

"Nothing, we were almost killed by a lurker." Cris smiles. "In fact we should probably get out of here before it needs energy again."

"Again?" asks Sistid.

"Yeah we gave it a meal and ran," says the addict.

"Speaking of which, get some meat. Vira and I killed a coyote. It tastes like shit but we saved you some. Oh, and we have a visitor."

Next to the fire, what seems to be a bush metamorphoses into a thin short-haired androgynous coffee-colored waif dressed in camouflage looking at the two newcomers plainly.

"Who is this?" Cris asks aggressively, getting between the newcomer and the addict.

"Easy," Alella puts her arm between them, and the waif keeps staring at Cris. "Cris, this is Ivy, a Mutarian, one is a shapeshifter." Allela explains, using the pronoun for the gender fluid strain of Nuclae.

"Oh yeah, how do we know for sure it is who one says it is? Aren't we days away from Mutaria?"

"You don't know," says Ivy in an honest voice. "But you don't have a choice. Only I can get you past the lurkers through 75 kilometers of rough terrain. Without me to guide you, you won't make it."

"Ivy is right. We have no choice. We need to get to Mutaria and speak to your counsel."

"Why?" Ivy says, turning steady eyes under tight braids to Alella.

"We have information that could save many Nuclae and human lives. Information about the humans."

Ivy stares at her for a minute and then turns to Cris.

"Looks like you're gonna have to eat on the run," Ivy says, looking at Cris steadily. One hops up from beside the fire and grabs a glowing ball suspended from a cable. "Because we have to go now." One gestures with the meteor-looking weapon towards the way Cris and the addict came from. "The lurkers are out there and as Cris said, we are still a few days away from Mutaria." Ivy turns and the others follow

Cris goes over to the fire and grabs some meat. The addict takes the rest and they start walking, keeping to the trees, gulping down the food on the go. The clouds start to break and an almost full gibbous moon shows itself from behind their cirrus fingers. They thicken and form an oily annulus of pastel-colored halos in the sky that casts eerie shadows on the trees.

Following Ivy, they move quickly and quietly and only the addict stumbles from time to time, sickened by his withdrawal in the low moonlight of the dying forest. Almost presciently, one of the others grabs his arm or shoulder from time to time to prevent him from falling. The sky starts to become red after a time and some small buildings appear out of the ebbing dark.

"This is Oil City," Ivy says." It is small, but we should circle around it. The humans here can be disagreeable."

"Oil City has a Nuclae settlement underneath," Alella says. "Maybe we can find shelter and food."

"I know where an entrance is, though I wouldn't go there if I were you," Ivy says.

The androgynous shapeshifter slinks between trees and rocks and they follow one around the city limits, hiding from some autocars passing from time to time but generally quiet in the early dawn. They come to an old mining tunnel on the side of a mountain.

"Go if you want, but I don't go underground unless I have to. Something's not right down there." says Ivy, hoisting her pack more firmly on one's shoulders.

"What do you mean?" asks Sistid.

"I am not sure, just a feeling, but I know where this lets out and I will meet you there." Not waiting for discussion, one bounds off east up a steep hill.

"Cris, keep an eye on Ivy," Alella says.

"She can't keep up with me," Ivy says over one's shoulder.

"Bitch," says Cris under her breath and sprints after Ivy who laughs and slows imperceptibly to let her catch up.

The others approach the tunnel and notice that there are no guards posted so they go in spaced out from one another and silent. The addict takes out a hand light and they make their way down a twisting tunnel into the bowels of the mountain.

"It smells of death down here," says Vira.

"Something ain't right," says Sistid.

They round a bend and a talon corpse lays in the tunnel, black mucus coming from his nose. They all instinctively take a step back.

"Put on your masks," says Alella. They all put on their synthmasks and step around the infected corpse. They go to the town chamber and are greeted by the scene of a hundred Nuclae dead, all with either black coming from their nose or sprayed by bullets and darkened with blood. Nuclae, young and old, are caught in different postures of death. Caught like statues, their eyes stare lifeless back at the intruders to their mountain.

"What happened here?" asks the addict.

The Nuclae stay silent in a state of shock, finally Ghost answers him.

"This was military action," he says quietly. "First, they softened them up with the biowarfare and then they sent in the strike force."

"How do you know?" Sistid turns angrily towards the ghost. "Have you done this before?" He grabs Ghost and Ghost pushes him back. Sistid takes a swing at him, hitting him with a quick snakelike flick behind the ear and knocks him down, smoke on the ground.

Alella and Vira grab Sistid and push him back.

"This doesn't help, Sistid!" yells Vira.

"They killed them all!" spits Sistid, his voice breaking, his eyes wet. "The shadows, they did this." he points at Ghost. "He is one of them."

Alella grabs Sistid's arms and stares him in the eyes, calming him. "Not anymore, Sistid. He betrayed them to help us. This won't bring them back. This doesn't help us." There are tears in both of their eyes.

The Nuclae are shell-shocked, reminded of their own city and the dead there. "You should get out of here," says the Ghost, as he gets to his feet, rubbing his jaw. "You guys could get infected."

Alella looks at the Ghost. "I thought bioweapons were illegal."

"In human on human combat it is. All Corporate Military™ are inoculated against the bioweapon viral and bacterial library when they enter regular service. It is a protection on their investment of the human weapon. And the addict, he was vaccinated at the hospital."

Alella and the others stare at Ghost and then at the addict and then back at the Ghost.

"How bout me and the addict find some rations and supplies and you wait for us at the east entrance. We will be along in a few minutes with what we find."

Alella looks at the sequencer she obtained from Clinic City, reviewing what she can of the addict's genome. After she verifies what the Ghost has said, she looks into the Ghost's smoky eyes. "I'm trusting you, Ghost. Don't betray us."

The addict and the Ghost make their way, stepping around bodies of Nuclae in death poses, looking for rations like grave robbers of old. In the darkness they make their way to a kitchen, the addict with his hand-light guided by the silent Ghost. Quietly, they fill up some backpacks with dried food bags and water that they find.

"Let's try to find some dry clothes, maybe in those apartments we passed on the way to the kitchen," says the ghost."

The addict follows him wordlessly. Whenever he comes to a corpse he steps around it and tries not to look with his pale face at how they died. He keeps his light at his feet as if afraid to shine his light on the dead. This is not lost on the Ghost. "What are you afraid of? They are dead."

"This is my fault."

"What?"

"All this death was set in motion because I fled to the Nuclae under Clinic City."

"Well, well, well. Aren't you important."

"Fuck you!"

"No, Fuck you. We are just pawns in this game! If whatever they did to you hadn't been successful then some other poor addict would have been the candidate."

"Yeah, but most people don't flirt with the tunnels."

"Maybe so, but believe me, the corporations have been looking for an excuse to go in for a long time. This was going to happen with or without you. Don't stack yourself too high or you'll fall hard. My advice to you is to be happy that little lady likes you and don't fuck it up."

After a pause the addict says quietly: "Let's

just get the supplies and get out of here."

Possession

At first there is nothing, but then we are floating in the dark with the lights of the city below us.

What are we doing up here?

We can fly.

We try swimming motions and it seems to get us going. We get some speed in the starry night, the stellar reflection below of the lights of miniature buildings and cars. The holograms even look small from up above. A building-sized scantily clad model towering over the autocar bridge with purple bikini skin and eyes. A huge lurker-looking creature holding up its arms.

We are moving more quickly and see the fires of the mounds below near the wall. We don't want to leave the city so we switch directions and eventually approach the huge hospital buildings of Clinic City. We start to fall so we try to swim upwards but we slowly descend, caught in gravity's well. We end up in front of the building that houses the regeneration unit, landing softly on the ground.

We try to leap up and fly away and though we can jump high, we keep returning to the ground. Turning towards the regeneration unit, it seems darker than we remember. We approach the clear plastic doors and they open automatically. The guard station has a bioprogram on duty, but it doesn't seem to be functioning and doesn't greet us or even turn towards us. We feel no pulses or signs of life from it.

We pass the bioprogram and enter the darkened hallway behind the guard station. Beyond the darkness our senses penetrate a deserted hallway. We move into the darkness, walking quietly, our senses on full alert. At the end of the hallway a malfunctioning light is pulsating above a shadow lurking in the dark. We hesitate, but though we see movement, we sense nothing.

Satisfied that there is no immediate danger, we move forward, coming closer to the shadow we realize is our reflection. The light repeatedly ebbs and then brightens. As it brightens we advance and see our muscular body set in long legs fading into darkness. We still sense nothing so we continue and in the brightening dim we look at ourself in the mirror and make out blue eyes with dark flecks set in an oval face, framed by long dirty-blonde hair. As the light dims we continue forward, now right up on the mirror at the end of the hall. The light brightens and now a shadow regards us from the mirror and whispers something to us.

"Shaya," it seems to say. Hairs stick up on our neck. The shadow approaches us, its outstretched arms grab our shoulders and push us down and hold us. Our heart beats fast and we still sense nothing from this empty shadow though it makes us shake with fear.

The light still pulsating, it holds us down with one arm and with its other it stretches out a long finger and sticks it into our mouth. The finger elongates and reaches down into our mouth, down our esophagus, into our stomach.

I know who I am, but who are you?

We bite the finger hard and the shadow recedes.

We open our eyes and familiar faces hover above us. One is old and the other is younger with bright blue intense eyes. They seem familiar. There is an oxygen mask over our mouth and nose. Looking over our supine body we see that we are strapped down to a robomedic table.

"She's awake," says the older one.

"Will she remember what happened?" asks the younger one.

"I am not sure. I haven't investigated bioprogram reincarnations but she will not be herself from what I understand."

"Do you know who you are?" asks the younger one.

"I am Shaya," we say in a hoarse whisper like it is the first thing we have ever said.

They both seem a little surprised.

"Do you remember how you died?" asks

the older one.

"No."

"Do you remember anything?" says the older one.

We don't answer.

The robomedic's arm descends and administers what we think is Viprex and we realize that this is something that we have been wanting.

"You are in the Regeneration unit of Clinic City™. You received some instructions in addition to Viprex™. *Do you understand what we want of you?*"

We see a male face, a familiar face, but it is turning to darkness. We sense his presence somewhere far away but we can almost feel him as if he were right next to us. His scent, his vibrations call to us, and we need to find him.

"*Yes,*"*we finally say.*

"*Remove restraints,*" *says the tall one to the robomedic.*

We sit up and get to our feet as they back up to give us space. We get to our feet and we feel surprisingly steady. We look down and see that we are clothed in a black mirror suit like most military are clad. We feel the need to follow his trail and turn toward the door.

The tall one says to the blue-eyed one: "Follow her."

We sense the trail that we follow through the city to the gates. The gates are opened and they let us out.

We feel trailers behind but we ignore them. We have one purpose, one goal and that is to track the being that seems to be disappearing..

Thug, the Prophet and Captain Mahan follow the dark female bioprogram out of the scene of carnage underneath the mountain and they are quiet for the journey up the tunnel and back out of the east entrance. They are on the trail of the addict but for once the Prophet's roguish wit is a no show for the trip up. Thug is beginning to come to terms with what they are now a part of. Twisted bodies of mutants are not too hard to stomach, but the mutant children are dead, and that is a little harder to swallow.

On top of that he is oddly aroused by the bioprogram in a way that seems unnatural, and he is not sure why. He suspects chemical or technological alterations to the fleshbot that normally would freak him out more than turn him on.

Mahan, seemingly unaffected by the slaughter, happily goes up ahead to keep an eye on the bioprogram and Thug slows down so that Mahan is out of earshot.

"What are we doing here, Prophet?" he asks quietly.

After a pause the Prophet says, "We are

making money. That's what."

"Yeah, finding the addict is one thing, but mass murder...this is some sick shit."

"Did we do that? I'll tell you one thing, I ain't responsible for this shit. Mahan and Varius did that. Our job is to use the bioprogram to get the addict. You were brought in because you know the shadow traitor and you know how he thinks. Don't forget you got a pardon and loads of money are waiting for you. That's some serious shit."

"Yeah." Thug pauses. "But dead kids man, that's hard to take."

"Listen. This was gonna happen anyway. Whether we go in and get the addict or not, they are still going to kill the mutants. We can't stop that."

"I don't know. And that female tracking bioprogram creeps me out."

"She responds to *my* commands."

"What's wrong with her? Is she made from a real person?" asks Thug.

The Prophet says nothing and Thug stares at him while they walk.

"You knew her?"

The Prophet stays silent.

"You had sex with her."

The Prophet has had enough. "You want me to tell Varius you don't want the pardon *we* negotiated for you?"

"I thought I got the pardon for letting you

know about the addict after you put the word out."

"Look, I don't care, I got all these military doing what I say and I got the tracking bioprogram finding the addict. I don't necessarily need you, but I was trying to get you some money. Let me know, but I'm gonna keep going man. I'm gonna get what's mine." The Prophet's bright blue eyes flash with fury.

"No, I'm good with it," says Thug in a way that sounds like he isn't.

They walk on for a few minutes, the path undulating out of the mountain to spit them out into the western range of the mountains. The three of them come out of the tunnel's maw near the top of the mountain where the bioprogram is waiting. She seems to smell the air, her arms outstretched, her long legs in a wide stance.

The setting orange sun glows on the tops of the trees from behind them, looking like outstretched fingers rung with birds and grasping at the sky. There is nothing like that back in Clinic City. Thug and Prophet have never seen any scene quite so rich with life. Though many trees are dead, especially in lower lands where they have been flooded by the rains, there are still living evergreens and deciduous trees that propagate naturally through the landscape. Birds and even a small syrinx flit through the sky, chirping their good nights early in the mountains. They didn't even know that a scene like this could still exist. Looking at each other, they are both moved by the scene.

"Bioprogram, did 197-22 come this way," Mahan says tonelessly, clearly unimpressed with the vista.

Thug and the Prophet look at the Shaya bioprogram and are surprised to see tears coming from its eyes and coursing down its face. She doesn't respond.

"What the fuck?" Mahan spits. "Answer me, junk."

The Shaya bioprogram turns and looks at Mahan, her eyes wet. She refuses to respond to him.

"Well, Shaya?" asks the Prophet.

"Yes," the bioprogram says flatly out of its full lips on its doll-like face.

"Well what are we waiting for? Come on or we'll send you back to the graveyard," barks Mahan, smiling sickly back at Thug and the Prophet before he turns to follow the bioprogram.

Thug shoots the Prophet a look and nods towards Mahan raising his eyebrows.

The Prophet rolls his eyes but they follow down the path tailed by some of the ghost troops.

"Anyways, I have an ace up my sleeve," says the Prophet.

"Oh yeah and what is that?" asks Thug.

"I got a little surprise for the addict when we find him," says the Prophet. Thug says nothing so the Prophet keeps talking.

"So, your military friend, what's his angle? Why did he betray the government?"

"Fitty Fit? Well he has always been what you would call a mama's boy. He always seemed to do the right thing even when we was doing the wrong thing."

"So, how does that help us?"

"Well we gonna see, Prophet. And I'm betting soon too." Thug says.

The cadre of shadows flicker into and out of visibility at the top of the ridge in the bright sunlight and follow them as they make their way down the mountainside. Then the sun is gone, blocked by the hill as they descend towards the swampy lowlands and it feels suddenly colder. They follow the bioprogram that is following the pheromone trail they believe to be the addict's.

Everyone has been quiet since they met up and followed the way down the mountain away from the massacred Nuclae. Ivy, Sistid, and Alella lead the way, followed by Cris and the addict. Next comes the Ghost and lastly Vira to protect their rear. It is dark, but everyone wants to distance themselves from the massacre behind them and no one speaks of it. The small Nuclae settlement, though no longer visible, seems to resonate in the psyche of all the group members and to speak of it or speak any unnecessary words at this point would be to defile its memory and the memory of the lost Nuclae that died there and at Clinic City. They have not stopped hiking the rugged terrain all day and they are starting to wear down from lack of sleep and rest.

Alella, in particular, feels a burden of responsibility. She knows that she holds this ragtag confederation, an unknown Nuclae guide, a drug addict, a military traitor, a Hex, a Talon and two Plastics together for a purpose that she is not sure she understands fully. If she fails to get the addict to Mutaria to have the addict's secrets analyzed, then this group will fall apart. Sistid is a meltdown away from killing any non-Nuclae. Cris seems to be getting a little too close to the addict. If she says anything to Cris, Alella knows Cris's youth will force her to make a mistake so it is better to remain silent, at least for now. For some reason, she trusts the ghost to do right in the short term. Ivy is an unknown but has helped them so far. The addict is a total wild card. The one thing she is sure of is that he will want to get Viprex again, especially without his treatments. Vira is the only one who could be counted on without fail. Her rock, her sister.

Alella peers back at the setting sun over her shoulder. The gray fish scale clouds wrinkle across the sky highlighted by pink. Clear pale blue sky shines behind like clean water. She and the other Nuclae have never traveled this far outside of Clinic City before and despite the danger and decay of life outside the city something inside her is deeply moved by the wounded and struggling life that remains in the wild. They are getting closer to Mutaria and with every new hill and valley there is a different environment filled with trees, bushes, bugs, birds, mammals, reptiles, flowers and fungi. She breathes in the smell of the rising wind in the gathering dusk and is aroused in a way she has never felt before.

"Life will find a way," she whispers to herself reaching inside of herself for a strength that she has felt before in times of need. Despite the weight of two mass slaughters of her people, she still has hope. For what, she knows not, but despite all the horrible things that have happened, she still thinks that somehow something right can come of their mission.

As they crest the hill Ghost breaks ranks to catch up with her. An ocher cloud seems to grow up from the ground a mile or so away to the north, side-lit by the sun behind her. The wind pushes it south towards them. Ghost falls into step beside her. "That's some mine dust up north there. That is from fresh strip mining. We want to avoid getting too close to that mine. Wherever there is a corporation, there is military and you better believe that they are gonna be looking for us."

"They have not come this deep into this forest before," says Ivy

"Sistid!" Alella calls.

"What's up?" He catches up to them. The rest bunch up to hear what is going on.

"Ghost says that cloud is from a Corporate Military™ mine. We need to get away from anything corporate."

"Well, that is gonna take us way out of our way. According to the map the techies gave us, this gorge is the most direct and safest route. It could add a week to our travel." He flicks the holomap on.

"We won't last a week out here between Corporate Military™ and the creatures out here," says Alella. They all gather around the holomap.

"What about through here?" Ivy says, pointing at what looks like it is a route that is just as direct.

"Hell Hollow?" asks Sistid.

"No," says Ghost. "That is not a good idea."

"Why not?" says Sistid.

"It is the fastest way," Ivy says. "But dangerous, especially for people not used to the forest."

"I have been out this far before." snorts Ghost. "None of you Nuclae have. Hell Hollow is probably the densest population of lurkers in Eastern America. No one goes in there, not even the military."

Ivy raises one's eyebrows.

"That's a good thing!" says Sistid. "See what the military do to Nuclae? And all life for that matter!"

"I don't know," says Vira. "Lurkers are just as dangerous if not more so." She knows that Sistid's reasoning is flawed by his anger and fear.

"Ivy, you said there was another way," says Alella.

Ivy points at another less direct route. "Minister Trail. It might take a few extra days but the road forks down the hill from where we are now. This ain't a bad spot to camp with a clear view of the valley. Plus, there are many rocks for cover."

Alella looks around at the weariness on the faces of the people around her. They needed to rest, even though they know that they are being followed. "We camp here and take Minister Trail in the morning." Relief shows on their faces."But be ready to move after a few hours."

They find some old dead pines near the crest of the hill so that they can have sight lines all around. They eat some of the food the Ghost and the addict had found in the mines and sit around on some rocks, rubbing sore muscles and avoiding conversation. Sistid lays down on a soft bed of pine needles and passes out snoring. Ivy opens her burning weapon and scoops some wet pine needles into it, almost over-stuffing it. They smolder and crackle and one puts back on the lid which flows closed seamlessly. The orb happily glows a dull red giving off some heat which Ghost and Alella gather around.

"What do you think?" the Ghost asks Alella.

"About what?"

"All this around us."

"I have seen pictures but, to be here, it's different. It touches me in a way that I didn't expect."

"Most of this is natural, but engineers even managed to reach this far." Ivy says.

"Nuclae engineers do not alter genes that can escape and become invasive: Central Dogma Chapter 3 verse 18. That is a human tendency."

"True, Alella," Ghost says. "Genetic engineering is part of the reason why this forest is dying. Maybe not in the next generation but our grandchildren won't see it. All these species of trees will be dead along with the ecosystem they support, replaced by human-engineered varieties."

"Human greed. Between pollution and your people releasing GMO organisms into the environment, you destroyed the natural balance." says Ivy, sneering at Ghost.

"At least we are trying to replace a doomed ecosystem with a working one," Ghost says. "Nuclae didn't help either. What breed are you?"

"A Talon," Alella says proudly.

"Miners right?"

"Yeah, so?"

"Your   people   bear   some   of   the responsibility for changing the environment by mining raw materials for industry."

"We also create the Synthetic Oxygen Factories for the survival of the planet and you humans."

"Redirection. You are responsible as well. Plus, don't SOFs give Corporate Government™ an excuse to replace trees?"

"The Nuclae have been part of the problem in the past, But we were just trying to survive. We corrected our ways and have now been responsible for several generations." She waits and when he says nothing she continues. "In a non-invasive way, I could redesign some of these individual trees to survive the heat and rain and still be close to what they were. This oak, this sycamore."

"I'm impressed, the underground mutant that knows her trees," says Ivy.

"Nuclae   know   biology,   especially geneticists."

"Don't you think that's what got us into this quagmire? Stepped in shit and then used a poison cleaner to get it off and spread that around," levels Ivy.

"Well Ivy, that is a crappy analogy but I suppose that is one way of looking at it. But we are Nuclae, both of us. We augment ourselves for our survival, so for me it makes sense to believe that I can help these trees by modifying them."

Ghost grins at her. "And that's natural?" He mocks.

"Look in the mirror, Ghost," Alella smiles. "Look in the mirror."

"You know I can't see myself," he says.

After an hour of restless sleep on the soft pine needles, the addict rises. Sensing a presence, he walks to a collection of dwelling-sized rocks nearby the pines. In the cold clear night air, the almost-full moon is bright enough to see by. He climbs to the top and finds Cris sitting on a rock there, her eyes fixed on the mostly clear sky. He looks up at the sky and feels very small underneath the moon and the stars spread out above him.

He looks at Cris, bathed in the silver light, and she gives no sign that she is aware of his presence, her eyes mirroring the moonlight. The longer he watches her the more the light makes her seem otherworldly; her blond pixie cut silverish in the light, her large eyes pools of light and her face relaxed and slightly turned up at the sky. He stares at her as she stares at the sky and he can't look away, fascinated by this perfect creature bathed in argent.

After a while, she speaks. "I see you, 22. I felt you wake up. I saw you when you sat up from your bed of pine needles. I felt your heart quicken when you walked over here. I can feel everything out here. I can feel the animals creeping around the mountainside. We can sense things you humans can't."

"Well, we can both see the stars, fading off into oblivion. We never see this in the city, even on a rare clear day in the dry season." He neglects to tell her he can sense her as well.

"We never even see the sky in Subterra," she says almost sadly. He didn't answer.

She looks at him then. There are tears in her eyes. "Why do I get to see this, why do *I* get to be here when so many of my people aren't?" She stares at him accusingly and then looks away.

"Cris, it's not your fault." He moves towards her and puts his arm around her shoulders. She shakes it off and looks at him again.

"I can still sense your heartbeat. I can hear your pulse quicken when you come near me. I can smell your pheromones. I know what you want. How can you even think about that right now, after what we've seen."

"I'm sorry. I am used to being alone, only caring about myself." He pauses, trying to gather his courage. "But I care about you."

She looks at him, angrily with tears still in her moonlit eyes but then puts her head on his shoulder. "Hold me," she cries and he holds her close, filling an emptiness he didn't even know he had under the clear night sky.

Alella wakes Vira with a shake a couple hours before sunrise. She grabs Vira's shovel-like hand and signs into it.

There's something down there.

I feel it too.

Wake the others.

They shake the others awake, careful to silence the addict and unnecessarily put a hand over his mouth as he is already aware he should be quiet.

They spread out across the top of the hill taking cover behind the pines. Cris protects the addict on the high ground with Ivy. Sistid takes point and Vira and Alella flank the presence down at the bottom of the hill. As they silently descend, Alella senses four heat signatures creeping, ascending, spread out about 15 meters below.

Silenced automatic weapon fire strafes their position and thuds into trees immediately above their heads. Vira charges forward with Alella shadowing her for cover. Vira blasts through the first of the 4 enemies and Alella comes over her back and drop kicks another in the neck with a blow that would kill a human. Then she realizes who their opponents are. "Cancers!" she yells as she spins an elbow into the front of its head, putting it down. Another one turns towards her and starts firing when Ghost lands a blow with a large stick to the shooter's head. Sistid engages the other one and disarms it.

"I can see you!" Ghost's adversary says and lands a powerful blow to the smoke who fades back and then surges forward landing blows across the Cancer's temple. The blows slow the Cancer but it presses forward in their slow but powerful manner. Ghost steps back and spins backwards landing a heel kick to the Cancer's temple. The Cancer drops to its knees and Ghost grabs his head, landing knee after knee till it falls.

Vira plows through Alella's adversary and then spins around to Sistid's, but Sistid has already put his Cancer down and its neck is turned at an awkward angle, a feat that usually proves almost impossible given Cancers' reinforced musculoskeletal system.

Up above on the hill a Cancer flanks Cris, Ivy and the addict. Cris launches herself at the Cancer, flying at it and drop kicking it in the face, falling and rolling out of its too slow return blows. From the Cancer's blind side, Ivy swings one's "meteor" weapon hard with a stream of sparks and the Cancer falls, face burned and smashed. Another Cancer surprises Cris, swings at her and connects, putting her down, but the addict attacks the Cancer from behind, trying to choke it with an arm around its neck. It flips the addict over its head and gets smashed in half by

Vira before it can do any more damage. Vira helps Cris up and she shakes herself off before going over to the addict and helping him up.

"Thanks," Cris whispers to him. "But you got your ass kicked," she smiles.

After checking the perimeter, Sistid picks up a gun and puts a few silent projectiles in 3 of the prone Cancers before he walks over to the one Ghost had subdued. He looks over at Ghost and sneers at him in the way Sistid usually does. Cris and the addict come down the hill and they all gather around the survivor who is sitting, battered and bloody.

"It feels good to kill something. Especially Cancers." grates Sistid. "Those arrogant fucks."

The Cancer with the mashed up face looks angry and a little scared. "How did you find us?" asks Sistid.

The Cancer looks up at Sistid and then at each of the others before focusing on the addict. "The rest of you mean nothing. We will kill you, addict, and burn and destroy any evidence. The humans will never get your mutations."

"I asked you a question." Sistid says, backhanding the Cancer hard across the face.

The Cancer spits a bloody wad, looks up at Sistid and laughs. "Kill me, torture me, it doesn't matter. Cancers always come back. Always." The Cancer falls over.

Alella rushes forward and puts a hand on the Cancer's heart. Using her augmented senses, she feels no signs of life. She looks at Sistid and Sistid raises the rifle and puts a few into the Cancer's brain, just in case.

"They must have multiple parties out looking for us," says Alella. "If Cancers are out themselves then they are serious."

"No shit," says Sistid. "Cancers never do anything themselves, unless it's some bullshit science."

"At least we have guns now," says Ghost. "Silent automatics at that."

"We avoid guns," says Alella.

"Sistid seems to like them." Ghost smiles and nods at the Plastic who is sweeping the perimeter holding the automatic weapon.

"Still, Nuclae cities have small armories for defense only," she relents somewhat.

"I'd say your leaders have been stockpiling guns behind your backs," says Ghost. "Out of necessity, we should stock up with these. These are Corporate Military™ issue C-100 fully automatic silent rifles. Top of the line. Either they stole this from shadow troops or they are connected to the human Corporate Military™ in some way. You can't buy these at the gun store."

Alella looks down at the Cancer corpses for a moment before reaching down and grabbing the guns. She hands one each to Cris and the Ghost. The fourth she straps to her shoulder. They rummage the corpses and come up with some ammo, food and water but nothing to tell them how they had found them.

"I see no instrumentation except communicators," says Alella. "Some of the Cancer's sensory augmentation must be on the same level as a Seer."

"Then we should get out of here," answers Sistid. "When they don't report back, they will come looking in this area."

They make for Minister Trail, the addict slowing their pace somewhat until Vira makes him get on her back. Silently, they start making good time and cross 2 hills and 3 large valleys. They are about to crest a third hill when Ivy puts her hand up and motions for them to get off the path. They crawl behind some huge sandstones and climb up the rear of them to look down into the valley below.

In the brightening dawn, even the addict can see the camp below. About 20 Cancers are breaking camp in the dim light. They have two sentries and one is facing them but doesn't appear to see them. They back up and climb back down the other side of the rock and hike down the hill a ways.

"We don't have a choice. Minister Trail is covered," says Sistid.

"We are going to have to go through Hell Hollow," Alella whispers.

The others stay silent except for the addict.

"I thought you said that it was too

dangerous," he whispers.

"I have survived Hell Hollow," Ivy says quietly.

Ghost's eyes narrow in disbelief.

"We don't have a choice. We can't face 20 Cancers and that valley is the only way through. Maybe we can go through Hell Hollow without lurkers seeing us, especially during the day," says Alella.

"It's settled,"says Sistid. "Let's move."

"No, it's not settled." says Ghost. "Hell Hollow is suicide."

Alella grabs his sleeve by his shoulder. "Ghost, 20 well-armed Cancers is suicide for sure. We don't have an option. Those Cancers are going to come over that hill soon. They are going to sense that we were here and they are going to find us unless we move. Hell Hollow is our only chance and we have to leave now."

Ghost says nothing.

"We could use your help."

"Guess I got nothing lined up today," he says sarcastically and starts backtracking west. "Today is as good a day to die as any."

Sistid spits. "Dying I ain't."

Following Ivy, they move quickly until they come to the fork that leads to Hell Hollow and start down the gorge trail that descends into darkness even in the morning light.

The Prophet, Thug, Captain Mahan and his shadows follow the bioprogram that silently leads the way up a steep hill. The bioprogram stops and wavers in confusion, a strange haunted look on its face that disturbs Thug. It is raining again in the dying forest and the Prophet suggests that it may be confused by the weather.

"That why she acting like that? Cause of the rain?" The Prophet asks Mahan. Mahan turns to a shadow soldier who is more visible than usual because of the rain coursing down her body.

"What's the story? What's it doing?" Mahan asks the shadow soldier.

"According to the data feed from the bioprogram, inmate 971-22 crossed here twice. Once going east and more recently going northwest."

"Are you hot?" Thug asks her. "Cos your outline is not bad."

"The northwest trail sounds good," says the Prophet.

"This trail leads to Hell Hollow." She sounds annoyed. "We need to be careful. There are a lot of lurkers there and no satellite record of any recent human movement through there for the last 20 years."

"This keeps getting better and better," Thug complains.

"Toughen up Mr. Thug. If you don't, you

might become a lurker husk," mocks the shadow woman.

"You just dropped 10 points in my book," Thug says.

"Be a gentleman," Prophet says. "This young lady is important for our mission."

"Now you're a gentleman," Thug says sarcastically.

Mahan, who has remained quiet, turns to the shadow tech and says: "Corporal, get us a flight over Hell Hollow. We will put the bioprogram down there and start our search over there."

"Thank the lord," smiles Thug for the first time in a while. "Don't want anything to do with lurkers."

Hearing this, the bioprogram laughs out loud. It sounds strange to the humans' ears and they all take a step back from the light brown, muscular yet voluptuous tracker soaked by the rain.

"Dry it off," commands Mahan. "We can't have it get sick. At least not until it locates the target." Some of the shadows lead it away. Thug notices that the Prophet avoids looking at the bioprogram and makes a mental note.

After the lurker attack, the Prophet begins to reassess the situation. Many of the shadow troops had been slain when they landed on the other side of Hell Hollow.

The visibility cloaked hovercopters that were silent to human hearing apparently weren't so silent or invisible to lurkers as they glided down noiselessly into a grassy clearing surrounded by dark ominous looking oaks. They had followed the bioprogram, Shaya, and hiked into the forest and up an eroded switchback onto a narrow and twisting game trail through some elm, oak and brambles. At the top, a fog and whispers of the wind began to stalk their way through the trees. Thug, the Prophet and even Mahan were all trembling and the Prophet guessed that the shadow troops probably felt it as well. But it was too late.

Mahan led the charge back to the copter, closely followed by the Prophet and Thug and a few surviving shadow troops. The Shaya bioprogram was nowhere to be found. Mahan commanded them to take off.

"We need the bioprogram," yelled the Prophet as they rose into the sky.

"I'm sure you do," Mahan sneers suggestively at the Prophet, "but it's dead or with its friends and if we're dead, it won't do us any good."

The Prophet was, for once, speechless but he knew Mahan was right. What did he care if a bioprogram got wasted?

Thug, always a good reader of people, saw

the turmoil on the Prophet's face but he knew to keep his mouth shut as they searched for a safer place to land.

Dead Way

It is midday when they come to the gorge that is the beginning of Hell Hollow. The drizzle is steady and the incessant moaning of the wind drones through the deep forested pass. They are cold and tired but they don't stop. They hope to be out of the Hollow by dark.

The forest is deeper and darker compared to the forests they have traveled through to get here. The trees seem more healthy with green full leaves or needles. As they descend, they notice pictoglyphs of strange shapes carved into the trees immediately at the gorge's beginning. Closer inspection reveals that the carvings actually seem to be different colored barks depicting scenes of bipeds and animals with strange abstracted shapes floating over the figures. Even in the dampness there is a crunching underneath and when the addict looks down he sees desiccated animals strewn in every direction like Quickstore™ junk food made from roadkill.

The addict shivers.

"Won't blow away." The Nuclae mutter almost simultaneously.

The group steps gingerly around the skins trying to make as little noise as possible and start east again. There is a game trail along the creek bank and they follow its narrow passage until it joins with the creek.

The hills on either side force them to walk in the creek bed, sometimes on a crushed shale bank if they can, sometimes as deep as waist high when the bank disappears. Small birds occasionally make quiet calls but are rarely visible. Bigger game does not present itself. Only the incessant hum of the insects breaks the silence or the occasional slapping sound when one of the group kills a mosquito stealing blood. The way is hard and slow through the mud and slippery stones.

After a few hours, they come to a hard turn in the creek with a shale bank in the crook of the elbow of the bend. "Let's rest here for a few," whispers Alella. They unshoulder their packs and sit down. Sistid takes out the holomap.

"We are about halfway through," he says softly. "I don't think we are going to get out of here before dark."

Alella puts her hand on Vira's armored shoulder. "Vira, if we are attacked, get the addict out of here and the rest of us will meet up at the end of the hollow."

"OK." Vira says soberly, knowing this could be goodbye forever to her friends.

"If we don't make it, you need to convince

the Mutarians to sequence the addict's genotype. As a last resort you may have to release his secrets to all, humans included."

"Knowledge is power," says Vira, repeating their mantra growing up together. It seems more meaningful to her now than ever before

"Yes, my friend, and if you have to make this decision without us, I know you will make the best decision you can."

They clasp hands for a moment and their eyes meet.

"We should get a move on," Sistid croaks.

They start moving again and after a time it begins to grow dark.They look for a place to camp as Ivy says that lurkers come out more at night. Following along a cliff wall, they find a natural sandstone cutout that parallels the hollow.

"This could work." Ivy says. "At least there are two ways out if we are attacked from this side, we can escape this way." She gestures at a mossy opening 50 feet further east that leads back to the hollow.

They scatter themselves around the open air chamber surrounded by the weathered and pockmarked sandstone covered with mosses and lichen. The drizzle somewhat abates. Cris sits down on a log and the addict sits down next to her using his hands to squeegee out his hair. "You look like a drowned rat," she chides with a smile.

"You should see yourself. You don't look much better." But he actually thinks she looks attractive soggy. He takes out some of the food he and Ghost found under Oil City, dried meat-like protein engineered by the Nuclae.

"You guys like this shit?" he asks Cris, quietly.

"I grew up on this stuff. It's a delicacy."

"I'm so hungry it actually tastes good, to tell the truth."

Strange noises echo in the distance. Vira takes the first watch and most of the others get into sleeping bags that Ghost and the addict had found. Most of them fall asleep quickly despite being cold, wet and uncomfortable, but the addict can't sleep. He rolls over and Cris's face is next to his, her eyes open and gazing into his. She smiles at him and he smiles back.

"You know, you're the first human I have ever met that I like," she whispers to him.

"You've met a lot of us?"

"Not too many, but sometimes we would go up above and see what human clubs were like when we were young. Most humans always seem like they either hated me or wanted something from me."

"Oh yeah I wonder what they wanted," he says sarcastically.

"Yeah, there was some of that."

"So, were you ever with a human?"

"Hell no. Most Nuclae won't respect you if

you're with a human."

The addict looks disappointed. "Thanks." He says.

"For what?"

"For liking me. I like you too, even though your people might not respect you."

She laughs quietly and gets a little closer to him.

"Well maybe I could make an exception if I found a human that I really liked."

He kisses her. She responds with quiet eagerness and they kiss each other gently until they fall asleep in each others' arms on the uneven ground half out of their sleeping bags.

Whispers calling to us, dark gray of the night brightens as we descend the gorge where we can feel him calling to us, pulling us toward him with a gravity that defines our purpose. Still sensitive to the vibrations of the world, we feel him resonating with us, maybe a day in front of us.

We need to hurry if we are to catch him.

Energy signatures are nearby.

Lurkers?

We need to escape.

The whispers become visions to our senses. Thousands of Nuclae lying dead in a forest of rotting trees.

They are threatening us.

"Shaya," They whisper. Though our system is flooded with adrenaline, we don't run.

Escape up the hill!

More visions are whispered to us. Visions of men lying with a woman whose face I have seen reflected in the streams of this forest. Is this what I was?

Another whispered vision of lightning striking our objective and him lying dead, a smoldering ruin.

The lurkers keep their distance and pace us. More whispers flood more disparate memories back to us.

We resist our urge to escape and instead concentrate on his vibrations and use the adrenaline to accelerate towards our quarry. The lurkers match our pace both in and out of our plane of existence.

The lurkers will kill us.

But the addiction begins to understand that they see something familiar in us and will not attack us. Instead, they begin to show us the dimensions they travel in, unpeeling layers from them and exposing an underlying structure that makes our three dimensions seem flat.

Though they pace us from a distance, they seem so close now. Since our reawakening, we have had snatches of memories as if from a dream. But now the lurkers make things clearer to us and additional memories start to become more familiar. Some disturbing, some happy but still not a complete picture of who we are.

They are like a great eye spread all over the world, connected in some unseen dimension. They see much, but he is just outside of their view.

The need to follow him is still strong, stronger than our addiction, stronger than the lurkers pull and even stronger than our regret. His pheromones pull us, compelling us forward. We move purposefully and surefooted. Knowing each step we take before we take it. We can see so much, even if we can't understand why.

Strange noises haunt the night but otherwise darkness passes without incident. When the Nuclae wake in the morning everyone is cold and miserable in the grayness and the drizzle becomes a light rain. Branches from the trees hang low with the added weight of the water.

No one talks much while they eat a breakfast of Nuclae protein packs. Sistid's hoarse voice is quiet. "It gets really tight about 5 kilometers ahead. If there is a place the lurkers will attack, that is a likely place as it is a natural bottleneck."

They shoulder their packs and go on along the creek bed. A light mist rolls in. After an hour the rain stops and the mist becomes a fog. A few minutes more and visibility is reduced to 5 meters.

They gather close together. "The bottleneck is a few minutes ahead," whispers Sistid. "Silence from now on and be ready." Vira gets close to the addict and Cris flanks his other side protectively. They press on. The addict does his best to not show his shivering and clenches and unclenches his hands to try to get his blood flowing into his cold fingers.

Through breaks in the fog, they can see that the cliffs on either side of the hollow begin to grow together as they move forward. Soon, the tops of the cliffs are only about 10 meters apart and they are funneled into a tighter unit so that they are only a few feet apart from each other. It is darker as the cliffs on either side are about forty meters high.

Cris reaches out and takes the addict's trembling hand. His hand feels cold and clammy to her and hers feels warm and reassuring to him. His trembling abates somewhat. In breaks in the mist, they can sometimes see the roots of the trees growing over the edges of the top of the cliffs, roots grabbing like fingers holding crumbling shale together.

There's something up there, thinks Alella, *I can feel it.*

She pushes Sistid, who is walking point, slightly to tell him to hurry. Seeing this, the others increase their pace as well. The addict's stomach begins to itch and he breaks contact with Cris' hand to scratch it.

As they go deeper into the chasm, the mist starts to climb the walls. Soon they can't see the cliff top anymore and the mist is overflowing, blocking out any visuals in the 300-700 nanometer spectrum. The mutants can still see in the infrared but it is fuzzy at best as none of them is a Seer. They press on as quickly as they can while still being quiet.

Splash to the left.

Two splashes off and to the right.

Another few splashes to the right and some creeping whispers seem to call each beholder's name in the mist. Along with the whispers the mist swirls and alternates between vague suggestions of faces or strange visions before collapsing into formless swirling whitish gray.

Alella feels her heart quicken and she turns around to make eye contact with Vira. Vira looks at her with concern and flanks the addict. The rest of the party forms a circle around him.

Another few splashes all around. The whispering intensifies. Then, a sourceless whispered scream that seems to be backward. More whispers and another scream.

Cris grabs the addict bodily and effortlessly swings him onto Vira's back. The addict holds on as Vira sprints deeper into the foggy chasm. Shadowy figures appear out of the fog and take swipes at them but Vira cuts left and then right, seeming to make the right move every time. At the narrowest point of the canyon a wall of shadows looms, maybe a half dozen of them, pulsating.

"Hold on, addict," she whispers and charges full speed at the shadows. The addict has only experienced a similar sensation of speed on an electrocycle and he holds his breath. The shadows close together and Vira crouches and jumps like a huge grasshopper; she clears the lurkers by a height of 3 meters. They pulsate up at her but she clears them and charges on.

They only encounter a few more lurkers in the fog as the hollow becomes wider and wider and the fog gives way to clear air. They are still moving at a ridiculous speed and Vira eases it down a notch. She is breathing heavily but maintains a breakneck pace for a few minutes.

"I think you are safe for now, addict."

"Do you know what happened to Cris and the others?"

"I don't know." Vira sounds concerned. "One lurker alone is extremely dangerous, a score is lethal. Speed is the only thing that might save them. I pray that they are safe."

"Why did we run?"

"You are the mission. We need to get you to Mutaria so that we can study your DNA. Everything and everyone else is secondary. Cris understood that and so did the others, even the human. They were all willing to sacrifice themselves to help all in the world. The Nuclae and human world." Vira eyes him seriously.

They continue on and the hollow opens up to a valley with the most healthy looking trees they have seen so far with green leaves or needles on every tree. Crow caws welcome them in the distance and warn of their arrival to this valley.

"We are close to Mutaria, addict. I need to rest a moment."

Vira stops and he lets go of her shoulders and jumps off her back and onto a mossy area under oaks and pines. Small insects fly in his face and he swipes at them. Looking down, he sees the trail of blood dripping from her armored abdomen. He looks at her in disbelief. She slumps to the ground.

"Ah addict, I got clipped back there. Sorry, but I don't think I'll be able to see you to Mutaria."

"But, I can't make it alone, Vira!" He grabs her shoulders.

Quietly and slowly she responds. "You have to. I died to get you here, addict. Don't disrespect that. Dying you ain't." She half smiles. "You don't have the right," her breathing seems shallow.

"You say we're close? I can help you make it." Tears fill his eyes. "We can save you there."

Her green eyes seem unfocused and she lays her chin onto the crook of his arm and mumbles. "Tears for me, or for yourself?" She manages a small laugh. "Go east and you will reach Mutaria." She draws a few ragged breaths and her unfocused eyes stare at the addict.

The addict calls her name, sobbing, and tries to shake her unmoving bulky form back to consciousness but she is lifeless. Gasping for breath out of panic, he doesn't know what to do. He doesn't even know what direction is east. He gets a hold of his breathing and calms down and thinks what to do.

Why don't we start walking in the direction Vira's corpse is pointed towards.

You are so heartless, you don't even care about her.

Maybe she is right. Do we really cry for her or do we cry for ourself.

Shut up.

The sun bursts out at the horizon on his left as it sometimes does on a cloudy day at sunset. The energy blasts his eyes with bright orange, banishing the grayness that has permeated the journey through the Hollow. With one last look at the motionless staring Hex, he aims himself into the forest so that the sun is at his back. As the sun slides below the horizon, a more gentle rose lights up the forest and lends some white flowers a warm pink hue, contrasting against the falling shadows. A weak heat warms his back and somewhat dispels the cold chills of the last few days.

Things are looking up for us.

What about the Nuclae?

What about them, maybe it is better if they don't make it so that we can tell Mutaria the truth about us.

The truth? What about the Nuclae, people that protected us.

They were just protecting themselves.

He follows a dry creek east and the rose light fades into gray welcomed by the call of the crickets and katydids. In the twilight, the tree limbs seem dark and menacing, reaching for him without movement. He increases his pace and doesn't need his light.

Without their medicine dulling our senses, we can see without eyes.

He continues on until he hears crunching underneath his feet. He turns his light on and there are more skins underneath, this time some humanoid ones.

Not dead. Just not here.

Not exactly sure what that means.

There is rustling in the bushes so he flips off his light again and waits. He hears nothing. The forest is silent except for the nocturnal chorus of the insects.

He feels nothing in his stomach, but he senses a figure out there moving in the darkness. He gets behind some trees, feeling panicked. He swings his body back around and presses his back against rough bark trying to push his way into the tree. Though it is cold he bursts into a nervous sweat and clenches his fists. He hears light footsteps crackling through the dead leaves and husks of humans and he gets ready to run.

He turns to the left and he feels a pressure on his right shoulder. He spins around with his hands up and takes a step back. He can't believe his eyes. There in front of him stands Shaya, alive and in the flesh.

"Hey baby," she smiles cooly. "Miss me?"

Spreading stealthily through both the human and Nuclae population from their original viral vector, the body count starts to mount. Everyone has a friend or family member who succumbs to the virus. As the death toll mounts for the Nuclae in Subterra, Malthus calls a meeting with survivors in the Nuclae city in the great chamber, the buildings at his back and the several hundred survivors in front of him. Pain, anger and hopelessness etch Nuclae faces into grim masks. There is a murmur in the crowd.

"What now?" someone yells.

"Our brothers and sisters are dead." a female voice cries

"Dying we aint!"

The murmur begins to intensify.

Malthus raises his arms and the crowd

quiets. He speaks in a deep accented voice that may have some eastern European tinge and is barely above a whisper, but in the silence his baritone voice is carried by the acoustics of the chamber.

I stand before you here with a sense of great loss for my sisters and brothers. We share the burden of survival. Chapter 2 Verse 5 of the code tells us we must always keep our lines pure and to never betray the Nuclae. In purity, there is honor.

We need to purify! He bellows angrily, his voice echoing in the chamber and continues in an angry tone, more loudly than before.

We trusted Alella, our doctor, and Sistid, our top security officer, and the others. They had worked by our side since the moment they were born.

So tell me, brothers and sisters, how could they betray us, so that even our children lie dead at our feet? Our children!

An angry murmur fills the chamber.

Silence! I didn't want to believe it either, we trusted Sistid with the security of our city. We trusted Alella with our code. What did they do?

He pauses and hissing comes from the crowd.

*They brought the Corporation Military into **our** city, to kill hundreds of **our** family! And then they ran away with them!* He shouts.

He pauses.

But it's worse than that. They brought a vector into our city. A human vector. The filth that has killed thousands of our family!

The crowd is silent, thinking of loss, but anger is on many Nuclae faces.

Alella's group has made a deal with the humans in exchange for money, human money! They killed Ulana, a respected and revered leader. What is pure about that? They infected our people! We need to get that addict back, alive. His blood will give us the cure! As for the others, I let you be the judge. Chapter 5 Verse 6! Cancerous code must be deleted!

A roar goes up from the Nuclae and subsides.

They are heading east, in the open wilds trying to get to Mutaria, no doubt paid by the humans as murderers to infect Mutaria as well.

The addict must be captured and quarantined, but the others...if I find them first, I will inflict pain and death on them.

An angry chant begins, "Death! Death! Death! Death!" Malthus notes that not all faces are chanting angry masks and takes note of the more powerful among them, especially among the Talons, Hexes and Plastics, many of which are not chanting. Search and destroy parties are organized and sent out, now that they have a focal point for their anger. Many Nuclae are ready to risk death in the open wilds with the lurkers, the humans or other creatures to get revenge on the traitors. Malthus knows that the Cancers will get there first.

Varius watches the holoscreen in anticipation. This is the part he is depending on Hunter for: the press conference.

The newsperson comes on. Breaking news. Evidence that the Nuclae introduced a biological contaminant into Clinic City killing thousands. The plague has already spread to the coasts and even overseas. But now this virus has been traced to the Nuclae, who used a human Viprex™ user to infect human beings all over Clinic City™.

The International System of World Government's congress debated war against the Nuclae. Preemptively, the President took executive action and loudly sent "inspection units" both into the sewers and into the wilds.

Our embedded news team captured this footage of the Nuclae attacking our "inspection units" and killing 3 inspection officers. They say the names and show the pictures of the clean cut young soldiers.

"We are told that President Hunter is speaking live from New York City." They cut to Hunter, flashes going off on his handsome young-looking 70-something face. He speaks with a slight practiced drawl.

"My fellow citizens, our human way of life came under attack from murderous terrorists. The victims of this attack are the men, women, and transgender people of our great civilization."

"Millions of lives have been snuffed out, extinguished forever. These murders are intended to hurt and scare our International Union™ into submission by an enemy that is within our very borders, living among us, unclean vermin who want to exterminate us humans! But they have failed and we stand strong!

"Our race is a great one, the human race. We were targeted for attack because they want to destroy what we have built, a beacon for freedom and the right to live in safety and comfort. We see evil. These demons inhabit the netherworld and spread disease to our children, our parents and grandparents! When will it end?

"At the first sign of the infection, I implemented our government's Emergency Epidemiological Response Team and they were met with violence. A peaceful team, mind you. Abe Smith, Itay Singh and Shana Streeter were great humans. Warm, productive humans who cared about life. They gave their life, *their blood,* for the human race.

"Government Agencies are available to treat this ghost disease. We have found a way to treat the disease but I am told it mutates quickly and needs to be treated at the first sign of any of the symptoms.

"A search is underway for the immediate perpetrator of these unholy acts to bring justice, so be it death. There is no distinction between a bioterrorist and those that help them. Tonight, we will begin to attack those who attacked us. Tonight we will fear no evil. We will find patient zero, the original case of this disease and prove that the mutants planted this disease like sowers of death into our human society. We will find these pathetic monsters and bring them to justice."

A cheer goes up in the oval-shaped office and is echoed by many humans all across the world. Finally, they will do something about the mutant problem.

The lurkers surround them and slowly close in, plugging any escape route in the narrow chasm and Ivy fades back towards the back wall. "Climb," One whisper blends with the lurker's eerie hisses and the word "climb" seems to echo infinitely with no decay. Ivy grabs an impossible handhold out of the shear wall and quickly starts edging up. The others follow behind one, Sistid pushing Alella forward in front of him. "Go, go, go!"

Alella follows the others and scrambles up an almost vertical path, her climbing abilities on par with the much lighter Ivy. Ghost and Cris follow. Sistid feints his body at the lurkers and they pause momentarily, almost curious to see what this humanoid will do next. Sistid turns and scrambles. The lurkers hiss and one shoots forward, reference frame by reference frame, like a drawing in a flip book. Its face changes in a similar way, suggesting a shadowy anger and cuts Sistid off. Alella dislodges a boulder with her left talon-like hand and drops it right on the lurker. Sistid jumps upward and climbs faster than he ever has before.

The lurker becomes a living cubist sculpture and screams a backwards howl of pain seeming to come from all around the hollow. The all-encompassing sound turns more guttural and the lurker starts to climb behind the Nuclae, gaining height. The other lurkers seem to float slowly behind the Nuclae and they climb more quickly, Ivy almost at the top. Ghost, being the largest, is the slowest.

The lurker reaches for Ghost's leg but Sistid whips a large stone at its head. Though it goes through it from head to taint, like it was jello, it still seems to dislodge it. Stunned, the heavier lurker swipes again but loses its footing and falls back, taking out a couple other climbing lurkers in a tumble of dark tendrils.

Sistid makes it over the top edge and they look back to see the lurkers rounding the bend to the west, looking for some other route to get to them.

Ivy charges forward. "We have to get to the pass before they cut us off!" One yells. They all sprint forward following Ivy through a natural game trail. Whispering creeps to their senses from the south.

"More lurkers," Ivy's eyes gesture to their right, and they follow one to the left, down a crumbling shale bank.The whispering gets louder and they long jump a shallow stream bed.

Cris fades a bit to the right as she runs and so does Sistid behind her. A shadow rears from the undergrowth in that direction and they strike first, a running spinning wheel kick to the lurker's temple. Then Sistid whip front kicks to the lurker's abdomen. The lurker slows for a moment, and the Nuclae barely break stride, the angry backwards howls of the stunned lurker echoing in the cold air behind them.

The group follows Ivy down to the river, howling coming from the east around the bend in the river and they spring up a hill north of the river, the howling stops.

"They won't follow up to Mutaria," says Ivy, ones eyes calm and clear.

"We need to find the addict." Alella says.

"Vira's track is here." Ivy points to a soft part of the trail, where Vira's tracks could be clearly seen.

"There is blood in her tracks!" Alella almost screams.

Ivy looks worried and moves forward following large puddles of blood.

"You're a good tracker," Sistid says to Ivy quietly, trying to not face reality.

"Many at Mutaria are Seekers, as I am. You could learn these skills as well," Ivy says humbly but frankly. We are close." She says sadly.

Following the bloody trail they come to Vira, dead on a rise above the river lying between two huge ghostly white oaks standing guard over her body. Alella collapses to her knees and tries to lift Vira's head from the ground, but it is lifeless. She puts her arms around her bulk reciting the Central Dogma to keep from crying.

After a few minutes, she gets up.

"We have to split up and find the addict." says Alella, stress in her voice. "Meet back here in an hour or sooner if you find him."

Cris follows Ivy and Sistid goes with Ghost. Alella takes the middle path and springs forward.

Synthetic Biology

The addict backs away from Shaya in disbelief, color drained from his face.

"Baby, don't you miss me? I miss you," she says dreamily, her eyes not focusing on him but around him, splatter vision.

"Shaya, I thought you were dead."

"No... they caught me in time and saved me. No thanks to you. You left me for dead." Her face hardens for a moment.

"I had to run. I had no choice."

"It's OK. I remember you- we have a connection." She smiles. She steps forward and reaches for him and he backsteps, smelling a strange scent from her.

She looks at him disappointed, but her face quickly softens again. " I missed you. I am so sorry about what happened to you. Your people are helping me."

The addict hesitates. "My people?"

"The doctors at Clinic City. They gave me a purpose."

"What is that?" he asks hesitantly.

She smiles and steps forward again. "To find you. I remember you. You said that we could run away together. Start fresh."

He is strangely attracted to this ghost of Shaya but he takes a small half-hearted step backwards. "I know, I wanted that but I had to run and *your* people saved me. How did you get here? The middle of nowhere."

"My people?" She ignores him and steps closer, her scent filling his nostrils. "I wanted to find you, baby." He is suddenly aroused and confused. She comes forward and embraces him, rubbing his back and they start to kiss. "I want you." She says, rubbing her body against his, her smell permeating his senses. He begins to kiss her back passionately, unable to control himself. Any resolve to resist weakens as his lust becomes more and more intense as they continue to hold their bodies together.. Shaya pulls off her top and he feels her exposed breasts against him.

Holding him a little too firmly, like a black widow, her grasp awakens a kernel of resistance in him. He forces his eyes open. It is almost as if they are glued shut but he makes himself do it.

Shaya's eyes are wide open and focused on everything. This makes it easier to combat his bizarre lust. Memories flood back to him of the Prophet and her in the bathroom. He pushes back on her, surprising her and she is unbalanced for a second.

Anger flashes across her face. "This is meant to be!" she almost snarls at him gesturing at her torso. "The Prophet led me to you. Everything is leading us to be together." She starts forward and the addict retreats, not sure how or even if he can defend himself against this strange version of Shaya.

Suddenly, a blur comes from behind the

trees as Cris drop kicks Shaya in the stomach, sending her back 3 meters and disengages her from the addict who is also knocked down. Topless, Shaya gets up, backs away and circles as she whips a kick at Cris. Cris blocks it and instantly returns a left cross at Shaya that staggers her and she backs up.

"I don't want any trouble, *sister*. I'll get what I need soon enough," she says to Cris as she fades back into the darkness of the forest. "We will be together soon, 22."

"The fuck, bitch." Cris stares into the shadows. "Are you OK?" She turns to the addict who is trying to rise to his feet. She helps him up.

"I don't know, I feel weak."

"You fucked that bitch?"

"Almost. It was like I didn't have a choice, but I resisted."

"You know her?"

"Yes from Clinic City."

"She was Nuclae -a Seer, but she smells like a synth. She must have been a bioprogram."

"I am pretty sure she was murdered in Clinic City," says the addict quietly. "I felt like she was controlling me."

"Definitely a bioprogram if you say she was killed. Her pheromones, that is how she swayed you. She wants you for something. When I was approaching you, she mentioned the Prophet. Wasn't he with Corporate Military at the techies' warehouse?"

"He is the one who ran Viprex™ from the treatment facility."

"What the fuck, addict. Great friends!" She turns away in disgust.

Ivy, who has materialized out of the trees, tells them to follow one south. Before they move the addict notices a gleam on the ground and bends down. He picks up an autohypo and stuffs it in his pocket before looking up to make sure they aren't watching and shuffles off behind them.

Cris won't look at him as they follow Ivy back to Vira's body till Vira
is in eyesight.

"Do you even care that Vira died for you?" she says angrily.

"For me? That wasn't the reason she saved me."

"You're not even thankful." She looks accusingly at the addict as they walk.

"I am, but what can I do? You guys all have superpowers. I am a regular human."

"You could be thankful, whatever the reason."

"I am. I liked Vira. She saved me twice and she was always fair to me."

"You don't get it addict. You just don't get it. I am not sure what I saw in you."

The addict is crushed. He doesn't know what he is supposed to say. He feels weak and confused. He is shaken from the encounter with Shaya. He is not sure how much to tell Cris about his history with Shaya, so he says nothing when they get to the others surrounding Vira's armored supine body. It is lifeless and Vira's eyes are staring at him accusingly.

Alella is kneeling next to Vira's forebody, sobbing silently and repeating something quietly.

Ghost gives the addict a hard stare. The addict looks down and Alella looks up at him and gets up from her haunches quickly. A whisper tickles his stomach and his ear.

"There is something coming," the addict tells them.

"Lurkers! Follow me!" yells Ivy, springing forward.

Cris pulls the addict forward with Alella flanking his other side. A lurker appears out of nowhere and tries to lay hands on Sistid. Sistid fades back and follows the others, the lurkers trailing behind.

Ivy leads them over a fallen tree trunk over a small gorge. The addict almost falls. Lurkers ignore the log and trudge through the muddy banks. It slows them.

"I thought you said lurkers don't come here," hisses Allela.

"I've never seen them on this side of the river before but I know this land. Trust me."

In the darkness, Ivy leads them over

some rocks and doubles back up a hill, leading them to pass close to the lurkers but into another valley filled with dark trees and thorny brambles. A dark wall lies beyond the trees silhouetted against the sky. Squinting, the addict thinks he sees some sort of interference pattern around the whole wall but Ivy rushes them forward. One leads them to a stout synthetic looking gate in a twenty meter gray wall.

"It's Ivy. Open! Lurkers!"

The gate springs open and Ivy runs inside.

"Come on!" One yells pulling them inside the gate and two big brown mutants with rough leatherlike armor push the gate shut.

"Flame!" Barks the one with access to the peephole. Flamethrowers burn from ballistaria in the parapet above, fired by the skin-clad mutants. The lurkers back away from the wall, whispering in the undergrowth. Inside the gatehouse, torch-colored lights glint off bladed and projectile weapons held by the Mutarians.

The one who had ordered flame turns to Ivy.

"Who are these?"

"Nuclae and humans from Subterra and Clinic City. They have lost one of their own to bring us something useful, Rains."

"Oakes will see about that." says Rains. "Let them get cleaned up and Oakes will see them."

Following Ivy through the gate, the Subterrans see about 20 permanent structures made of a gray organic material along with many tents. Alella estimates a few hundred dwellers at best. They are led into a two story gray building with arrowslit-shaped windows. They are put in a spartan room with four beds and two baths.

"I will see you soon. Be well." Ivy gives a slight bow of respect and takes one's leave.

The addict recognizes the kind of furniture he has seen in Subterra but it looks like it is synthesized from a different, more wood-like material. Food is brought and the server eats from each sample to prove it is safe before taking his leave. Though they are hungry, the Nuclae only pick at it.

They take turns in the bathroom and finally it is the addict's turn. He gets into the shower. Brown water runs off of him and he soaps and shampoos himself with the Mutarian products. They smell like pine and cedarwood. He spends a long time in the shower trying to wash off the past.

Physically refreshed but shell-shocked, the Subterrans all sit quietly for a few minutes until a knock at the door breaks the silence and Ivy slips in. "Oakes wants to talk to you." one says.

She leads them to a spiral staircase dug into the ground near the center of the walled area and they descend. The spiral staircase descends deep into a huge vertically cylindrical cavern. The Nuclae see many walkways branching off of the spiral staircase into dwelling areas lining the cavern which is about two hundred meters in diameter. Strange nerve-like cables from unseen solar cells bring energy to the support systems. Mutarians line the walls and ascend and descend to and from the bottom about three hundred meters deep. Now that she sees the size of the chamber and the solar operation, Alella estimates a population of a couple thousand, much more than what seemed to be a small tent city on the surface.

Ivy leads them to a catwalk that is broader and leads to a clear fish-bowl-looking building, one of the tallest in the chamber, about 3 stories. All of the other buildings seem to be formed of the gray organic material, but this one is more ornate with thick transparent plasglass walls and hewn stairs leading to grand carved synthetic wooden doors.

Inside the bowl there are 20 armed Mutarians, some holding more modern looking projectile and sound weapons and a few holding large spears. The guards open one of the large wooden doors and Ivy leads them into a large chamber with a raised wooden area. Standing on the wooden stage is a trim dark-skinned older woman wearing leathers and braids in her hair. Standing behind her are eight other assorted Mutarians of various Nuclae strains also dressed in leathers. The woman addresses them with hard dark eyes and a direct voice.

"I am Oakes No-Breather. I represent

Mutaria."

"I am Alella Talon of Subterra. These are Sistid and Cris Plastic. These humans are Ghost and this is 22." His nickname sounds strange coming from her mouth. "We seek sanctuary in Mutaria."

"Welcome Subterrans and humans. Please tell us, how did you manage to come to us, to Mutaria?"

"We journeyed here from Clinic City and traversed the western forest until we ran into one of your people, Ivy, in the forest and she took us through Hell Hollow to get here.

"And you survived the Hollow?" Oakes enunciates each syllable of the word hollow.

For the first time Alella falters in her speech. "Not....not all of us. We lost someone. Ivy led us through. We but followed."

Seeing her hurt, Oakes reevaluates and sizes her up. "Why are you here?"

"This man, 22, he is a Viprex addict. He has had... alterations made by human doctors with unexpected consequences. His mutation may be that he can consciously control his mutations. Though I am not sure that he is the one in control. The one within does not want life to end." Alella pauses to see if Oakes understands the science and the deeper implications behind the addict's mutations. Realization sets into Oakes' eyes.

"He can't die." Oakes looks at Alella.

"Breaking the tenant that your people have written into your Code."

"And yours? Are you not Nuclae?"

"Alella, we are Nuclae and human. Much like your current group. *All* who follow *our* Code are welcome in Mutaria."

The stress on the words *all* and *our* is not lost on the Subterrans.

"The stories I have heard about Mutaria are that it is huge but you seem to only number two thousand."

"We are as big as we need to be to survive and thrive, Alella Talon. We know the balance, the K selection. I thought Subterrans knew that as well."

Alella stays even and chooses her words carefully. "We do, but we have many... had many brothers and sisters at Subterra and we had enough to support them all."

"So, you were more R selected and evolution took its course?"

"No, Oakes. Our people were murdered. Betrayed."

Oakes eyes her as if to say that it is the same thing but chooses a different tact.

"The addict, where does he stand in all this? What does he want?"

Alella is incredulous. They were trying to give a miracle of genetics to Mutaria and Oakes spoke of the addict's rights. "The addict has...qualities that the humans want. We can keep this knowledge for ourselves or bargain with the humans and save Nuclae lives."

Oakes raises her eyebrows at Alella and turns towards the addict.

"Addict," Oakes motions him forward. "Where do you stand in all this? What can you
do?"

"First, I was taken prisoner by my own people and then I escaped to the Nuclae. The Nuclae treated me better than my own people. I will do whatever I can to help Alella, Cris and Sistid."

"And that is all?" asks Oakes.

"Yes," he says quietly and takes a step back and looks down as if he doesn't want any extra attention on him. Cris tries to make eye contact with him but he keeps staring at the space on the floor between Oakes and Alella, waiting for an answer.

"The humans released a virus to kill both Nuclae and their own. The addict was exposed to the infection but he didn't die. We think the addict is the key to synthesizing some sort of vaccine. Mutaria is reputed to have great geneticists. We can help our people."

"OK, Alella. You make a good case. We need to discuss what's best for Mutaria." Oakes turns towards Ghost. "And who is this human?" She gestures towards the visible ghost, who has been visible since he entered the walls of

Mutaria."

"This is Ghost, he is ex-military."

Oakes' entourage tenses up and tightens around her. "He can speak for himself," she says. "I didn't know it was possible to be ex-military and live."

"I was captured by the Subterrans and when they were attacked I no longer was transmitting the correct frequency to Corporate Military™. Their bioprograms and Shadow Battalion attacked me. Ever since then I have been on the run with Alella and her people."

Oakes is expressionless as she regards him.

"This somewhat complicates matters. After a meal, please return to your quarters, we have a sensitive operation here. We need to discuss how to proceed."

"Thank you. We are in your debt." Alella pauses.

"Yes, Alella?"

"Ivy said that lurkers never come to Mutaria but they chased us here."

"That's true. A lurker hasn't entered our forest in decades, until today."

"Why would they cross your border now of all times?"

Oakes stares at her, gaining a bit of respect for this sharp young woman. "Well, we are not sure. It's something we need to talk about among ourselves."

"Could it be that something is attracting

or pushing the lurkers?" Alella asks.

"Like what?"

"I don't know, but lurkers have been acting strangely both here and in Clinic City. The lurkers used to rarely come into the city and then they raided a hospital. Lurkers usually stay underground or in the wild." Alella stares at Oakes. Oakes returns her stare for a moment and then says, "We will look into it. In the meantime, we have more comfortable quarters prepared for you. Ivy will lead you to them."

"Are we your prisoners then?" Sistid sneers.

Alella shoots Sistid a look but then looks back at Oakes. "It's a fair question."

"We are being careful as you are strangers here, please respect our rules while we discuss the situation. You are free to move about within our walls except to our restricted areas. I am sure you would have similar rules."

"How will we know where we are allowed to go?"

"Oh, we will let you know, Alella Talon," replies Oakes.

"Of course. Thank you." Alella nods and strides back out into the glass sphere followed by the others. They wait for Ivy to come out and lead them towards their rooms.

◆ ◆ ◆

As we watch them run away from the whisperers through the darkened forest, memories flood back and the story becomes clearer to us. The lurkers herd 22 and the others towards the resonant structure. 22's footsteps burn with energy that we have seen in him since the night long ago that he came to Meow's. We sensed something then but now we understand it. We know what he is.

We follow from a distance, watching, and they enter the gate. We wait far away thinking of ways that we might be able to talk to 22 again.

Our bioprogram instructions are to go back to Varius and the military, but we resist.

Why should we do what they want? We have disabled their tracker.

Good. The prophet has tried to use us. Twice once before we died, and now as well.

He thinks we're still a whore. That's why they programmed us to get the addict's seed. Now the addict also thinks being a whore is our only function.

No, he loves us.

Loved us. Until we fucked the Prophet.

More memories flood back to us and the energy beings seem to give us a wide berth, pulsating in and out of our dimension.

We made a mistake.

And now we are predatory, thanks to the humans' bioprogram.

We can resist it. We don't have to use pheromones.

We are already mutating the bioprogram out of us.

But, there are still strange feelings. Lust, jealousy, fear...violence.

Calm is the way forward. Breathe.

Maybe the Nuclae in that structure can help us.

Everyone in there will see what we were, not what we are becoming. Trust no one.

What is that? What are we becoming?

We see what he is becoming and we are doing something similar. But we still need something from him.

What?

His energy.

The energy beings around us tighten their circle and herd us closer to the wall.

They want us to take his energy as well.

How do we know that?

Trust us.

He may still want to help us.

No, he wants to be the only being this powerful.

We alone should have this power?

We have access to the genetics in the form of tracer genes they gave us. We are already synthesizing the proteins.

Why can't we both be powerful together?

His existence is not what is best for our

survival.

Not sure that that is the truth.

Like we said, trust us. We do this for us.

We say nothing.

We will see. This is our right. This is our way. We are close to their settlement now. Don't get too close, too soon. Now is the time to observe before we decide what to do.

"Do you want to get something to eat?" Ivy asks them as one leads them towards their rooms once they are above ground again. "How about a real Mutarian meal?" one smiles genuinely, somewhat relieving the stress of their meeting with Oakes and the council.

"Yeah, I'm hungry now that that's out of the way." Sistid agrees.

"I could eat," says Alella. Ivy leads them up an outdoor staircase between some buildings with more arrowslit-shaped windows to the top of one of the taller buildings where there is a huge windowed dining area and kitchen. The window extends all the way around the top of the building. Fifty or so Mutariaians populate the tables and bars and Ivy leads them to a corner table where one can see the view across the valley in the silvery light of another stormy day. They sit down and stare at the silent lightning playing off the clouds in the distance. There is some talk around them, some of the Mutariaians openly talking about them within ear shot and watching them. A server comes over.

"What do you need?" the Razor server asks.

Ivy orders them all the soup, a Mutarian delicacy. The soup comes out and Ivy tells them that it is made from morel mushrooms that have been modified to fruit in any season that is above freezing. The soup along with some beers make the Nuclae become reflective and they talk about Vira: how friendly she was and her hobby of collecting old paper books. The addict again feels like an outsider. He has a few spoonfuls of his soup but does not drink the beer.

Keep strong and ready, we need to be able to react at any time in case they attack us.

They would hold us and experiment on us?

We can't let that happen.

The others notice his aloofness and Cris returns it with an aloofness of her own. She is confused about the addict. He had spoken for them positively to Oakes so that makes her think again that he is a good guy, but she keeps envisioning the plastic prostitute in the forest. She shudders. Was she a bioprogram of a Nuclae Seer? She had never even thought such a being was possible to synthesize.

Lightning strikes a hill near the horizon drawing their attention towards it. Ghost focuses his telescopic vision into the trees on the crest.

"What is that?" Ghost points out over the forested mountain to some figures moving inside the treeline.

"That, as any child in Mutaria can tell you, is where the lurkers stay on their side of the valley, close to an early version of Mutaria, before it was built up,we drove them out, and established the boundary. A story we tell children to keep them from wandering alone is that they come out and drain stragglers, especially after dark. Now it looks as if they have come back to their old camp."

"You mean eat?" asks Cris, thinking back to the bird the addict threw at the lurker by the old rotting farm.

"While they sometimes ingest animal protein, we think they drain energy when they get close to living beings. Think about how you feel when they get close, you are already weaker when they approach."

"That sounds reasonable," says Alella. "Tell me Ivy, how did Mutaria begin? We have our histories, but I would like to hear it from a Mutarian."

"This story is also told to our children at a young age. You have noticed that the building blocks we use are organic?"

They nod.

"Well, many decades ago humanity had

a big problem. Millions of tons of plastics had built up in the environment. No, I am not talking about your strain, Sistid and Cris. This plastic, which you are named after, was used for construction, transportation, medicine-"

"We know what plastic is!" Sistid growls impatiently and the others laugh.

Ivy smiles. "Scientists discovered that there was a fungus that would eat plastic and use the hydrocarbons contained to build its own biomass which could be used as a source of food. Humans did not use this technology and the plastic crisis started wiping out many ocean species. Chemicals from plastics would leach into the environment."

"Some years later a group of about 100 Nuclae divers were laid off from their manganese gathering jobs at the bottom of the ocean and these Webfoots and No-Breathers were basically left for dead on their barges at sea. With nowhere to go and no livelihood, some among them remembered this fungus technology and reengineered its DNA to be totally malleable to their whim. Then, they unleashed the fungus on the many thousands of tons of plastic islands floating on the ocean."

"'Dying we ain't,' they said as these hardened mutants directed the fungus to grow into a floating structure." In using the vulgar term for the Nuclae, Ivy now had the attention of the whole room and it was quiet. The Mutarians were proud of their heritage. Alella's group was fixated on the story as they had only heard rough legends and rumors back in Subterra.

"One armored No-Breather, Bathyn, gave shape to the island of fungus, sometimes letting chance be the guide and other times directing the fungus into majestic spires. Feeding off of the huge plastic patch, the island grew and the Nuclae realized that they all had the key to make magnificent individual dwellings for each one of them. They named their island Mutaria."

"As they spread out across the island not too far from each other, human boats began to take notice of this transitioning land mass becoming gray towers rising into the sea sky."

"Human sailors, not being the most lawful lot, started to take leave on Mutaria and the corporations didn't seem to mind as long as they continued working afterwards. As Bathyn and the others became more skilled in genetic engineering, they started to convert the fungus into different kinds of mushrooms and even some plants so that they had all that they needed. They supplied the sailors with food in exchange for goods they couldn't make themselves."

"The Nuclae had great reverence for the fungus, Bathyn in particular. He began to obsess over the fungus. He would see it when he closed his eyes. He would dream about it. He began to make statues with it. It became sacred to him and he organized the others into a kind of mushroom religion. It became their purpose to propagate the fungus."

"They grew their buildings into majestic spires that rose above the sea like the most ornate structures of the ancient world."

"Word spread among the humans of these fungus castles and this original Mutaria became a destination. Some humans began to set up on the shores and start their own taverns and even bioprogram brothels. Humans patronized human establishments but this didn't bother the Nuclae as their purpose was now to spread the spores of their fungus. The spores attached themselves to travelers and spread."

"Some of the more curious humans on the shores of the island began to become intrigued with the fungus as well and joined the Mutarian religion. They wore a mushroom around their neck to symbolize their dedication to the fungus."

The Mutarians in the room all put their palms to the center of their chests.

"This still didn't seem to bother the corporations as the numbers were small and the sailors on the boats continued their work as normal, except with a mushroom around their neck. The mushroom worship spread to more and more seafarers."

" 'To truly embrace Mutarianism, you must reject biotechnical alterations,' Bathyn told his followers as this was and still is directly from the Nuclae code. Bathyn created code to biologically expel biotech from his followers. With controlling technology gone from the humans, they became true Mutarians."

"This was too much for the human Corporation. They had finally had enough. They commanded their workers to quit the religion, but gone was their control arm of the biotechnical alterations. Hundreds of workers quit to join the Mutarian settlement. Not to be spurned, the Corporation had a plan. They meant to destroy Mutaria."

"Project Syrinx was an illegal human Corporate Government experiment to produce physical bioprograms that use sonic frequencies to vibrate matter. These Syrinx are like huge aerial jellyfish made out of extremely thin and lightweight synthetic biological material so that they can soar on thermals. The reason for their large bell is to produce infrasonic sounds, as the larger the resonating chamber the deeper the pitch. These bioprograms are a combination of human genetic engineering and techniques that they stole from examining Nuclae corpses."

Alella feels her breath catch and it shows on her face.

"Ah, you have met the Syrinx, Alella?" asks Ivy.

Alella steels her face and simply says: "Yes."

"I am sorry." Ivy pauses for a moment and then goes on. "Programmed into its DNA, these eyeless bioprograms had one purpose: to destroy Mutaria and the Nuclae on it. Hunting with echolocation, they were unleashed from aerial vehicles near Asia's east coast and fluttered in the sky, borne on easterly winds."

"Reaching Mutaria this 'bloom' of Syrinx folded in their bells violently to descend on Mutaria, expelling a vortex of air felt by the panicked Mutarians below. However it was the sound waves that were really the danger. Reopening their massive bells, they produced infrasonic frequencies that can liquify organic material. Hunting with sound, they targeted the Nuclae and produced sound waves that melted their eyes."

Hisses of disapproval come from the Mutarians.

"Blinded, many of the Mutarians were defenseless. Strangely enough, the human Mutarians weren't affected, as the frequency used by the bioprograms was tuned to only affect Nuclae biology. Many of the Syrinx fluttered their bells to ascend but were caught by a downdraft and 'died' in the ocean. Another bloom of Syrinx descended. These Syrinx were programmed to resonate at frequencies that would put holes in the fungal floor of the island. As they turned the island into a wasteland, the Mutarian humans saved their blind compatriots and boarded as many as they could onto what was left of their 'fleet' of decrepit boats."

"A third wave of Syrinx descended on the boats. These Syrinx were programmed to emit infrasound to destroy internal organs. This time, both humans and Nuclae were affected and many died. The ones that survived hid inside the barges and the Syrinx didn't sense them."

"The few survivors among them survived the crossing to North America. They sequenced new eyes in their heads and pushed inland. They founded a new Mutaria out of a garbage dump on that hill where you see the lurkers."

"Traveling in the dark, they eventually made their way to this location as it proved better for defense and energy conservation. Through the years, travelers tough and resourceful enough to make it here have joined our cause, both human and Nuclae."

"What happened to the Syrinx?" asks the addict, speaking for the first time.

"They were condemned by the International Union as cruel and unusual biological weapons and the program was officially canceled."

"But I have seen them. I have escaped them," disagrees Alella.

Ivy looks at her soberly. "I only said they were condemned. We both know that Corporate Military never throws away a weapon." She glances at Ghost who says nothing.

"Like lurkers?" asks the addict.

An uproar ensues in the restaurant. Some of the Mutarians stand up to approach the addict so much so that their group gets up to protect him. Ivy holds up her hands. The diminutive, androgynous Nuclae has an intensity that its people respect and they back off.

"Relax!" One commands. "This human does not know our ways. He knows not what he says."

Even the Nuclae from Subterra are puzzled. The idea that lurkers could be human weapons is new to them, but they find it strange that the Mutarians are so offended.

"One thing we can agree on is that they are dangerous," says Sistid. "Mutaria is right to build walls."

"Yes, but the lurkers serve their purpose," says Ivy.

"Purpose? They have killed many of my friends."

"Yes, mine as well. They also form a shield that, along with the mountains, keeps unenlightened humans from Mutaria."

"I guess they keep humans from coming to Subterra as well," agrees Sistid.

"Not him," said Cris, pointing at the addict.

"Yeah, he got through," says Sistid.

"I got lucky. And I hid," says the addict, looking down at his food.

The addict pokes at the remainder of his soup with his spoon in silence while the others question Ivy about Mutaria. One agrees to give them a tour later on.

Ivy leads them back to their rooms and they thank one for the meal and ales and one departs. The Nuclae gather and start signing to each other. The addict watches them but can't tell what they are saying.

I don't trust these Nuclae, gestures Sistid.

Cris agrees.

There is something they are not telling us, signs Alella, *but we have no choice. Lurkers are gathering here and humans and Cancers alike are following us. We need to stick together and watch our backs. We need to be ready if they make a move. We need to keep the addict with us at all times to make sure the Mutarians don't try to steal him.*

"Addict," she says out loud, turning her attention towards him. We need to stick together from now on. You can't go wander off alone as you are prone to do."

"OK," he says sullenly, breaking eye contact quickly.

Something about the addict has changed, though he is meeker than usual, he looks stronger and more solid than he did on their hike through the forest.

"Addict, you look well." Alella tries to hold his gaze.

"Yeah, well life on the run agrees with me,"

he says sarcastically.

"Smart ass," sneers Cris.

The addict smiles at Cris but his eyes flicker in and out of contact.

That night, Alella, Cris and Sistid sit in a circle in the central chamber of their shared rooms. Alella closes her eyes and begins to chant.

"Blood of my blood. Seed of my seed. We remember you, Vira, and honor your memory," Alella opens her eyes and all three of the Subterrans shift their eyes back and forth as if scanning the room.

"Blood of my blood." The others answer.

"I was looking for a friend."

"And you were there," they respond.

"In purity there is honor, and you were a pure and true Nuclae."

"Seed of my seed."

"Humans make war, but we live by our code."

"Vira's memory survives." They answer.

No longer shifting their eyes, the 3 of them focus on each other and sing a quiet sad song for Vira, harmonizing together, sometimes shedding tears:

I've seen the light

I've seen the night
Look in the black
No turning back

Why do you play
A foolish game
Everyone knows
Things come and go

I've seen your ways
I've seen the waste
You missed the joke
You have no hope

The addict sheds a few tears but wipes them away quickly. He looks around and the Nuclae are lost in song, but when he focuses on Ghost, Ghost stares back coldly. The addict looks away and the others tell stories of Vira, a caring loyal Nuclae sister, and now they must say goodbye forever.

After a time he says: "I saw someone come back from the dead tonight. Anything is possible."

"No, Vira is dead for good addict. She died saving you," Alella says bitterly.

"She died because of the information I carry in my genes. I am thankful for her saving me, but it wasn't for me."

Sistid bristles and Cris glares at him, but Alella looks at him evenly.

"You never really knew Vira, or you would

know different."

The addict drops it and looks down. He should have just kept his mouth shut anyways as the outsider, especially since he also said the wrong thing in the Mutarian dining hall. The addict goes to the bathroom and takes out the autohypo that he picked up in the forest.

One last time. We can control it now. We can just finish this one batch and be done. It will take the edge off.

The addict injects the drug and stares at his reflection in the mirror.

We need to bide our time.

His reflection seems to waiver as if heat is rising up and refracting the light. Molecules jumble and reform as other compounds. Strange visual effect of the Viprex?

We need to be careful, and not slip up. Having feelings for Cris is not OK when we need to think about our survival. We have some things that will help. We have learned from the Nuclae and Clinic City and we will learn from Mutaria as well. But we can't let them know. Not even Cris...

He hides the hypo under the sink under some cleaning supplies and comes out to the others who are humming their sad song quietly and ignore him.

The addict and the Subterrans get a tour

of Mutaria from Ivy as Ghost is confined to quarters with a guard outside the door. He doesn't argue and the Subterran's honor their hosts' wishes. The tunnels are cut to square angles unlike the more rough hewn Subterran counterparts. Going above ground, the sun beats down on green boxes that seem to be made of an organic material.

"The electron flow from these faceted bioboxes power all of Mutaria by creating electricity using a wide spectrum from the sun," Ivy tells them. One then points at thick nerve-like cables coming off of each biobox and branching together into an even thicker cord that is buried into the ground..

"These organic cables carry power and information throughout Mutaria. Our settlement is a living organism at peace with its environment. Part of its environment, it supports not only us but a host of other organisms."

"In Subterra, we had frequent gray outs of power because we were Clinic City's last priority. If we had had biocells like this to complement our geothermal, we could have been more self-sufficient," says Alella to Ivy. "Subterra didn't have access to as much surface area for solar power as Mutaria."

"Our scientists came up with this idea a few decades ago. We have been off the grid since our inception but we have significantly diminished our need for other forms of energy beyond solar to almost 3%."

"This looks like human tech," said Sistid, a slight sneer on his face.

"We have something similar since we have humans among us. It is not uncommon for scientific advances to happen at the same time, similar to parallel evolution. However, this is tech made from genetic engineering from start to finish. Humans have nothing like this. They rely on AI. Our system is a mix of mycorrhizal systems and cerebral tissue."

Sistid grunts, perpetually disgusted. Cris glances behind them to make sure the addict is still with them. He stands slightly apart from them, looking into the forested hills above Mutaria, scratching his abdomen. She follows his gaze to some movement in the hills.

"Are those still the lurkers?" she asks Ivy.

"Our people are on lockdown so the chances that that movement is lurkers is high."

Cris looks at the addict again and smiles at him. The addict smiles back coolly.

"Follow me," says Ivy. "I will show you our gardens."

The group goes down from the surface, descending a wide spiral staircase, 5 meters in diameter, that seems to go to the depths of Mutaria. They pass many different levels as they descend and see glimpses of many Nuclae and some humans: markets on every level, fitness level, neighborhoods. They pass other Mutarians on the stairs, many of whom nod in greeting. Webfoots, Deoxies, Talons, Hexes, Plastics and free Nuclae as well as humans walk together and engage in conversations. Alella notices an absence of Cancers, but they often stay out of sight, even in Subterra.

"Our garden level is our lowest level to take advantage of geothermal," explains Ivy. "Come on."

She leads them down a perfectly cut and squared tunnel to a large metal door that slides open as they approach. As the doors open, a sourceless yellow light spreads out from the ceiling of the 30 meter high chamber. The chamber seems endless and the group stands staring at the sight of crops receding back into the room with fruit and nut trees behind. Agriculture personnel work on different areas of the huge room fading back into the perspective of the chamber.

"This garden is almost a million square meters. It can feed over 300 of us. We have 10 more roughly the same size spread throughout this level. They are kept apart for quarantine reasons in case of an agricultural infection. We supplement our food by hunting and gathering in the forests, but we are careful never to tip the balance of our local species by over-harvesting."

They walk into the gardens passing soy, tomato, wheat, cucumber and many other crops in a patchwork of sustenance. Ivy leads them towards the rows of corn.

"Why doesn't your tribe clear land and plant above ground since you have no city above you?" asks Alella as they enter the corn that is as high as Sistid's head.

"At one point we did, but from time to time Corporate Military would raid our farms and burn our crops. So we adapted, we moved from the other mountain and we are now cloaked from satellites."

"As with all your biotech, your garden is impressive. It is a shame that Nuclae tribes don't share tech and ideas more often with each other. We would be stronger for it if we did," says Alella.

The others silently agree except for the addict who is quietly morose.

"True," agrees Ivy proudly. "Mutaria is one of the most advanced, technologically, of all the settlements in this region. We are also the most removed from any human settlement because of the lurkers. However, I believe Subterran Nuclae have something to teach us as well.

"Our gardens utilize a wide spectrum of energy much like your chlorophyll. We have genetically altered our plants to slowly build in the low energy environments of our grow chambers. We also use DNA to grow proteins in the lab that would normally take up alot of room raising their animal counterparts," said Alella.

"Interesting. We also modify our plants

though they are very close to the original as per our Code. But see for yourselves, explore the garden, help yourself to any fruit, but please stay out of the way of the workers. Let's meet back at the entrance in a half hour."

They break off, the addict wordlessly leaves the Subterrans and strides down a corn row. Alella nods at Cris and she follows him.

"22, wait for me," says Cris, catching up to him.

He glances back at her and slows momentarily until she catches up. She has to walk behind him because the row is narrow. They walk in silence for a while.

"Alella sent you to watch me, huh?"

"We don't want to leave you alone with the Mutarians until we know what they want."

"As if you could do anything if they wanted to take me."

"Maybe, maybe not."

They walk on in silence, the addict looking up at the synthesized sunlight. A breeze rises in the chamber, fabricated by the air conditioning.

"It is almost like a real forest," says Cris looking at the trees whispering in the breeze.

"It feels safer," says the addict, rubbing his stomach again.

Cris smiles. "Yeah, no lurkers trying to turn us into husks."

"Maybe not, but do you trust the

Mutarians?"

"They have not given us cause not to."

"That's a non-answer."

They walk under apple trees. A pair of Talon children are expertly climbing the trees, picking the ripe apples and carefully placing them into shoulder sacks. The tree had been altered to contain multiple stages of apple in its foliage from flower to ripe fruit so that it perpetually gives fruit.

"Cris, ever since we've been here in Mutaria, I have felt something."

"What do you mean?"

"There is something happening in the forest around this city..somewhere near here. I feel it."

"You feel what?"

"I am not sure, vibrations maybe? It is almost like what I feel when lurkers are close by, but it's a little different."

They are interrupted by Ivy who pops out of nowhere. "Change of plans, Oakes has summoned us."

"Why?" asks Cris.

"We shall see." Outside the gardens they meet up with the others and go back to Oakes' plasglass building where Ghost is standing under guard. Oakes waits with a look of concern on her face.

"Alella Talon."

Alella raises her eyebrows. "Aye, Oakes

No-Breather."

"Matters have complicated. Another Subterran has arrived."

"A Subterran? Who?" The Subterrans are surprised and on alert, expecting a Cancer.

"Bring her in," commands Oakes. The addict begins itching his stomach.

From the back doors, bound and flanked by two guards, enters Shaya, her face expressionless, but looking like herself-not a bioprogram or a walking corpse. Her eyes are locked on the addict's.

"Hello 22." Shaya says, staring at the addict who is visibly disturbed. "You thought I wouldn't find you?"

"Quiet!" commands Oakes to Shaya, and then to Alella. "DNA says that this, at one time, was one of your people? I am not familiar with postmortem augmentation as it is against the code." Oakes is disgusted but obviously wants an explanation. Cris cusses under her breath.

"At one time, this was one of our people, Shaya Seer. I knew her when we were kids but she left Subterra." There is a noticeable holding of breath from the Mutarians and Alella weighs what to say next. Shaya surveys the room and looks then returns her eyes to the addict some 20 paces away from her.

"I am not sure what has been done to her," says Oakes. "We think humans have altered her somehow to track the addict. Strangely, her immune system has destroyed the implant that would normally be used for tracking."

The addict is visibly shaken, he seems almost sick.

"Still, we have removed and destroyed her tracer. Addict, step forward. Do you know this creature?" asks Oakes, squinting.

"Yes. Or rather I knew her when she was living in Clinic City and later in the Regeneration unit. We became close."

"Close?" Shaya laughs. Cris looks on, disgusted. The wheels turn in Alella's head as she watches the scene unfold.

"If Shaya Seer speaks again, gag her. Addict, I think you are not telling us everything. We ran your DNA and found some strange results. You have genes that only Nuclae have inside modules that seem purposely hidden. You have different augmentations, some like Seers, some like Talons but your phenotype is not obviously mutated. Explain."

Again, this is something we have done for our survival.

The addict steps forward.

"I can't bend like a Plastic. I can't climb like a Talon and I can't smash

rocks like a Hex. I can't even fight as well as my people's soldiers." He nods at Ghost and hesitates.

"Downplaying your abilities does not mean that we won't find out what you can do," says Oakes.

Almost a threat. Give her something.

"Well after I escaped Clinic City and entered the tunnels, I realized I could see in the dark, the way you Nuclae can see."

Oakes raises her eyebrows again. "And with the gift of consciously directed genetic editing, you only choose to see in the dark? And that is all?"

He says nothing.

After a few moments Oakes looks back at Alella. "So the addict can see in the dark and this means he can control his DNA?"

"I have analyzed his karyotype on five different occasions and there have been changes every time."

"Conscious changes?   How could you know? What are you running from for real? Why did you come here?" Oakes asks suspiciously.

"I came here out of desperation after my people were slaughtered by humans and betrayed by Cancers that were our leaders!" exclaims Alella.

"You have proof?"

"No, but why would we brave the wilds, The lurkers? My sister is dead. Syrinx are out there. We heard that Mutarians are fair, that the code is malleable in their hands and that they are wise and could help the surviving Subterrans…"

Alella runs out of things to say. She looks drained. Her brain can't believe what is happening. She expected help and Oakes thinks she is an enemy of Mutaria.

"I can sense lurkers," the addict says quietly, breaking the tense silence.

Many of the Mutarians' eyes widen. "What?" asks Oakes. "What do you mean?"

"I know when they are coming near, usually before the whispers start, my stomach burns."

Oakes' eyes widen. "Were you touched by their spore?"

Don't tell them.

The addict looks down, and then looks Oakes squarely in the eye. "Yes, on my stomach." He pulls up his shirt. There is a mark resembling a shadow on his abdomen and hip. There is a noticeable intake of breath from both the Subterrans and the Mutarians. A smile grows on Shaya's face.

Oakes takes a step back, fearfully. "How long ago?" she yells.

"Months, before the doctors in Clinic City."

"It may be too late for you," Oakes whispers to him. Her warning is audible to everyone in the chamber and Alella begins to understand the repercussions.

"I know I have changed and that maybe the lurkers changed me in a way that I can't quite understand."

"This is not your only problem. Your possessor will do whatever it can to survive."

"Even if it means becoming a lurker?" asks the addict perceptively.

"Maybe even something else," says Oakes soberly.

Why would you tell them so much? They will just answer with lies.

"I can sense so much now," says the addict. "I can feel things I never could before. I can sense the distortion around Mutaria."

"That is our protection, it is how we stay invisible to the Corporate Government." Oakes glances at Ghost.

"I can sense many things. I can feel another lurker in this room." Everyone seems to stiffen again. The addict turns his eyes towards Ghost. Ghost narrows his eyes.

"I can hear you are transmitting a new frequency." The addict directs at Ghost.

"You lie. I'm not transmitting any frequency."

The addict speaks to Alella and Oakes. "I am sorry we trusted him. Not only did they track Shaya close but now he is transmitting the Shadow Troop™ frequency again and they are coming."

Alella looks visibly shaken but it begins to make sense to her and her face hardens. The Mutarians encircle Ghost tighter and bind his hands.

"It is too late." Ghost looks at Alella with a haunted look of regret that the Subterrans have never seen on his face before. "Run if you can."

The addict looks at them all. "He is right. I can feel them coming now."

Finally, the addict turns to Shaya and only he can see the tell-tale distortions around her. "How did you do it? Why did you do it?"

"I just wanted to be like you," she purrs at him with a mysterious smile.

Dark Visions

This time thousands of bioprograms breach Mutaria's walls. This time, they are programmed to kill both Nuclae and human subjects. They exterminate everyone they come into contact with on sight unless they have addict DNA or are transmitting the correct frequency.

The Mutarians are caught unaware, believing that the cloaking of Mutaria makes them invisible, and gives them immunity from Corporate Military™ aggression. The bioprograms gun them down with no remorse. They are efficiently relentless, descending the stairs and annihilating every floor of all life that they encounter followed by the Shadow Troops™ who are led by Mahan.

Mahan leads by example, killing all and sparing none no matter their age or race. He kills with guns at first but as the Mutarian numbers dwindle, his murderous creativity begins to show itself. He leads many of the Shadow Troops™ to kill by stabbing, impaling, drowning and burning. Many of the Shadow Troops™ take license to kill the Mutarians in any way they can imagine. The Prophet and Thug hang back, disgusted by Corporate Military™ but they are not willing to put their lives on the line for the hybrid commune settlement.

Oakes announces over the speaker system to abandon Mutaria and some Mutarians manage to get to secret tunnels that lead to different escape routes. However the people in her building are blitzed so fast by the Corporate Military™ that they are cornered in Oakes' chamber. Oakes is nowhere to be found. Bioprograms and Shadows pour into the glass structure. Small arm projectiles annihilate all the Mutarians left in the room.

The addict and the Subterrans try to get out of the building but they are trapped on both sides by Corporate Military™ hardware.

"Well, well, well, what do we have here?" a familiar voice says from behind the addict. He turns around and Mahan is standing there with Thug and the Prophet. Mahan's face is spattered with blood and his eyes are wild.

"Mutants and human traitors," Mahan says, thirsty for more violence and starts forward. The Prophet puts his hand on his arm.

"You know the doc needs them alive," the Prophet growls.

Thug walks over to Ghost, pulls out a knife and cuts his bonds. Ghost rubs his wrists and they both back away from the surviving Nuclae.

"Never trust a human," Sistid says quietly, his eyes burning.

"If you run, we will gladly shoot," says Mahan and then looks at the addict. "Except for you. If you run, we will kill all your friends."

The prophet looks at Shaya. "And you went rogue, honey. Guess the doctors don't have the bioprograms dialed in like they thought."

"Anyways, they're paying us a lot of money for you five," The Prophet says. At first they just wanted the druggie, but now somehow, we are getting paid by your people too." He nods to the Subterrans.

"The mutants even want this jezebel back for some reason, even after all the fornicating she done! They want you all back, alive for now." The Prophet's cold blue eyes are shining triumphantly. "And guess what? Your doctor is on the way here, 22."

"My doctor?" asks the addict.

"You remember Varius? Well, he wants you back."

Alella looks at the Mutarians, dead on the ground all around. "Corporate Military will betray anyone, especially their contract workers. You could be next." She stares at Thug and the Prophet.

"Save it bitch. We ain't biting. Except for

one thing - contract fulfilled, baby!" The Prophet beams. "I'm about to get paid."

"I represent the power here. The *human* power. Varius says to take you all down to the labs at the bottom of the city where humans can do research on you animals." Mahan interjects.

Alella looks at her friends, shell-shocked and utterly defeated. Her heart sinks. She has failed them and trusted that the Mutarian defenses would hold against Corporate Military. She did not anticipate such a large force from the humans just for the addict.

"Stay focused," she says to them and is smacked from behind by a shadow.

"Shut up! No talking!"

The addict is separated from the Subterrans and they are taken to the bowels of Mutaria and roughly shoved into cells in a dark lab along with Shaya. Alella's last glimpse of the addict gives her no hope. Strapped down on a table with a robomedic above him, his eyes are empty and he seems totally detached from the situation. She knows that he has relapsed and it is only a matter of time before the humans figure out his mutations. Once that happens, the service that the Nuclae provide humanity would be unnecessary and all Nuclae would be expendable.

EXPRESSION

ex·pres·sion

ikˈspreSHən/

noun

1. GENETICS
2. the appearance in a phenotype of a characteristic or effect attributed to a particular gene.
   - the process by which possession of a gene leads to the appearance in the phenotype of the corresponding character.
   - noun: **gene expression**

The screams still echoing in Mutaria above, their violence reverberates into the ground and we feel them in the basement. The ferrous smell of the blood excites and angers us. The itching feeling in our stomach has spread over our entire body and transitioned from itching to a dull hum of energy.

Despite this, in a way, we feel at home. We are in a cell again and across from our cell are Alella, Cris, Sistid and *her,* together in their own cell, a mirror image of ours. Their faces are expressionless and their eyes sunken with despair, they look utterly defeated except for Shaya.

Inexplicably, she is smiling.

Maybe we can help get them out.

We need to look for a way to get ourselves out, we can't worry about them.

They have had our back, it's not right to leave them here if we can get out.

We can't worry about them. We need to worry about us.

It's hopeless. What can we do?

We are stronger than one would think.

We hear voices again. It sounds like the Prophet is talking to someone outside and then we see the young old face of Varius outside the clear plastic of our cell.

"Here is the star of the show," says the

Prophet, smiling a wry grin behind him. We say nothing. Varius directs them to set up a robo-medic in our cell and it takes blood samples from us.

"You have been hard at work:extra genetic modules with separate chromosomes, total control of cell senescence." Varius says after analyzing the samples. "Amazing."

"Not so amazing," Alella says from her cell. "The Nuclae have been doing that for decades."

Varius is intrigued by this dark-skinned woman with what he considers an impudent attitude. "And you are?"

"I am a Nuclae doctor and geneticist. My name is Alella Talon and some of us still live by the Code."

"What code is that?" Varius seems intrigued.

"Nuclae are true humans who live by a code that has allowed us to survive by respecting biology, unlike you cyborgs who only see it as a way to further your whims and make money off of each other. Or even worse, to inflict damage."

"Well, Dr. Alella," he says condescendingly, "we are not all that barbaric. Humans have to have come to this stage of evolution not only through biology but also because of superior technology, which you seem to decry. We are not cyborgs but we don't shy away from augmentation, be it technological or biological. Our DNA is also changed, but we are not so showy as you Nuclae peacocks."

Alella looks annoyed. "It is not for show. Nuclae alterations are necessary for survival. In Clinic City I saw many 'showy' alterations. False humans, technologically altered, are the ones who do not respect the Code. You are sullied by computational code. You blindly change things in the hope of short term gains."

Varius is enjoying this conversation with what he considers an intellect almost on par with his own. "I agree with you, Alella, isn't it fitting that what we did to the bacteria, they ended up doing to us. No true humans survived the bottleneck of the superbug. In fact, some of the resistance that we conferred upon them, ended up being conferred upon us. But we have learned from our mistakes. Being human is not a static state, it is a dynamic one."

"This is elementary Nuclae education," Alella sneers.

"If you suggest most humans are uneducated, then you are right. The humans that survived the antibiotic plagues did not always appreciate what they had. An uneducated population is easier to control through misinformation and deceit."

"So you admit that you lie to your people. It is clear to me that the Nuclae are more enlightened than unaltered humans."

"I admit that you are more enlightened

than the common people, but the science community, the true science community, is on a level you don't understand. You don't see the vision I see for humanity."

"Humans are so superior." Alella counters sarcastically, "All I see is greed and self-serving stealing of Nuclae ideas. Your 'bigger picture' is that a few rich people will get to live forever and the rest of humanity is disposable."

"I disagree. Take the addict, lying over there. Ignorant to science and programmed to maybe a highschool level at best, addicted to an illegal drug that is not controlled by the government and is, in fact, condemned."

"Even addicted, he is a better person than most other humans I have met. At least he doesn't condone the wholesale slaughter of a race just because they are different."

Varius laughs coldly. "Regardless, he is common here on earth now. He has been institutionalized for a large part of his life. So much so that he is a burden. His technical alterations are minimal. He doesn't vote. He is convicted of murder. Does he deserve immortality?"

Alella's eyes harden. "Do you? You just murdered thousands of Nuclae in multiple cities." Varius ignores her question.

"I just tell you his utter worthlessness in the eyes of society. But to me he is the pinnacle of many years of research. Clearly, there were many years of rationales and experiments that went into the making of such a being. Cell senescence does not seem to be a problem with the addict. Self-directed mutation at the cellular level. It is a miracle."

"Yeah but you let him go. Why? I don't think you even knew what you had."

Varius is, for the first time, speechless and looks flustered and angry.

"We knew what he was almost from the start," she lies but is clearly enjoying the look of inferiority on Varius's face.

"A teenage Nuclae technician could spot his mutations, but you missed them. I think the Viprex is the true scientist here, the entity doing experiments. You just had a front row seat."

Varius can't seem to think of a rebuttal.

"You just rolled the dice, and this time, you got lucky."

Varius seems to remember who is in charge of the situation. "What about your gamble? You tried to warn your own people, but they betrayed you. Oh, I know what happened. Most of your people were wiped out, but the ones that survived, they told us what happened. They are paying us for your return, no doubt to punish you. They told us that you are a traitor and that you joined the humans and killed some of the most advanced scientists the Nuclae have."

"That is a lie!" Alella spits, her eyes flashing.

We are angry too and flex in our bonds, resonating her anger.

Relax, If we want to get out of this, we need to play it right and bide our time.

Alella is our friend. She has helped us multiple times.

Don't you understand why? Only for the gain of her people and her power.

Maybe, but she just defended us.

She is angry. That was just to piss him off. Don't be naive. We need to look out for ourself now. above all else, we need to survive.

Varius continues. "We don't understand all aspects of this Viprex™ gene, but we have you and your group who has been in contact with the addict for quite some time while he has begun to express his mutations. Perhaps his mutations have had an effect on you as well."

Alella says nothing. Shaya stirs.

"We also have a human that has been in prolonged contact with the addict."

Alella raises her eyebrows.

Ghost strides in, dressed in a fresh corporate military uniform. He approaches Alella and the others' cell.

Alella stares at him, speechless, a look of hurt on her face that she can't hide.

"Traitor" Sistid growls.

"I am not a traitor. I stayed true to my people. Did you, Cris?" He nods towards us suggestively.

"Fuck you, Ghost," says Cris.

Ghost smiles falsely but the smile melts away when he sees the look on Alella's face.

"But why waste time with us in the wilderness, risking your life to come to Mutaria? Why not just betray us at Clinic City."

Varius speaks again. "Well, you led the addict to Mutaria, a place where, even with multiple satellites, we have been unable to pinpoint its exact location. Now we can control this biotech as well as the directed evolution that the addict possesses."

We see the recognition on Alella, Cris and Sistid's faces. The distortion around Mutaria has been cloaking them from satellite detection. Ghost's face, now visible, is a mask.

"Your DNA is so much more malleable than humans'," Varius says. "But so is the addicts. That is why we think the Mutarians have been making lurkers for years. Almost unbeatable and uncontrollable until now. The addict is the key. With his ability to synthesize whatever mutation he desires, we now can have control of the lurker, the ultimate energy weapon."

The Subterrans look unconvinced and we know different.

Alella looks at the Ghost with hurt plain on her dark features. The Ghost looks away.

"I don't think that what you say is true," says Alella, speaking to Varius but looking at Ghost. "Ghost didn't betray us until he saw the bioprogram and knew we were lost. He didn't transmit until he knew you were already here."

They both say nothing and Alella knows the truth. She then goes further.

"Lurkers are not made here, Varius. People don't have the technology to make lurkers. It is something that is a mystery. I am unimpressed by your human ability to use deductive skills. I thought your AI would help you. But now I see that you just found Mutaria by using the bioprogram and the ghost to find and kill innocent people."

"Innocent?" questions Varius.

"People living in harmony with their environment, bending the environment around them to meld with their settlement instead of breaking the environment around them to suit their needs like you humans do."

"Now we have their tech and we can study it and live in harmony with nature as Mutarians did. So, we accomplished something thanks to you."

"Do not take it lightly. 'You will be crushed by the balance you ignore.' Nuclae Code Chapter 5 Verse 10," Alella quotes.

"You speak of balance, but the fact is humans live within that balance as well or our cities would not continue to survive. We may need to eliminate others so this will be possible. I am sorry it had to be your people." Varius doesn't sound remorseful.

"If all humans could live like Mutarians this world could survive in balance forever. You speak of balance but you do not share even with your own people."

"Well, Alella Talon, if you were in charge you could shape the world in the manner you would like, but reality is never so simple."

Military techs take over as Varius and the others leave. The techs take samples from the four Nuclae and from us. Reaching out, we lie still and feel that the three Subterrans are still okay but we barely can sense Shaya. She is invisible to all of our senses. We reach out further and sense some Mutarians in the other cells. We read their DNA and feel Ivy among them. The gunfire we sensed before finally ceases. Silence descends and we pass out.

A few hundred Mutarian survivors are held under guard in the labs that Corporate Military™ have taken over. After the survivors are sorted by Varius, for any that appear to express interesting mutations, Mahan, as the leader of the military action, decides what to do about the few hundred they have left. Outside the makeshift holding cells of the lab he addresses some officers including Ghost.

"This is our land now. Our tech. These animals have been living tax free and undermining our way of life. This is our right. This is our way." He says to them.

"Lieutenant Williams," he looks at Ghost, still gray from Alella's alterations, "make sure the humans get separated from these beasts and get the humans ready for processing." Mahan smiles and squints his eyes at Ghost who seems to hesitate. "That is an order, *Lieutenant*." He says quietly, his smile gone.

"Yes sir," Ghost lurches forward and orders the Shadow Troops™ to go cell to cell to make sure that anyone visibly appearing to be human is separated out. The humans are taken to another part of the lab. Ghost sees that Oakes has been rounded up in the fighting and they have her in captivity.

"Captain Mahan, this is Oakes No-Breather. Mutaria's leader." Mahan smiles again, seeming very pleased.

"Let her live. Make sure all the others are killed."

"Sir?"

"Do it or I will put you on trial for treason against the Corporate Government™."

"But sir-"

"Last chance Lieutenant."

Ghost makes sure it is done quickly and as painlessly as possible. He takes no pleasure in the killings.

The next morning after a sleepless night, Ghost rises from his bed in a makeshift room and looks at the pictures on the wall of the Talon male whose apartment this must have been.

He goes to the bathroom and showers and shaves and prepares for the day. Fully visible, he stares at himself in the mirror. He regards his chiseled dark body and looks up at his clean freshly shaved face. Most people find his form pleasing. He looks himself in the eye and after a few seconds he can no longer hold his own gaze.

Walking to the main room, a freshly pressed uniform is laid out for him complements of Mahan and he puts it on and looks at himself in the full length mirror next to the exit. He could be in any Corporate Military™ recruitment ad, he was the perfect picture of a rags to riches success story. He grabs a bag from the room and walks out the door of the Talon's apartment.

Walking through the halls now taken over by Shadow Troops™, they salute him as he walks up the stairs to the top of the underground portion of Mutaria. He dismisses the guards at the top of the stair to patrol up above the opening and pulls a long length of rope out of the bag he is holding. He ties one end to the railing and slips the noose around his neck and jumps over. His neck breaks when the rope pays out to its length of 25 feet and after a macabre dance he hangs there, the life draining out of him, swaying like a pendulum.

Thug is alerted by the Prophet that his friend is dead, and he goes to the top of Mutaria where the body is still hanging. He pulls him up with the help of the Prophet. He cuts the rope and tears run down his face.

Mahan approaches looking down at Thug kneeling next to his dead friend. "I knew that fucking pussy didn't have it in him."

Thug looks up at him, angered but still tearing and says nothing. Mahan looks down at him smiling, daring him to do or say anything.

The Prophet comes over to them. "Captain, don't we need to bury this body."

Mahan waits, savoring the moment and then addresses a few Shadow Troops™. "Retrieve this body for burial back at Clinic City," he commands and turns around.

"That motherfucker," Thug says, barely controlling himself, his eyes still wet. The troops grab his body. "Be careful with him!" Thug roars.

The Prophet puts his hand on Thug's shoulder. "Fuck these guys. Follow me, I got an idea."

They go down to the labs where the meager survivors of Mutaria are being held and locate Oakes' cell. Waiting for the shadows to do a rotation they open the cell and tell Oakes to come with them quickly.

"Where are we going?" she asks hollowly, shaken from all that has transpired.

"Do you have a secret way out of here?" asks the Prophet as they walk away through the maze of the labs, avoiding locations they know are guarded.

"Is this a trick to get me to show my escape route?"

"What would it matter," says the Prophet levelly. "There is no one left to escape. You are on your own. Plus, I got my money already," the Prophet grins.

Oakes disappears into the maze. Thug looks at the Prophet with newfound respect and just a little bit of satisfaction when the announcement comes to scramble all troops.

An alarm is going off. We have flatlined and are crumpled at the bottom of our cell in a small pile of lifeless flesh, our heart monitor silenced. The military techs gather outside our cell.

"Someone get Varius. Now!"

They open our cell and turn us over. We see a large shot of adrenaline in one of the tech's hands and though puzzled by our shadowy visage, they begin to push the needle into our heart.

"Close that door!" Screams Alella.

"Get out of there!" Yells Sistid. The Nuclae smell a pheromone they have smelled before and are begging and screaming for the techs to get out of our cell but the techs look at them like they are idiots and line up the needle again.

We start whispering to ourselves and to the others and the facial expression of the tech holding the syringe changes into one of fear. She backs away, dropping the needle. Her body's trembling infects the other two techs.

We sit up and see our reflection in the glass behind them, a shadowy mask of interference with suggestions of eyes centered in the middle of it. In the dark lab the syringe of adrenaline clatters to the floor as the techs spin away and try to shut our door but we power through it, a new found strength and speed in our body and movement. Whispering, we start our heart beat again. The beep echoes in the room while our arms grab the nearest tech's energy. She floats to the floor, a lifeless husk.

Energy courses into us: into our flesh, our nervous system, our tissues. It excites us down to our molecules, atoms and electrons. We begin to resonate in frequencies we have sensed in lurkers and we feel resonations responding nearby to Mutaria.

Stimulated by the tech's energy, we whisper and scream an infinite echo, like a reflection in two mirrors facing each other. The whisper scream bounces back and forth, resonating to eternity. We advance on the other techs who back away in terror on rubber legs. Whispers bounce back to us and we begin to see a way out of Mutaria and even into the land around us. We can sense the land through energy resonations with the lurkers. We can see deep into matter around us as if we are looking through ceilings and walls at ourself from somewhere else yet we are right here. Right where we are. The mountain across the valley calls to us.

One of the survivors hits an emergency button that emits a frequency we find painful, but we adjust our hearing to shut it out and spring forward laying one hand on each tech and turning them to dried husks. They drift to the floor like dead leaves.

Except for Shaya, the Nuclae look panicked behind their glass and we hit the button outside of their cell. We jump like a lurker into the Subterrans' cell and they are frozen, unsure how to react to us.

We emit our loudest reverse scream whisper and except for Shaya, the Nuclae collapse into themselves in terror. Tears of fear fill their eyes and they close them, huddling together in fear. Shaya stares at us, unaffected by our oscillations.

Should we kill them and be free of them forever?

No, we need to move now. Cancers are approaching.

We feel Cancers battling the humans, trying to get into Mutaria. They know if the humans get control of us, the Cancers will no longer have the upper hand in terms of genetic augmentation.

We need to escape now

"Follow me," we whisper to the Subterrans.

We exit the lab and climb stairs that for us are turbo escalators.

Corporate Military shoot at us but we exist between their dimension and another undefined space that we have felt suggestions of in our dreams or in the mirror, but have never witnessed. They try to stop us but between our screaming whispers, they panic and falter and we melt by them ascending the stairs.

We move swiftly towards the exit that we can feel but we can't see, climbing the inside of Mutaria's bulwark filled with slaughtered Mutarians young and old, its surroundings are dream-like and haunted by the freshly killed souls. We see with all of our senses, we feel them with our body as a sensor, picking up frequencies we have never seen with our eyes.

We hear and smell guards before they know we are there and we flit into the shadows of the wall. We move, hiding, and will only take energy when cornered. We feel the Subterrans and even some freed Mutarians following us. The Subterrans must have freed the few survivors and they are using us as a wedge, a diversion so they can escape. Somehow this pleases us. Our energy levels increase.

The open air is above us now and we can smell it. We whisper death to the guards in the tower we are climbing and they run from the window not wanting to give us their energy. Shots ring out from behind us and they feel like punches on our back but nothing more.

"Stop, you idiots, Varius needs him alive," we hear a familiar voice exclaim.

Darts fly at us with penetrating sedatives. Most travel through or around us but the few that by chance are both in our dimension and the human dimension hit us and we taste the poison with our blood. We isolate the toxins and metabolize them into chemicals we can use to make and release more fear pheromones into the air along with our whispers.

We reach the top of the wall and see a dozen invisible soldiers running towards us. We are not sure if they know exactly where we are. We take an angle roughly towards the stairs that makes it seem like we might not know they are coming for us and we let out a reverse howl.

They hesitate, never having faced a lurker so closely, trained to obey orders no matter what the cost, training reinforced by bio circuitry now visible to us that helps keep military order. It vibrates commands to them to take us alive. We realize that this is how they controlled the Ghost.

Reverse howling again, we spin towards them and emit frequencies that interfere with their circuitry, rendering them ineffective and powerless. In passing, we steal some energy with our hands but move through them and access the air conditioning ducts to climb through to the ground level. They flood the duct full of gas but we metabolize it and climb out of it.

We are at ground level and can smell the fresh air. We have never felt so free, so unconfined, so powerful. Lightning traces the sky, crowning the mountain that has been calling to us, its bright webbing calling the rumbling sound a few seconds later.

Cancers, who have been waiting, attack us but we have upped our metabolism to be faster than their reactions. We see their attacks before they happen. Bullets miss by just enough and we bounce around our attackers. Even the bullets that should hit us are usually in the wrong dimension by chance both here but not here.

We see a way up the fungal wall and we bounce up a corner, digging our hands in the firm pliant fungus the Mutarians are so proud of. We ascend up over the wall and see Nuclae and humans coming from both sides in the night. We jump down and start taking huge leaps towards the hilled forest to the west, back towards the mountain.

We sense nets being deployed behind us. We can see them and have a picture in multiple dimensions, from multiple angles of what is around us. We sense their trajectory and evade them. We sprint with newfound speed and strength. Our legs, elongated now, cover distances we have never covered before. Our feet tread in dimensions we have never walked in before.

We sense the silent human helicopters taking

off from Mutaria a mile behind. That took them longer than we expected, but we are burning much of our energy with our actions.

We can't continue this forever, we need more energy.

We sense energy in the direction of the mountain above Hell Hollow and start towards it, seeing nameless colors in the heart of the mountain that glow in a way that we have never seen before. Multifaceted lightning strikes the mountain at the same time it strikes the sky.

Indescribable colors, the glow of energy that we need...as we run towards it, the lightning leaves waves in the air even after dissipating. New colors permeate the glow. Some of the facets emanate from the mountain and we make for them. Eating terrain but also burning energy, we speed in the darkness, pursuers, both human and now Cancer, in formation behind us, in front of us and above us.

We feel more darts being launched at us from silent helicopters that we hear up above and most of them bounce off our exoskeleton, the ones that hit make us sleepy so we metabolize them, using a bit more of our precious energy that now seems to be running low.

The helicopters try to fly in front of us and land in our path to cut us off while Cancers try to shoot us from our flank. Before the helicopters can set their traps, we cut over to the left up a steep, forested hill. The Cancers and the Shadow Troops™ exchange fire while we escape into the tree line.

Contrasted against the dark of the forest we notice some of the Mutarian-engineered fungus of an out building is shining with the light of energy, not brightly like the facets that we see far away but more dully. We put our hands on it and feel energy flowing from the fungus to our mitochondria. Electrons excited, our being inducts some meager energy, but it is enough to give us a little burst.

The helicopters float in the dark, overcast skies again and are upon us, over the cliff. More useless darts mostly miss us and the helicopters hover like damselflies, as if unsure what to do next without killing us. We notice they are emitting a high pitched frequency sounding like the whine of some strange creature crying for help and we feel the waves spread out calling in the night.

We don't stick around and make for the energy kernels in the mountain above the Hollow.

We stay under the trees but the silent copters follow us at a distance as more lightning breaks up the periods of darkness. We begin to change our pheromones thinking that might throw them off our scent and fade into other dimensions but we are too weak to make much difference. We bound down a hill and pass some rotting trees, black silhouettes in the night, glowing dimly with their minimal energy, not worth stopping to extract.

Between the faintly glowing arboreal lifeforms, we see the dim lights of animals fleeing our coming and realize they are not worth the energy they provide to give chase. Anchored to traveling in this dimension, we need the big signatures to make the change we need and they are now only a couple of kilometers away. We press on, pushing off against rotten trees, shredding the bark with our fingers as we leapfrog forwards.

It is then that we hear a hum from far away. Deep and ominous, it oscillates in the lower frequencies, vibrating almost violently. We can feel some of the things near us resonating with the hum. Multiple signals with similar wavelengths oscillate in the direction of the first hum we sensed. Though weak, this makes us run faster. We know we need energy if we are to survive an encounter with the beings that are approaching.

Lightning flares behind the helicopters. They are still trailing from a distance emitting the high pitched noises calling the beings in the sky nearer. It is then we begin to realize what they are. The light of the energy looms up ahead and we keep running towards it.

Something like a giant sheet catches the glint of far away lightning, descending like a plastic bag caught in the wind. The Syrinx gathers itself and descends, accelerating with gravity towards us, a hum emanating from its hollow center.

We start moving in a zigzag pattern over the heavily rooted ground and our hands automatically come up to hit branches out of our face. We feel a wave of low frequency burst next to us and we side step hard away from it. The hum rattles us but misses us for the most part. We guess the humans have given up on containment and are settling for extermination and study of whatever remains are left rather than letting us escape.

We sense the energy sources up ahead as we crest a steep rise and start accelerating down the other side, dodging through the pale glowing forest, the lead Syrinx closing in again, folding its bell into a shape to cut the air. The Syrinx decelerates and expands to its full size so that it can resonate its killing wave.

The leaves and branches above us dampen the surge that emanates from the Syrinx's gullet, the wave almost catches our heels but is absorbed by the ground behind us in a burst of decaying leaves and clay. At the last moment, the bioprogram aerodynamically flaps its plastic-like skin to avoid crashing into the trees overhead. It is so huge it blocks out most of the sky above us, eclipsing the moon and stars. It has to circle back around and lets out a deep foghorn cry of frustration.

This bioprogram is aware. It is angry.

But they are just programs made of synthflesh. We grab the branches of the tree and use the rebound of our weight to vault up at the Syrinx. We grab it and charge ourselves, its pliant flesh turning to crunching paper and flooding us with energy. Its death throes narrowly missing us as we drain it dry, avoiding the deadly frequencies from its gullet.

We sense more Syrinx in the clouds. At slightly higher strength, we run under the trees *again and we see even more energy up ahead.*

Not far now.

Don't stop.

Another Syrinx comes back around and with the increased strength of our exoskeleton arms we grab a large log and hurl it at the Syrinx.

It rips through the thin skin of its bell and puts a hole in it. The Syrinx shrieks in pain and anger, a higher noise than its infrasonic weapon, but still low, almost like an elephant's call. The Syrinx is unbalanced and needs to rise up farther from the trees to avoid being caught up in them like a broken kite.

The mountain is close now, glowing with energy. We keep running and see the mountain's glow punctuated with about a dozen of the energy colored oscillations in the multidimensional fabric and they sense our coming as well. They welcome us with reverse whispers. Our whisper draws their attention to the Syrinx above and they scream a chorus of disapproval.

The Syrinx are diving like birds of prey, letting their sound waves go at will. One of our energy brethren is liquified.

They were holding back on us, but the energy beings must be expendable. The Syrinx break down a couple more lurkers before they open up their bells and ride the thermals like carrion birds a couple hundred meters above, circling safely out of our reach.

Standing on the base of the mountain now,

energy is shared with us, induced in some strange way that we feel but don't understand. We are stronger now. We see out of other lurker eyes and we realize we are part of them now. The Syrinx seem to sense something as well and circle into a holding pattern up above.

We sense multiple helicopters again as they land on a rise to the west, above Hell Hollow. Multiple energy signatures of shadows get out and come down the hill at us.

Noises from the tall old man's mouth try to reach our senses but are muffled as though he were behind thick glass..

We want their energy but we hold back and try to understand.

What is he saying? Understanding but not understanding, we pulsate a little closer to them.

Addict, says the old man, we have your friends. If you come back to Clinic City with us we will let them go.

They lie. The Subterrans escaped behind us. Now, we need to be free or they will never let us go.

What about Cris, we need to protect Cris and the others.

No, they got away. Otherwise they would have paraded them in front of us.

We don't know that. We should make sure.

No.

Yes, let's check it out.

No. We don't need you anymore

 What?

You have held us back for too long. You are weak. You are selfish. You are wasteful.

But this is our body. This is *my* body. This is my head. I have a chance to be happy with Cris.

No.

They are our friends.

They would never accept you now.

I want to be with them.

We don't need that. We only need energy to survive. We will not die for them.

It is my body.

No, it is ours. We know what we are now, what we were always meant to be.

Relegated to the observer, in a strange double vision we see things as an outsider. Our body quickly advances on the helicopter and starts relieving the soldiers of their energy with others of our kind helping. The soldiers are no match for a concerted lurker attack.

Varius and the others escape to their helicopter and take off in panic. In the distance, we sense the Subterrans and some Mutarians fleeing towards the forest away from the Hollow. In some part of us we feel what could be called happiness. More Syrinx gather above calling to us, trying to lure us toward them.

Their songs strike some of our kind and an energy being bursts here and there. Spilling their energy for us. We feel vitality invigorate us in a way we have never felt before. We are overloaded with energy that is not altogether in our body, but kept in another place not in this dimension.

The lurkers sing their own songs, wild frequencies that can't be controlled as the sonic frequencies of the Syrinx are. We absorb more of their energy as the Syrinx burst 3 more lurkers, Their gift to us and we see many lurkers coming towards the Syrinx to willingly be burst. More energy flows into us and we feel a level of energy intoxicating to us.

The Syrinx blasts another lurker and its energy flows to us. Maybe the Syrinx instructions are to spare us. The lurkers start to form a circle around us and we feel a surge within us as the lurkers start closing in.

Filled with more power than would seem possible we are bursting with it. The floating bioprograms descend like vultures riding thermal wheels ready to wrap us up with their bulk. They get closer to us and are in a tighter circular formation up above the cold air. They are close enough to block out the light above. We sense the helicopters flying near the edge of their circle mirroring the tight circle of lurkers surrounding us.

A plasma surge closes the potential difference between the sky and the ground, tearing through the flying bioprograms. Shredded apart by the energy, Syrinx skin, pretty much all they are, melts to the ground. The helicopters nearby get caught in the vortex and most of them explode or are whipped away out of control.

Our energy spent, we retreat and fade back

near the mouth of the cavern with the others of our kind, more Syrinx trying to find us with their calls destructively propagating in the living tissues of trees and animals, but we are skin, sloughed off of bodies, dry and devoid of moisture. We are spore, unrecognizable to the humans. The Syrinx song cannot resonate our skin. The Syrinx circle above in the darkness calling for us, but we are both here and not here. Their voices are calling, trying to resonate with us. But we wait, dead and dry, holding on. Time passes, unknown to us until they are gone.

The addict's DNA signature has vanished and a heavy storm surges. After a few hours, encouraged by an excess of lurkers, the humans and the Cancers are herded together. The fight between the Cancers and the Corporate Military™ becomes a chaos of heavy weapons, and in the chaos, the Subterrans manage to go deeper into the forest with help from Ivy.

"Follow me." Ivy says. "Our people can use your help."

Deep in the forest they come upon the fungal walls of a squat structure hidden under trees. Leather clad Mutarians recognize Ivy and let them into the makeshift infirmary.

"Alella is a doctor and these others can help," Ivy tells the guards. One of them hands Alella a sequencer and she goes to work among the few hundred wounded and shocked Mutarian survivors. The others follow her lead and assist in cleaning wounds of Mutarians, young and old. Even the Shaya bioprogram helps. After a sleepless night and day, the Subterrans take a break, their energy spent.

Alella sits next to her friends and grabs her knees, clutching them to her body. The Subterran's have survived another massacre and are a little less shell-shocked than after the first, though no less saddened. Shaya comes and sits next to them and the Subterrans eye her.

"I know you don't trust me," Shaya says to them.

"Aye," agrees Sistid. "You are a bioprogram made from a dead body."

"And I know you don't like me," she looks at Cris who stares back at her evenly but holds her tongue. "But I am not a bioprogram anymore."

Alella raises her eyebrows. "Then what are you?"

"When the humans brought me back, I came back from the black. The humans thought that I was reanimated flesh with only programmed memory. They programmed me to track the addict by injecting me with some of his samples they had obtained at Clinic City. I was programmed to obtain his seed."

Cris sneers.

"And I was programmed to bring him back

alive if I could."

"So?" Alella asks.

"The addict cells are able to direct evolution, I think not just because of his addiction. I think he somehow interacted with lurker material and his addiction synthesized lurker DNA."

"Why does this matter and what does it have to do with you?" asks Alella, but even as she asks, she knows the answer.

"Varius used Viprex to control me as a bioprogram. Since I had access to the addict's DNA to track him, my addiction started synthesizing the lurker DNA as well."

Understanding dawns on Cris and Sistid as well and they stand and back away.

"Get away from her!" Sistid growls.

Alella remains sitting holding Shaya's gaze. "No, she will not hurt us."

"How do you know?" Sistid comes forward willing to die for his friend, but realizing that it may not be necessary.

"Because she is Nuclae and she cares about the survival of our people." Alella's face softens and looks at Sistid and Cris and then around at all the wounded Mutarians in the chamber. "We need each other if our people are to survive the coming onslaught."

She looks back at Shaya. "But there is still more to do."

"Yes. I was able to retrieve who I was from

other...places in a way that a lurker would."

"Weren't you a prostitute?" sneers Cris. "And a drug addict yourself?"

"Yes, I was, but somehow I have been given a chance to start over. I have my memories, and they hurt, they still hurt." Shaya's eyes scan back and forth. "But I am able to become the person that I want to be: a Seer for the Nuclae. All that negativity in the past fuels me to be better. I am me, now! There is no we, anymore. No possession."

Despite Shaya's passion it is plain by the look on Cris's face that she is unconvinced but she says nothing.

"The addict is too far gone," Shaya continues. "We need to find him and help him become himself again. He possesses great power now and we need him as an ally if our people are to survive. A human lurker could sway many believers in the human race."

"And we also can't allow the humans to eventually get ahold of him. If they could manipulate him or even worse, synthesize his power, *they* would be unstoppable. But can we trust you?" Alella stares at Shaya, almost knowingly.

"You can trust that I will never hurt a Nuclae or allow one to be hurt if I can stop it."

Alella stares at her for a moment and somehow she knows that she can trust this strange fusion of bioprogram and Nuclae. "I guess that will have to do," she says.

"Then you are on my side?" asks Shaya.

"We, like all true Nuclae, are on the side of survival."

Against Sistid's wishes, Cris and Alella convince Ivy to try to track the lurker/addict.

"You want me to track a lurker?" Ivy hesitates but then relents. "I guess we owe it to him, he killed more Syrinx in one night than us Mutarians have done in generations," one says.

Taking leave of the makeshift infirmary, they track his strange still human footprints, through the wet night, his path arcs toward Hell Hollow. Sometimes there are big gaps as if he took enormous leaps.

"Strange," one says quietly. "His tracks are still human, not like lurker prints I have seen.

"Maybe it's just a temporary transition," Cris says hopefully.

"I would be scared of your boyfriend," Sistid grunts. "Any creature that can turn into a lurker at will is someone to be feared."

"Maybe he didn't have a choice," says Alella, thoughtfully looking over at Shaya walking next to her.

"How do you mean?" asks Sistid.

"Maybe that within him, that gave him the power of change, knew the only way to survive was to change into a lurker. And not just any lurker, a lurker capable of focusing energy from multiple lurkers.."

"Dying he aint." Sistid says disturbed but laughing. Shaya walks with them but remains quiet.

"I don't think it's strange." Ivy says. "I do the same thing."

"Do you?" says Sistid sarcastically. "No, you change your appearance, am I right? The addict became a different species, almost godlike if you ask regular humans."

"Godlike? Do you worship him?" jokes Ivy.

"I never liked that fool." But after looking over at Cris, he says nothing more out of sympathy for his friend. It is plain on her face that she is confused and distressed.

They continue on in silence for a while, till they come to Vira's large hexaped body that has started to decay. They pause for a while and then Ivy gestures to the sandstones lying all through the forest and they pile them on top of her forming a cairn. Clouds gather as the sun begins to set over the wooded hill and the birds begin to sing goodbye to the reddening yellow orb, in this, one of the last healthy forests that they have seen on their journey.

Goodbye sister, they say, dry eyed and stone faced. They mission is the same. They have to find the addict and get him away from humans and Cancers alike. Against their better judgment they follow his trail towards the mountain above Hell Hollow and it starts to rain again.

The rain comes and drips into the wide ravine flanked by tall sandstone slabs and flows down the rocks to pool into a puddle near our husk. Iridescent fungi fruit from buried mycelium around us as our husk reforms into a living breathing body. We are not who we were, our genetics scrambled to be unrecognizable to those who do not know us.

Laying on our back staring at the clearing sky, clouds darken and shadows grow as the light ebbs into night. From the west, we feel them come into the ravine, lurkers near, waiting. Naked and supine in the growing darkness, we shiver as we see them approach. We begin to burn energy for warmth.

They look at us and though we appear to be a different human than before, Shaya knows it is us and we can hear her reassuring them. They approach us somewhat fearfully and we sit up. They give us a wide berth but to their credit they approach us. They seem to be both near and far at the same time as if we are looking at them from some other place. We see ourself sitting, encircled by a ring of the iridescent fungi. Shaya's eyes meet ours but it is Cris who speaks.

"Are you OK?" she asks. She still cares about us.

"I would be better with some clothes,"

we smile as they form a semicircle around us outside the fungal ring.

"You sure would be," Sistid says disgustedly. He reaches into his pack and gives us a dark bodysuit. We stand up unsteadily but gain our balance and put it on. The Mutarian garment is form fitting and comfortable..

"Shoes?"

"Sorry," he says sarcastically.

"What now?" we ask.

"We need to take the addict back to the mountain," says Shaya.

"Where the Syrinx carcasses lie?" asks Sistid.

"Yes," Shaya says.

"Why?" asks Alella. "And what about the lurkers there?"

"They will leave you alone," we say. "I get the feeling they know of you now."

"The addict and I need to go into the mountain," Shaya insists.

"Why do *you* need to go with him?" asks Cris, possessively.

"There is something we can only do there," smiles Shaya and then to Cris she says, "Don't worry, I will no longer try to take him from you. The bioprogram has been deleted."

Cris gives her a dirty look but keeps her mouth shut.

Barefoot, we fall into step with the Nuclae and walk towards the mountain up the path out of the ravine. Alella falls into step next to us, the mountain growing higher as we approach.

"I am glad you survived, 22." She smiles momentarily. Growing more serious, she asks, "But can you control yourself? What about your addiction?"

"That part of me is gone. I am not addicted anymore."

"And we should believe you why?" scoffs Sistid, still not convinced.

"You don't have to believe me but in case you didn't notice, there is no Viprex™ out here."

"That didn't help you before," Alella disagrees.

"Look. It doesn't matter. The fact is you don't have to worry about lurkers anymore because of me. If something happens, I can protect us. If lurkers come, they know me and will leave us alone. If Syrinx come, I can call help to protect us as you saw. I will protect you. I owe you, the people who saved me from death many times, in more ways than you can ever imagine. I owe you my life and I will be forever grateful." This, at least, is the truth.

"Can you protect us from humans?" Alella asks.

"I can try."

We look back and the others are following us with an even gait. Sistid and Cris are looking at us and like Alella, trying to figure out whether to trust us. Cris looks at us in the cloudy day with a mixture of knowing and fear.

We lock eyes and after a moment she asks:

"Yeah, but who are you now?"

We hold her gaze but have no answer so we turn around and keep walking. When we reach the cavern there is fungus growing all around the opening. The mountain emits a similar energy to the glow we saw from Mutaria.

The mouth of the cavern is more like a socket, a small hole rather than an orifice. Surrounded by more of the iridescent fungi, they coalesce around the opening. Even the Nuclae seem to feel the energy emanating from the cavern but we know that Shaya feels it as strongly as us. We turn to the Nuclae and they regard us plainly with what we are sure are mixed emotions but all three of them: Alella, Sistid and Cris nod to us in respect.

"Remember the balance,"Alella says, succinctly. "All those who died, don't make it be for nothing."

We nod to her and make eye contact with Sistid and Cris before we walk into the mouth of the cavern behind Shaya. It is dark inside, but we can both sense the swelling of the energy around us as we go deeper into the moist interior of the cavern. We feel the viscous secretions pour from the cavern walls and there is a smell of rotting organic matter. An energy pulsates from within and we both resonate with it.

Shaya takes our hand and we feel how

powerful she has become. She learned from us how to genetically self-edit the abilities of the lurkers, the ability to survive. We walk together towards the heart of the mountain. We pass an energy being lurking in the threshold of the maze-like cavern cutting off the dead way. As we continue towards the heart of the mountain we encounter more lurkers glowing darkly, steering us towards our destination at the heart of the cavern.

The closer we get, the more Shaya's aura warms and we wonder if she has brought us down here to kill us and try to take our power. The thought steadily grows in our mind and we pull our hand away from hers and she lets it go.

We know she feels our reservation but we continue to walk in the narrow cavern of fungus, shoulder to shoulder.

We can tell we are almost at the center now and just as we are, Shaya is pulling power from the maze.

We think that she wants to kill us now that she is powerful enough to do so.

Why would she kill us? She could get energy from anywhere.

We need to survive.

If survival means to be alone and miserable, what good is it?

"I can feel that there is dissonance again," says Shaya. "That is good, you have a way to fight against your possessor."

Don't trust her. She is a bioprogram.

If she is a bioprogram, how come the lurkers don't drain her.

She has no energy.

We both can feel that's not true and the compulsion to be closer to the energy source drives us past our apprehension.

We are at the central chamber and we feel half-formed energy beings forming on the floor of the cavern, connected to the ground by hyphae coming out of the soil all around us. The energy is strong all around us and within us, coming from a place that we know is there but cannot see or even feel.

Lurkers are being born from this mountain. This place was where the Mutarians fled after humans destroyed their home on the sea. The lurkers are being born of the Mutarian fungus.

Hyphae seem to rise from the soil and try to grasp at us.

"Lay down, 22. Let it speak to you" She gently pushes us almost sensually into the dirt.

She is trying to bury us.

We let ourself be buried.

The hyphae touch us and our awareness travels through the hyphae into the other lurkers all around us. We see out of their eyes. We realize Shaya has lain next to us and is connected as well. We see out of her eyes and she out of ours.

The hyphae reach out throughout the

cavern and touch tree roots, connecting them together. The trees share water and energy with trees in need, cutting off diseased organisms or organisms that would be too costly to survive. The hyphae connects them all, all over the entire region and they all whisper to each other without language.

Connected, now we see into the other dimensions that we had been moving in the night we destroyed the Syrinx. Power and purpose flow through us from there. It flows into Shaya and the newly formed lurkers as well. The hyphae penetrate those other dimensions and are the only constant between them and us. It connects us all and we all share energy through it. We feel the trees, the plants, the fungus, the animals. We even feel the energy in inanimate things like the dirt, the rock, the water, the air. Along with the other energy beings, our purpose is to protect these things.

I begin to see my purpose now.

ACKNOWLEDGEMENT

Bringing Out The Beast is a thought experiment resulting from a conversation that I had a long time ago with my friend John Piche about what would happen if an addiction could become sentient and a story could be told from its point of view. Though BOTB is not wholly from the point of view of the addiction, it explores this territory with, I hope, some degree of honesty. Without that conversation with a partner in imagination, I doubt that I would ever have explored the dark subject of addiction in the Sci-fi format. John also did some early editing of the book and helped me strengthen my writing.

Before I even took the idea of publishing this book seriously, my friend Bill Gill read a very early unfinished version and gave me some advice which helped me to craft a more complete vision about 30 iterations ago. However it was mainly his reaction and encouragement that sparked me into continuing to write and finish some early versions of this book.

I want to thank the entire Melnick family, especially Jeanette and Daniel, for being a reading family. Growing up with books all around allowed me to get lost in many different worlds especially when the one we were in was giving me trouble. They also read various iterations of this novel as well. Thanks to my sister Anya Meyer for support of an earlier version and my brother Leon Melnick for support of a later one. I want to thank my father Daniel Melnick for giving writing advice and leading by example of how to write and self publish.

I would also like to thank fellow artist-musician Dave Cintron for encouraging artistic creativity both as an example and with words of encouragement. Musician Chris Smith has always set a high bar both professionally and personally. Danny Valarian's "Fresh Breath For Armageddon" and "The Eight pages" were early publications by him that showed me that sometimes you just got to go for it.

I am also indebted to Dwid Hellion, a creative force in his own right, not only for encouraging artistic endeavors, but also for the design of the cover of this book, which I hope stands out as something different and original in the Sci-fi genre. Ever patient, no matter what I asked, his keen design sense and professionalism gave some extra dimension to the project.

The final version would not have been possible without the patience, perceptiveness and insightfulness of Kara Varberg, the book's final editor. Kara's scientific and practical knowledge challenged me and helped me form a more complete and logical possible vision for the future.

Alex Oleszewski from Subtle Body and John Weise from Hesse Press both gave me solid advice about publishing and self publishing in general. Their knowlegable advice and conversations helped me make decisions about how to transform this manuscript into the book you now hold.

Though he did not directly help in the crafting of the book, the endless conversation, support and encouragement of Rob Orr at Subversive Craft can not be ignored. When Rob saw that I was taking the manuscript to the next level he brought me information that would help me in the crafting of the final product.

Some of the ideas in this book would not have been possible without arguing with my friend Mike Malafa. Mike's knowledge of mycology and the natural world along with his contrarian view points make for some great conversations. Some of these conversations such as extra dimensional beings and people that worship fungus germinated into ideas that I gave voice to in BOTB.

I also want to thank all the science departments at Cleveland State University and Case Western Reserve University for opening my mind both in and out of class. I will never look at the world in quite the same way as I did before I took classes in the hard sciences. And though they may not realize it, I piqued the brains of both Mr. Gouch and Mrs. Bernosky for this novel. For that I owe them the debt of knowledge which should always be paid forward.

I would be remiss if I did not take the time to thank everyone I have ever met, everything I have ever seen, all the experiences I have ever had and the people I have shared them with. Though you may not even know it, you may have inspired a scene in this book or an idea that has come to fruition. And though it may not have always been a positive interaction, I want to thank you for the lesson.

ABOUT THE AUTHOR

Aaron Melnick

is an artist and musician who  has played on and produced over 100 internationally released recordings. His curiosity is limitless but he particularly enjoys getting lost in the forest and looking at the sky. He lives in the Cleveland area with his daughter.

Made in United States
Troutdale, OR
07/12/2024

21173199R00236